$EA WEED

$EA WEED

A NOVEL FULL OF HEARSAY

Liv Hawkins   Frank N. Hawkins, Jr.

$ea Weed is a work of fiction. Names, characters, places, and incidents either are the product of the authors' imagination or are used fictitiously, and any resemblance to actual persons, living or dead, businesses, companies, events, or locales is entirely coincidental.

PALMETTO
PUBLISHING
Charleston, SC
www.PalmettoPublishing.com

$ea Weed Copyright © 2024 by Liv Hawkins and Frank N. Hawkins, Jr.

No part of this book may be reproduced or transmitted in any form or by any means, electronic or mechanical, including photocopying, recording, or by any information storage and retrieval system without the written permission of the authors, except where permitted by law.

Copyright Registration: TXu 2-440-752

Hardcover ISBN: 9798822965058
Paperback ISBN: 9798822965065
eBook ISBN: 9798822965072

Cover design by Daphne Hawkins Moss

For our family who put up with us while we wrote this book.

And special thanks to our special friends around the country, and particularly in the Keys, who provided important advice and ideas. You know who you are.

This book is dedicated to the remarkable collection of Americans and others who lived in the Florida Keys in the early 1980s. They were a tribe like no other with unique lives and endless tales, some of them believable.

$ea Weed - The Cast

Starring

Florida Keys, early 1980s – A very special place in the world. A sunny and somewhat remote dot on the planet that defined laid-back. Home to comfortable flip-flops, brilliant blue skies, gorgeous fiery sunsets, America's most beautiful waters, great fishing and diving and rules to be broken. A rough-and-tumble paradise that some claimed was going to pot.

Co-Starring--
a colorful group of misfits

Johnny Bussino - tourist on his solo honeymoon in the Keys. Will he finally find love?

Juan Zamora - bartender at the Tiki Shak. A greedy moment can launch a book.

Hibiscus Dubicki - wannabe model, part-time waitress at Conch on the Bay restaurant, also part-time at the Pink Flamingo owned by her parents, Stan and Patricia. She's Marilyn Monroe lovely but even more ditzy. Why is it so hard to make the right decisions?

Micki Wilson - chef in training at Conch on the Bay. Daughter of newspaper publisher and editor Michael Wilson. She can fry up a sweet and spicy conch fritter like no one else.

Chuck Feelers - relocated from East "Bawstin." Owner of Peter, Dick and Willy's bar. A shady past and a bright future? If you can make it in Tavernier, you can make it anywhere.

David "Deep Dive" Rogers - self-absorbed owner of Deep Dive's Snorkel and Dive Adventures and captain of *The Reel Upside*. Too bad he's not as humble as he is handsome. Loose lips sink ships.

Shep Smith - part-time mate on *The Reel Upside*, EMT, exterminator and reptile breeder. He and Josephine have big plans for the future.

Josephine - A real snake in the grass. She doesn't play fetch.

Barry Baron, Jr. - son of Barry Baron, Sr., owner of the "Septic Baron" sewage service. Wannabe tattoo artist. Friend of Juan, Deep Dive, Micki and Hibiscus. Talk about deep shit.

Belle and Tinker Wilkie - identical twin daughters of Earl Wilkie. Boom-booms up! They've got it going on.

Sam Wilkie - manager of the One-Eyed Pelican Fish and Bait House general store. If he had a neck, he could wear a tie. But check out that fancy Hawaiian shirt.

Earl Wilkie - gangly younger brother of Sam Wilkie. Father of the twins. Employee of the One-Eyed Pelican. W...w...watch him wiggle his mermaid ta...ta...tattoo.

Tiffani Wilkie - Sam Wilkie's only child. She wants nothing more than a Disney wedding. Package #1.

Carlos Suarez - Cuban refugee. Looking for Key West and his brother Jorge.

Pearl Wilkie - mother of Sam and Earl, owner of the One-Eyed Pelican Fish and Bait House. A true Scorpio. Deadly stinger included.

Roo Baron - sister of Barry Baron, Jr. At least she can count. Inherited the common sense gene her brother lacks.

Enrique Zamora - Juan Zamora's dad. What does Neptune, God of the Sea, have in store?

Carmen Zamora - Juan Zamora's mother. Before cougars were a thing.

Michael Wilson - publisher and editor of the Keys Express newspaper and father of Micki. All the Florida Keys news that's fit to print and a lot that isn't.

Rico Valentine - Colombian drug dealer and cartel operative based in South Beach. Consequences for stirring (the) pot, indeed.

Felize Mendoza - Medellín-based head of the Mendoza drug cartel. The big guy.

Manny Mendoza - sixteen-year-old son of Felize. Always happy to put your money where your mouth is.

Stan Dubicki - father of Hibiscus. Co-owner of the Pink Flamingo souvenir shop. An original nudie burger. More meat, less dressing.

Patricia Dubicki - mother of Hibiscus. Co-owner of the Pink Flamingo souvenir shop. A real blossom herself.

Kimbo the Bimbo - Micki's high school nemesis. The dastardly kissing bandit.

Betsy - friend and coworker of Hibiscus and Micki. Please pass the eye drops.

Eddie Lambert IV - He should have listened to his mother.

Peggy and Shaman Paul - longtime friends of Stan and Patricia. It's all about the trip.

Special Guest Star-

Joseph "Bum" Farto - Legendary Key West fire chief convicted of drug distribution. Whereabouts unknown.

1

GOODBYE TO YOU
~ Scandal ~

"Dead. He's definitely dead. But, as God is my witness, he deserved it. He really did. If he hadn't been such an asshole . . ."

2

DON'T STOP BELIEVIN'
~ Journey ~

"I can't believe she did it."

His words slightly slurred, Johnny Bussino peered back into his Tiki Juice, a tourist favorite of the legendary Tiki Shak of Islamorada, a beloved bar if ever there was one.

It was the kind of place where customers were occasionally heard saying the ketchup was better than the burger. It was the kind of place where you felt you might be carried off by the palmetto bugs if you somehow slipped to the floor. It was the kind of place where most tourists never caught on or even really cared about "locals' prices" for drinks and food, which kept the place regularly stacked with the island folk. Well, that and the scantily clad girls strutting around the stage.

The Tiki Shak was authentic Keys. You know, old Florida.

Decades earlier, the land for the Paradise Isle Resort had been literally scooped out of the ocean floor by a family of farsighted, mangrove-hating entrepreneurs from North Dakota, creating the location for the Tiki Shak bar, a restaurant, a motel and a commercial dock.

It was the perfect location. Fresh salty breezes constantly blew in off the Atlantic, providing a cooling element on sultry summer ninety-plus-degree days. In winter months with temperatures in the seventies, it was a true sand-in-your-toes style paradise. A simple place with its own culture and a set of rules meant to be broken.

Behind the bar, a sign flashed: "Beer! So much more than a breakfast drink."

But on a day like today, beer wasn't the right call. Johnny swirled the red-and-white straw around his drink as though he was looking for something, perhaps a moment of clarity, a bit of cheer or the small mosquito that he flicked out of his cup with his finger. This was, after all, his honeymoon. But, alas, minus the honey. She was currently shacked up somewhere with Vinny "The Moose" Tiganelli, who was probably banging her right now like a loose screen door flapping on a windy day.

It didn't matter to Johnny that he and his boy, Vinny, had been best friends since third grade. Vinny got the girl. Johnny got a prepaid solo trip to what the brochure called "The Fabulous Florida Keys." He stirred his drink before sipping it again. The paisanos back home would all want a Tiki Shak keepsake plastic cup, he thought. The cup's grinning spiny lobster holding a rum runner would give 'em something else to talk about.

Only days earlier, he had been expectantly waiting at the altar of Our Lady Star of the Sea on Staten Island. With a cigarette dangling out of her mouth like a piano player in a saloon, Helen the organist was solemnly pumping out the classic wedding entrance theme as the guests anxiously waited for the glorious romantic moment, the arrival of the beautiful bride in her startling and certainly over-priced lace wedding gown. The enticing odors of freshly cut roses and lilies, incense, Drakkar and Marlboros filled the church.

His crew was all there. His mom. His dad. His beloved nonna and nonno. His brother, Salvador. His sisters, Maria, Theresa and Angela. Father Eugenio. His well-to-do about-to-be in-laws. His aunts and uncles, cousins, everybody. Everything was perfect.

Except that it wasn't, at least for him.

After an eternally long wait with multiple refrains of Felix Mendelssohn's memorable march and feet aching from his rented patent leather shoes, it finally dawned on him and shocked members of the wedding party—Rita was going to be bedding someone else that night. It was the ending of *The Graduate* all over again. C*azzo!* His bride had bolted.

An hour later, a humiliated Johnny was on his way to JFK more than ready to board his Pan Am flight to Miami. Everyone else partied at the already-paid-for reception like a freebie night at Studio 54 sans, of course, the bride, groom and best man.

"Yo, Juan, another one of these," said Johnny. He waved his cup, his heavy gold bracelet reflecting the multicolored spotlights flashing around the room and onto the thatched ceiling.

Bartender Juan Zamora reached into the refrigerator next to the sink for the pre-mixed container of his signature mango passion fruit rum runner, which he called Tiki Juice. Over the past few years, he had made and sold countless gallons of it. Mixed in a blender with ice, each frozen drink was topped with a Bacardi 151 rum floater and garnished with a bright red cherry, a slice of lime and the predictable small multicolored umbrella.

Johnny looked at the stacked and empty, grinning lobster souvenir cups on the bar in front of him. He would soon have a great collection to take back and share with the boys, except of course for Vinny, that *pezzo di merda*.

Juan's customer with the perfectly gelled dark hair, sad eyes, thick gold chain and bracelet and oppressive cologne was running up a pretty good tab. He would need food soon. Otherwise, Juan would be mopping up a fresh round of partially digested Tiki Juice.

The mug certainly didn't look very happy. Johnny barely seemed to be enjoying the parade of Islamorada Tropic Bikini girls shaking their gorgeous bottoms for the clientele as they strutted on the makeshift stage.

"Yo, dude. Look around you. What you gotta be so down about?" Juan inquired as he nodded and smiled in the direction of the sea of bikinis.

Juan turned away from Johnny and patted a wooden sign. "There are only two things a man can't resist—a beautiful woman and a cold beer," the slogan boldly stated in bright orange lettering.

"Isn't that the truth?" Juan asked the dejected out-of-towner.

Johnny shrugged his muscular, overly-tanned shoulders.

The Tiki Juice had loosened up the jilted bridegroom enough so that his attention was finally captured by the gyrating bikini contestants. Indeed, something had caught his eye. One part of the sign was true for Johnny—a beautiful dark-haired woman.

3

GIRLS, GIRLS, GIRLS
~ Mötley Crüe ~

Free-flowing alcohol, low standards, stupid jokes and dumb ideas were par for the course at the Tiki Shak. Saturday night did not disappoint. It was a good if not boisterous evening.

The smoky haze gave the place a dreamy look. Beyond the smell of cigarettes was the odor of stale beer and sweet traces of females. The Key Largo K-Mart did well with its line of Love's Baby Soft perfume—described as "cool and fresh as a gentle summer breeze."

Juan was happy to see many of his regulars had shown up for the Tiki Shak's ever-popular monthly Islamorada Tropic Bikini contest, where the women wiggled, jiggled and paraded for the monthly prize. Happily, it always drew a big-spending crowd, yelling and making suggestive catcalls. The girls laughed at the attention and played to the crowd as they pranced around in what were certainly the most barely-there bikinis that could be classified as legal. It was quite a show.

The bikini contest was just one of the periodic attractions for tourists and locals at Paradise Isle Resort, along with various fishing tournaments. Many of those who showed up to see the boats displaying prize-winning catches ended up at the bar with the captains and their mates looking for prize-winning catches of a different kind.

Juan's cash register chirped its own happy sounds as the party mood intensified.

Two of Juan's favorites were in the competition tonight. Aspiring model and free spirit Hibiscus Dubicki and her bestie Micki Wilson.

A visitor from Georgia, with a well-groomed bi-level, enthusiastically whistled and clapped as curvy blonde Hibiscus sauntered down the runway. A red hibiscus flower tattoo peeked out just above the pink cord holding the bikini bottom to her hips. The tropical flower was the handiwork of her good friend and aspiring tattoo artist Barry Baron, Jr. It was one of his finer works of art. The deformed dolphin tattoo on her friend Micki's foot wasn't.

The man from Georgia adjusted his glasses. He had never seen a tattoo on a lady before. Lured in for a closer look, he liked what he saw. Hibiscus blew the man a kiss.

"Jesse, you see that?" He elbowed his friend in the ribs. "She likes me!" His interest and excitement for contestant number seven intensified as he downed another cup of Tiki Juice.

"Seven, seven, seven!" he shouted, clapping like a drunken seal.

As an Islamorada Tropic Bikini contestant and former winner a few times over, Hibiscus, a striking dollish-looking girl with blue eyes and rosy cheeks, knew how to ignite the crowd in her favor. The more she revved up the audience, the more likely she had the competition in the bag.

Hibiscus had fine-tuned her flirting techniques to suit any situation. She applied a more family-friendly, toned-down version at her waitressing job at a local restaurant, Conch on the Bay. Nevertheless, she generally drew frozen stares and glares from wives and girlfriends and generous tips from their men.

She loved the easy money, the free drinks and tempting opportunities. But her main draw was the possibility of being discovered. There was always the chance that modeling agent and scout John Casablancas would be in the audience, ready to sign her to his agency.

Her friend Micki Wilson, an occasional contestant, was drawn in solely for the $200 prize. The highly anticipated Conchy Tonk Festival was days away and perfecting her conch fritter recipe, with fresh ingredients, was not cheap. Her "go-too," inexpensive canned conch, wasn't an option unless she wanted to snag fourth place in the Best Conch Fritter category again. She was determined to place first this year.

For bartender Juan, silently rooting for Micki had other implications. In high school they had been in a perpetual on-again, off-again relationship, but it finally fizzled after Juan was caught kissing her former bestie, Kim, during a scandalous game of Truth or Dare.

The smooch with Kimbo the Bimbo, as she was rechristened by Micki, crossed a never-to-be-crossed line. Territorial invasion was a cause for war. Since then, Micki and Kimbo had settled for an uneasy truce. Juan was demoted to being just a member of the friend pack as he continued to quietly have his hopes.

"Let's heah it for these beautiful ladies! C'mon, folks! You can do bettah than that." Head judge and Keys fixture Chuck Feelers, imminently conspicuous with his orangutan-colored toupee and hearty Boston accent, egged the crowd on between sips of scotch. His low-buttoned shirt accentuated his graying ginger chest hairs and a chunky gold necklace with a seventeenth-century Spanish coin recovered from a local shipwreck.

In his late sixties, Chuck imagined himself as a member of Sinatra's Rat Pack but had settled for owning Peter, Dick and Willy's, a dive bar popular with locals. His monthly role as contest judge was not only entertaining but a way to promote himself while providing what he deemed a public service to the community.

"Chuckie, you're so cute." A young lady in a shiny fuchsia bikini bent over to give Chuck a kiss on the top of his head, her breasts sandwiching his pointy red nose. He had no complaints. Being gobbled up by an ample pillowy bosom was an added perk of the head judge position.

4

IT'S HARD TO BE HUMBLE
~ Mac Davis ~

Further down the bar were remnants of Coral Shores High School's classes of 1975 and 1976. They were a tight-knit group eternally bonded by a good deal of foolishness, bad decisions, all-night binges, drunken fishing trips, pretty girls and, well, not-so-pretty girls.

Sucking on his sixth "celebratory" Coors of the night, David Rogers, owner of Captain Deep Dive Snorkel and Dive Adventures and captain of *The Reel Upside* felt alive, re-energized. Thanks to a little secret.

"What's with the shit-eating grin?" Shep asked.

"Huh? Whaddya mean?"

"What are you so smug about?"

David Rogers swayed to the music and kept smiling, showing more teeth. Mischief twinkling in his eyes. "Lighten up. Life is *gooood*, man." He boxed his buddy, Shep, on the chest and started humming the "We're in the Money" song.

"Get off me, freak." Shep pushed him. Something felt fishy.

Captain David Rogers, known locally as Deep Dive, believed he had the striking good looks of a leading movie star. From his viewpoint, a real stud. In reality, he was a cocky know-it-all, considered by some to be the ultimate definition of a narcissist. And viewed by others to be just a plain ol' asshole.

He had graduated from Coral Shores High School a few years earlier than his close buds and Tiki Shak regulars, Shep, Barry, Micki, Hibiscus and bartender Juan. He regarded himself as a legend for his past antics, most notably for once streaking naked across the auditorium stage in his mother's bouffant wig during an academic achievement awards ceremony. Good memories.

But the monotony of everyday life was eating away at Deep Dive. The days, weeks and months with his customers happily splashing around in the water around his boat had begun to blend together into one long, tedious way to make a living. He was tired of dealing with moronic scuba and snorkel tourists, which he labeled "tourons." The dive business had become all too routine.

Restlessness had crept in with a vengeance—until today. A certain "something" had reignited a rush in him he hadn't felt in a long time. He was back in the game.

During his high school years, while his school chums were satisfied with making the minimum wage of $3.35 an hour and unlimited free samples at Dairy Queen, Deep Dive had zero interest in serving Blizzard ice cream treats. His neighbor Harry served up something much more delicious.

With his newly installed CB radio antenna, a fishing pole and a cooler loaded with brews stolen from his dad, Deep Dive would drive his rusty pickup truck to Snake Creek Bridge. His assignment was simple. Keep an eye on the Coast Guard station below.

When a patrol boat headed out of the channel, his job was to broadcast a coded warning on the CB to alert shore delivery boats that trouble was coming. The multi-engined "go-fast" boats bringing in marijuana bales from larger vessels out beyond the three-mile limit had time to take evasive action and change their routes. The business generated enormous amounts of cash. In some instances, it was faster to weigh the bills instead of counting the notes by hand.

For a then sixteen-year-old, Deep Dive's reward was generally a "snap roll," a wad of cash held together by a rubber band. Not as tasty as an Oreo cookie Blizzard, but a lot more lucrative.

By his senior year, Deep Dive had moved on to a better-paying gig, but it carried considerably more risk. He would lie in the middle of the usually deserted 18-Mile Stretch leading into the Keys from Florida City. While on his back, he would point a flashlight straight up into the sky to guide planes flying in with their loads, hoping he wouldn't get killed by thousands of pounds of incoming ganja bales thrown out of the aircraft or be eaten alive by angry vampiric mosquitoes whose space he had invaded.

The jobs were not only exciting, but they enabled him to accumulate enough to buy his most prized possession, his dive boat *The Reel Upside*.

Many boat captains paid their dues as mates before assembling enough capital to acquire their own dive boats and equipment. But Deep Dive's unique employment helped him obtain his dive boat sooner than most.

There were persistent rumors about where his funds had come from, but as with so many Keys stories, they remained in the category labeled hearsay among those who didn't know him well.

Tonight, a reinvigorated and merry Deep Dive was distracted by an unexpected sideshow, a pair of unknown twins with big, feathered hair highlighted by Sun-In spray. Super short Dolfin shorts emphasized their long, gorgeously tanned legs. Their padded black bras peeked out from beneath their skimpy cut-off Rush concert T-shirts. He wolf-whistled as they walked by.

The two twenty something-year-olds were on the prowl, laughing, puffing away on Virginia Slims and mocking the contestants on the stage, who they rightly identified as rank amateurs.

Deep Dive wondered how anyone could ever tell them apart, except one was wearing red-and-white striped shorts, the other blue-and-white striped that at first he thought might have been painted on. Perhaps there were other distinguishing features hidden from view. His imagination was in overdrive.

Shep knew the "dirty dog" look in Deep Dive's eyes all too well. It was going to be a long night. He glanced at his watch. There was no way he was going to get eight hours of beauty sleep since he promised to play part-time mate on Deep Dive's early-bird snorkel charter.

Sunday was Shep's day off as an EMT. Assisting his friend on occasional charters put a little extra cash in his pocket that helped finance his reptile breeding side gig. Shep had concluded, dewy-eyed, that the exotic pet trade was going to be his big moneymaker because lizards and snakes were not only cuddly and quiet, they also were hairless and thus hypoallergenic. He tried not to show favoritism between his non-furry pets. But financially, iguanas were probably the way to go. They bred like crazy. More bang for the buck.

For personal emotional comfort, he was particularly close to Josephine, his pet Burmese python, who had reached eleven feet and now demanded more than three rabbits at a feeding. Shep's previous python, Isabelle, Josephine's older sister, reached twelve feet but sadly "escaped" into the Everglades, where she was currently breeding dozens of baby pythons, ultimately devouring mice, rabbits, possums, raccoons and even an occasional small deer or alligator, ridding the Everglades of its native wildlife.

Behind his back, friends would claim he was not the sharpest tool in the shed. What his enemies said was neither polite nor printable.

"You see that candy that just walked by?" Deep Dive asked Shep as he elbowed him in the ribs. "Daddy wants some."

"Good luck, buddy. I already tried."

Barry Jr. piped in. "You got this. Go get 'em, tiger." He took another drag on the last Camel in the pack, crumpled it into a ball and playfully tossed it at his close friend Juan, tending bar. Barry raised his bottle of Miller Lite, smiling lecherously at his friends as they refocused their attention on the bikini-clad contestants.

5

This Town
~ The GO-GO'S ~

Barry was best known as the spoiled son of the Septic Baron, owner of the leading sanitation company in the Upper Keys, boosted to prosperity partially by its captivating slogans, "Your Number Two is Our Number One" and, on one sign, "A Great Day Starts with a Good Dump."

It didn't hurt that the firm did a reliable job with a valuable service no one else cared to deal with. After all, there was nothing particularly sexy about poop.

"Another round?" Barry asked his friends.

"I gotta take a whizz." Deep Dive headed toward the restrooms, stopping briefly to try his luck with some hammered gals adorned in vulgar bachelorette party attire.

"You like these, huh?" he inquired as he playfully flicked his intended target's plastic phallic necklace.

"I do. Just not yours," she replied, turning her back on him.

With the message received, Deep Dive kept moving.

His strikeout did not go unnoticed by his friends. Shep and Barry snickered.

"Deep Dive's batting zero tonight." Shep grinned broadly and extended his hand palm side up toward Barry. "I called it."

"Dude, that's my last twenty bucks."

"Pay up, sucker."

"Hold up. I see my sister," Barry replied. Maybe she was in a generous enough mood to lend him some cash. The night was still young and he hadn't completed his evening rounds.

Barry was a true Conch, not a newbie "Fresh Water Conch." His family had been in the Keys since the nineteenth century, having migrated from the Bahamas. Those original Keys settlers made a living fishing, catching turtles, logging tropical hardwood trees and salvaging ships hurled by storms onto the reefs on the Atlantic side of the islands.

Among the successful wrecker families were the Barons, who also invested in pineapple plantations. By the early 1900s, it was estimated that eighty-five percent of the pineapples sold in the United States were grown in the Keys. It was a rewarding business until disaster struck from various directions. Hurricanes in 1905, 1906, 1909, 1910 and 1911 flooded the pineapple fields with salt, disastrously affecting production.

Disease also took its toll with a pineapple blight that damaged crops. The coup de grâce for Keys pineapples came with the arrival of Henry Flagler's railroad, which reached Knight's Key in 1908. Cuban pineapple growers began shipping their harvest to the Keys for shipment northward with Flagler. To encourage more trade with the Cubans, he gave them cheaper tariffs, thus pretty much finishing off the indigenous pineapple business in the Keys.

It was at that point that Augustus Baron dug the first septic tank on Plantation Key. By the early 1970s, the family had made a small but comfortable fortune installing and draining septic tanks. Everyone had to have a septic tank. It was not totally accurate to describe their business as a monopoly, but practically speaking, if you had a structural excrement problem, there was no one else you were going to call but the Septic Baron himself, Barry Sr.

Nevertheless, Barry Jr. felt he was ahead of his time. He fantasized about becoming a famous tattoo artist in defiance of his dad's desire that one day he would take over the family business as the poopmeister-in-chief.

"Barry," his daddy would say, "who in the hell would want a tattoo? They look tacky, low-class. Hell, how could you possibly make a better living than suckin' people's shit out da ground? I better never see that chicken scratch on you. Got it?" For now, Barry's developing artwork would be featured on others only.

He continued to make his way through the revelers in search of his sister.

Music blared through the smoky haze. The band played "Sweet Home Alabama" a second time. The crowd catcalled, cheered and yelled vulgar suggestions. The contestants loved the attention as they were encouraged to get ever more daring. It was not uncommon for a bikini top to "accidentally" fall to the floor, provoking more gasps and cheers, as it came time for a winner to be picked. Naturally, the victim of the wardrobe malfunction would immediately cross her arms over her chest with a naughty smile in a hilarious moment of faux embarrassment. More often than not, with a $200 success.

"Well, well. What a show tonight! A tough decision indeed." Chuck smiled and took a lingering sip of his scotch before making the official announcement. "And the winnah is . . . numbah seven! Hibiscus Dubicki! Congratulations!"

Hibiscus gleefully accepted the pair of crisp new Benjamins, savoring the scent and feel before waving them at the audience and making a big show of tucking them into the top of her bikini. There was something special about the smell of printer's ink on a $100 bill.

6

GOOD TIMES ROLL

~ The Cars ~

Micki and Hibiscus were living the quintessential Keys good life. Sun, fun and free-flowing booze with an occasional toke thrown into the mix. Hibiscus patted her bikini top and smiled. The $200 win was the perfect addition to the evening.

Hibiscus peered down at the various frozen drinks sent over by captivated admirers. "You want one?" she asked. Before Micki could answer, Hibiscus had moved on to a muscular distraction. "Hot patootie at two o'clock."

"Ah, no. He's all yours," Micki replied. "But I'll take one of those Rum Runners."

She removed the straw from the cup and licked it clean. "Whoa, that's got a kick. Juan sure turbocharged that one." Plucking out the cocktail umbrella, she tucked the toothpick end behind her left ear, showcasing the flower pattern on the circular paper. The brightly colored parasol highlighted the touch of green in her light hazel eyes.

The girls watched as a pelican flew past, effortlessly skimming the surface of the water. Micki and Hibiscus savored their surroundings, knowing they were living in paradise.

Home was a 365-day-a-year magical vacation atmosphere, which lured cold weather escapees and Miamians of all ages who also wanted a taste of nirvana. Who could resist the combo of holiday vibes and bars with knockout views?

Locals drove easily along the Overseas Highway, bordered by the crystal-clear waters of the Atlantic and Gulf of Mexico. The traffic was generally light to virtually nonexistent except on public holiday weekends and at the beginning of lobster season, when visitors arrived in droves, fully equipped with nets, snorkel gear and tickle sticks to battle it out with locals for the most productive dive spots.

It was the best of the early '80s. There was no better place to live than the gorgeous, dreamy rules-free playground of the Florida Keys. Sometimes it felt like you could get away with murder.

Behind the beautiful facades and great cocktails, many lived double lives. With the uptick in drug drops, newly acquired wealth had become commonplace. Folks wearing Timex watches on Monday might be spotted wearing Rolexes by Wednesday. But there was a simple unwritten rule in place—look the other way and zippity-zip the lips.

Micki had heard plenty of stories from her father, newspaper editor Michael Wilson. As the ultimate community bulletin board, his twice-weekly paper, the *Keys Express*, was closely read from Key Largo down to Key West.

There was no local TV. The closest TV channel, provided through a partially reliable series of antennas, was in Miami. There were two local radio stations, big country and Keys-flavored rock around the clock peppered with a few talk shows and fishing and weather reports. But for real information, the *Keys Express* was the primary source of news, police activity, local announcements detailing the latest deep-sea, reef, and flats fishing conditions, community events, yard sales and the sort of gossip that helped bind the community together. It was the primary link to the world beyond for so many diffuse and cloistered individual orbits.

As Micki's overprotective dad often liked to remind her, "The Florida Keys can be a sunny place for shady people. Don't get caught up in it."

It wasn't always easy in the "let the good times roll" party atmosphere of the Keys to obey all the rules. Micki tried to steer clear of "arrestable" offenses the best she could.

Micki's job at Conch on the Bay restaurant, known locally as The Conch, kept her busy and mostly out of trouble. She enjoyed the frantic challenge of slammed dinners and seeing new faces alongside the regulars. Glowing reviews and remarks about her cooking drove her culinary creations, most specifically the desire to perfect her well-known sweet and spicy conch fritter recipe.

Micki had started at The Conch while in high school and never left. Initially, she was waitressing, but eventually she ended up in the kitchen, where she created tropical flavor combos using the best of local products such as mangoes, Key limes, various species of fish, Florida lobster, stone crabs and, of course, conch.

Her dad was proud of her cooking talents but strongly disapproved of her foray into what he described as the "tawdry" world of bikini contests. For her, however, it was quick money, wearing a bikini and walking up and down a runway above a sea of inebriated Neanderthals. How was it any different from splashing around the highly popular Islamorada Sandbar on a weekend with locals and tourons looking for eye candy and a good time?

"What a night, huh?" Hibiscus asked Micki before taking a sip of her Goombay Smash, a drink sent over to her by the googly-eyed guy with the bi-level and tortoiseshell-rimmed aviator glasses.

"Those salivating drunk goofballs are like Play-Doh. Don't ya think?" Hibiscus took another sip.

"Pliable."

"Yeah, that. You can pretty much get them to do what you want with a smile and a shake."

Hibiscus giggled as she shook her hair seductively and smiled in Mr. Georgia's direction. His testosterone, on a hurricane scale, intensified from dormant to a Category 5.

"You know . . . it's just so obvious. A man's brain is definitely split in two. Half their brain is in their pants and the other half is in their head. Kinda like a devil and angel scenario. I'm telling ya, their crotch brain guides their decision making into the dumbass zone every time. Case in point—look who's coming our way."

Deep Dive strode up to the girls with a mischievous grin on his face, juggling three beers in his hands. "Hey, ladies! On me tonight." He handed Micki and Hibiscus a cold beer each, oblivious to the array of refreshments lined up on the table.

The girls could already tell he had a few brews under his belt. "What's all this about?" Micki asked suspiciously. Deep Dive was not one to buy a female a drink unless there was something in it for him.

"Celebrating!" A happy man is mindful that a hangover only lasts a day, but memories are forever.

"Oh, yeah? Hibiscus's win?" the girls inquired.

"Something else . . ." He flashed the smuggest of smiles.

"And?"

Deep Dive glanced around the bar. Should he tell them? What the hell? What harm would it do? He wasn't exactly the first guy to make a profit over stuff found floating in the ocean. Throwing caution to the wind, he told Hibiscus and Micki about his surprising discovery.

Micki glanced at herself in the smeary Paradise Isle bathroom mirror as she washed her hands. She looked over at the rotating cloth hand towel machine. It was at the end of the roll. There wasn't an inch of clean towel to pull on. She dried her hands on her shirt and grabbed her pale pink lip gloss out of her purse. Micki was thinking about Deep Dive's remarks at the bar after the bikini contest.

She wondered if there was any truth to Deep Dive's drunken revelation about finding square groupers tangled up in the hands of the Jesus statue at John Pennekamp Park. His tale seemed dubious, leaving her skeptical of his intentions.

Liquored up, Deep Dive was always a show. His self-centered one-man act was often far-fetched and comical. Would anybody be stupid enough to drop square groupers in a state park? And for the love of Pete, *if true*, why wouldn't he keep that little nugget to himself? Deep Dive was such a putz. Some tidbits you needed to hold close. Did he want some Colombian drug lord breathing down his neck wanting his stash back? For a find of that magnitude—discretion was rule *numero uno*. Micki wished she hadn't been a part of that conversation.

Hibiscus walked out of the bathroom stall. "Deep Dive is so gross. He's got some nerve entertaining the thought we would hop in the sack with him for a beer and"—she lowered her voice— "you know ... because he found something. Barf me out. What a gnarly thought. Shit, knowing his luck, he'd get busted and end up in jail. Who wants a boyfriend in the clink? I sure as hell don't. Who needs that headache?"

Micki couldn't agree more.

᭣ ᭣ ᭣

Micki and Hibiscus weren't the only ones Deep Dive tried to impress. He couldn't resist approaching a pair of sultry twins he had spotted earlier in the evening. He'd never seen them in the Tiki Shak. But they were certainly alluring. There was an air of mystique about them.

"Double your pleasure ...," he muttered to himself.

"Hey, pretty ladies. Haven't seen you chicks in here before. Buy you a beer?"

"Sure, Studzy, make it a Coors. In a bottle—not draft."

$ea Weed | 23

"Me too," said the other twin.

The twins loved beer, particularly when someone else paid for it. But it would produce nothing beyond enticing smiles. For them, Deep Dive was just another Keys boat captain, although admittedly he was cuter and younger than most. Still, in their minds, he was just a dive boat captain. They were aiming higher. Meanwhile, it was fun milking him for what they could get.

"Girls, you're looking at a guy who had a *biiiig* score today," said Deep Dive, trying to impress.

"Yeah?" said the twins.

"A couple of square groupers."

"Oh yeah . . . you runnin' stuff?"

"Nope. Just a find. Call it a gift from heaven."

The girls smiled, pretending they were interested. But he was not in the league they wanted to play in. Deep Dive wasn't going to score again today.

One of the twins reached into her pocketbook and retrieved a pack of Virginia Slims along with a matchbook from their family business, the One-Eyed Pelican Fish and Bait House. Deep Dive lit their cigarettes. The girls puffed away.

"Nice matchbook," said Deep Dive. "Let me give you one of mine—Deep Dive's Snorkel and Dive Adventures. My number's on it along with my pretty face." He gave the twins a wink.

"Sure . . .," the girls said indifferently.

After a few more beers and more than a few Sex on the Beach shots, it dawned on Deep Dive. He wasn't getting any more out of his investment.

Eventually, he strolled unsteadily back to the bar to sit with Shep and Barry. He had a big find. Yet the girls didn't seem to be impressed or even care.

"What's the world come to?" he wondered.

7

JOHNNY CAN'T READ
~ Don Henley ~

Even in a heavily tanned environment, Johnny stood out. His favorite white ribbed tank top accentuated a strange orange tan that had been produced with the lathering on of a heavy mixture of iodine and baby oil while baking in his Staten Island tanning bed, preparing for the honeymoon.

Some suggested he had overdone it. His skin looked like it was about to crack open due to his obvious overuse of steroids. He was as appealing as an olive left in the brine several years too long. In his own eyes, though, he was a bronzed Adonis.

His day in Islamorada had been quite something. For a few joyous moments he had forgotten he was on a solo honeymoon trip.

The spicy bikini contest and exciting boat ride had been good distractions. Both had provided a visual feast. The additions of the addictive Tiki Juice cocktails and a vacation atmosphere had a way of soothing feelings. Something Johnny badly needed.

Earlier in the evening a tall brunette with Aqua Net hair and a champion swimmer's streamlined body had caught his eye. Somehow contestant number three, by the name of Micki, reminded him of Rita, though admittedly Rita sported more of a pear shape and wasn't as tall. Maybe it was the way she tossed her head when she laughed. Maybe it was the way her perfectly proportioned smallish breasts lightly bounced or the way she moved as she twisted her body in her best come-hither manner.

For Johnny, boobs were a gift from above. They weren't ever meant to be man-made or too big. In fact, more than a handful was a waste. Rita's juicy little peaches were perfect. The *chooch* Vinny, on the other hand, had always been a bazoomba man. The bigger the better.

He was transfixed until the show ended and disappointed when contestant number seven, Hibiscus, was awarded the $200 prize to whistles and mixed cheers of delight from her fans and those who had bet on her and jeers from those who had placed their bets elsewhere. For Johnny, the prize should have gone to the girl who reminded him of the former love of his life.

Johnny snapped his fingers. "Yo, Juan, another." Further slurring his words over the raucous din and waving the empty plastic cup with the grinning spiny lobster, he deeply inhaled another Marlboro before blowing a large smoke ring. His best bar trick was his ability to not only create a perfect smoke ring but add another ring inside it.

"Can you believe it, that sewer rat Rita left me standing at the altar? And who did she take off with? My best friend Vinny! Oh, fuck . . . fuhgeddaboudit." He didn't want to think about those two anymore. They disgusted him.

The second smoke ring was well placed. But attempting to add a third ring, he failed, once again. One of these days . . .

"Coming up," said Juan, as noncommittal as possible. He had learned over several years running the bar not to get too interested in a customer's personal problems. He wasn't a priest or a shrink, just a bartender. This guy was approaching the potential nuisance level. But so far, his tips had been in the generous zone. And he wasn't really that obnoxious or hostile. Yet. Just boringly repetitive.

"Hey, how do you like the Keys so far?" It was time to change the subject. Juan couldn't endure another second hearing about Rita and Vinny.

"Well, I went on a boat trip to John Pennekamp Park today."

"You actually made it out? I heard the dive boats gave up their charters for the day." Juan was surprised. Blustery wind and choppy seas made snorkeling treacherous, especially for an inexperienced tourist.

"Shit. The captain tried to cancel the trip. I told him we were going. I didn't care about no weather. Capiche?"

It never failed to impress Johnny how easily cash, positively spread like creamy peanut butter on a delicious piece of focaccia, could produce a satisfying outcome. Johnny wasn't going to take no for an answer. After all, he had traveled all the way from Staten Island.

He had enjoyed a herky-jerky jaunt on the water even if it was spoiled by a heavy summer squall. Occasionally the sun had peeked through the clouds, very typical weather for the Keys on a summer afternoon when the weather could turn on the unexpected arrival of dark clouds.

Although he didn't get into the water, he had never experienced anything like the ride out to Key Largo's world-famous reefs on *The Reel Upside*, a Crusader 34. The fiberglass-hulled boat was showing its age, but it still enabled Deep Dive to reliably cater to tourists looking to share the wonders of the magnificent coral and colorful tropical fish in the gorgeous gin-clear Keys waters.

So as Father Eugenio had recommended, he was able to reach Christ of the Abyss, a four-thousand-pound underwater statue submerged twenty-five feet down in John Pennekamp State Park, the world's first underwater state park. Robed and barnacled, Jesus, looking to the heaven above, gazed at him with outstretched arms.

Johnny made sure he got a prayer in before returning to Paradise Isle. *"O most holy heart of Jesus, source of every blessing, bless my family. Make me humble, patient, pure, and obedient to your will, protect me in the presence of danger. Comfort me in my pain . . . And while you're at it, infest Vinny's tiny balls with painful pus-filled boils."*

Being out on the waters of the Florida Keys in any kind of weather was pretty cool for someone whose previous idea of vacation fun had been Brooklyn's Coney Island. Yes, New York had water, but not like this. It was the kind of aquatic Caribbean landscape Johnny had dreamed of.

Juan placed another Tiki Juice in front of Johnny and slid some saltine crackers his way. "Here you go."

"What a trip it was, even with the rain and the whitecaps," enthused Johnny. "Shit, it made me puke up my eggs and bacon." Bartender Juan was halfway listening, pretending he was paying strict attention, following the well-worn path to bigger tips.

"That boat was dope. Never been on one like that before. So, I'm out in the ocean with that guy driving." He pointed over to Deep Dive chatting up a couple of girls at the bar. "He sure knows what he's doing. I told him to take me to the Jesus statue. Heard a lot about it. Even if the weather sucked for snorkeling, I still wanted to eyeball it."

"But it was worth it—seeing Jesus looking up at me like that. I was in the middle of saying a prayer when I saw the craziest thing. It was like unreal, man. I looked down and the statue was holding what looked like Nonna's net shopping bag with really big packages inside."

Juan's ears perked up. Did he hear that right?

"A net shopping bag with packages inside? You don't say." Johnny now had his full attention.

"Yeah, you know, like large meat packages from Sal the butcher inside a large net shopping bag." Johnny showed Juan the shape and size with his hands.

"Captain Deep Dive jumped right in the water and worked his balls off pulling the net right out of the statue's hands. Nuts, huh? Who the hell would want an old net with crap inside? He told me it was important to keep the park free of trash."

"Interesting." Juan often claimed he was not born yesterday. He understood immediately what he was hearing. Packages in the ocean. He knew they weren't filled with Sal's sausages.

Marijuana smuggling was big business in South Florida in the 1970s and early 1980s, particularly in the Florida Keys, where it was almost impossible for the cops to keep up with the increase in creative drug trafficking tactics. The flow of drugs competed with tourism and various forms of fishing as the greatest generator of Keys prosperity. Smuggling was run primarily by locals intimately familiar with the waters, fed by deliveries from Colombia and other points south.

Stray floating packages widely known as "square groupers" or "floaters" were dream finds. Easy money. Discretion worked to your benefit. The unexplained and untaxed newly acquired funds jump-started numerous local businesses. Many of these good citizens went on to become well-known business owners, swell neighbors, fishing guides, local political leaders—in fact, pillars of the community.

Juan topped up Johnny's drink without him realizing it. There was more to the story. Juan wanted to hear it. All of it.

Hearing a soft purring sound, Johnny momentarily glanced down to see Katie Kat, the bar's black cat, pausing briefly from her nightly tour of the bar to rub her back on his stool leg. He wasn't superstitious. Perhaps he should have been.

Johnny rambled on, droning on about Rita and Vinny, the *stronzo*, oblivious to the fact that the band had packed up and the bar crowd had thinned, leaving just a few hard-core stragglers.

It was well after midnight when Johnny, breaking through the confusing, booze-fueled fog in his head, remembered runaway Rita's biggest wish when they were planning their honeymoon in the Keys. Above all, she wanted to swim with the dolphins. Well, he would show her. He would be the one in the water with the dolphins. She could stick it.

"I gotta go," Johnny slurred as he clumsily dismounted the barstool, tossing money down on the bar.

It was late. The captain from Johnny's snorkel trip and a few other souls were left nursing one for the road. "I'm gonna swim with them dolphins," he muttered.

"Sounds like a great plan." A distracted Juan watched him sway out of the Tiki Shak, not thinking much about the stray remark. His mind was elsewhere.

Next door was Seas of Wonder—Islamorada's pride and joy. The attraction billed itself as an unmatched marine wonderland where visitors could swim with dolphins, engage with California sea lions, touch otherwise dangerous stingrays and even watch family-friendly entertainment with the sea creatures before exiting through the inevitable fodder-filled, high-margin gift shop where you could get a treasured small plastic starfish for your desk or kitchen counter for only ninety-nine cents. Collectible stingray refrigerator magnets, made in China, were only fifty cents.

Life is full of choices—along with moments when it pays to read the signage.

Well, Johnny went and did something that he shouldn't have. If only he had paid attention to the *"No entry/No swimming with the dolphins"* sign.

Equally important is timing. For Johnny, swimming with the dolphins and disturbing the alpha male dolphin Conan as he was engaging in "private time" with LulaBelle turned out to be horrible timing. A fatal choice, indeed.

The sheriff's office labeled it "an unnecessary tragedy."

The front-page headline in the New York Post read *"Solo Staten Island Honeymooner Killed by Love in the Florida Keys."*

8

SMUGGLER'S BLUES

~ Glenn Frey ~

It was almost 2 a.m. Deep Dive had snorkel customers in a few hours, just after dawn. "I'm calling it a night, boys," he said, gulping his last mouthful of brew. The group staggered out of the Tiki Shak and headed to their homes. Captain David Deep Dive saluted Barry and Shep before making his way over to *The Reel Upside* to kiss his miracle haul goodnight before turning in.

At a guestimated value of $30,000 for each package, he was looking at $120,000. An enormous sum. Enough to buy a bigger boat or take off and do something else. It was going to be a big-time celebration. He hopped onto the boat and emptied his pockets onto the table before stumbling over to the engine compartment, where he had hidden his impressive catch of the day. It took a moment for his eyes to fully adjust to the low light. Light so low he couldn't spot the square groupers. He looked harder. He still couldn't see the packages. Gradually, it dawned on him.

They weren't there.

That was impossible. How could the bales not be there? It didn't make any sense. Holy shit! Where the hell were they?

Could it have been the girls playing a bad joke on him? "*Nah*," he thought. Hibiscus and Micki were his friends. They would never screw him—literally or figuratively. Had he mentioned anything to the twins? He was hoping when his head cleared in the morning he would remember. The too-much-booze curse.

Had some jerk-off come aboard and taken them? Perhaps some local pukey smart-assed kids had just happened to check out his boat while he was celebrating at the Tiki Shak? No, not in the Keys. Not here in Islamorada. Locals knew better. In a small community, it didn't happen like that. Nobody ever locked anything. Not their houses. Not their cars. They even left the keys in them. Not even an engine room holding four highly valuable square groupers.

"Shitballs!" he shouted to no one in particular. How could they not be there? Some fucking touron must have come aboard and taken them. "If I get my hands on the asshole who took it, I'll ... damn it!" As he stood up frantically, his head smashed against the engine room door frame. "Fuck!" he yelled, rubbing his forehead.

Deep Dive wildly waved his arms at the boys. "Shep, Baron, guys," he shouted. "Get your asses over here! I need ya, pronto!"

His two friends, still in hailing range, turned to see a frantic Deep Dive desperately waving at them and whistling. They trotted back to *The Reel Upside*.

"Hey, what's up?" said Shep. They had never seen their friend in such desperation.

Deep Dive breathlessly, "I ... I ... well, there's ... there's a situation."

"Whatchu talkin' 'bout?" asked Shep.

Deep Dive fumbled for words. This wasn't easy. "Something happened today ... really weird shit ... I mean ..." He was having trouble getting the words out. "I ... I, uh, I found something. On the Christ of the Abyss statue. Somehow it got hooked on his hands."

Deep Dive explained how he'd found the bronze underwater statue holding a large net containing four square groupers. Finding profitable jetsam was lucky but not uncommon in the early '80s Florida Keys. But the location was undeniably unusual.

"Rad . . . so, who did you tell?" asked Barry, masking his annoyance that his so-called friend waited until now to share news of his profitable find.

Deep Dive deflected the question. This was not the time to reveal his indiscretions. "Look guys, those packages are worth a lot. Do me a solid. Help me find 'em. I'll make it worth your while."

"Okay. I'm in." Barry high-fived Deep Dive. A few extra bucks in his pocket wouldn't hurt. Tattoo guns were expensive.

Under his breath, Shep muttered to Barry. "Notice how he didn't mention his find to us all night. But now that he needs us, he does. Super shady. Don't ya think?"

"Yup, I had the same thought. What an asshole move. Don't worry. He's gonna give us a good cut when we find the shit."

Greed is a particularly ugly monster. When it creeps in, mistrust can quickly form, even between longtime school friends, particularly as they each calculated how the square groupers could benefit or change their lives. They looked at each other, suspiciously wondering who now possessed the highly valuable pot haul.

9

BLACK SHEEP OF THE FAMILY
~ Rainbow ~

The wind-swept terrain of 1980s Big Pine featured a rich selection of native wildlife, including lizards, raccoons, wharf rats, small Key deer, an amazing variety of birds and tropical fish and a scattered population of a strange, unpredictable two-legged species mystically attracted to the green and bright blue coral reef waters that were as miraculously clear as a freshly filled bathtub.

Sparsely settled by fishermen, guides and those dedicated to avoiding the glare, judgments and rules of conduct imposed by civilization, Big Pine was very much a sanctuary. Located more than halfway down the Keys towards Key West, it was not everybody's idea of paradise. But it was perfect for anyone looking for a slower-paced life who loved to fish or to run loads of weed.

Overall, the lifestyle defined laid-back. A resident had once told a writer from the *New York Times*, "I can walk down the streets, and I ain't worried about gettin' mugged. My car's parked outside right now with the keys in it. And I ain't worried about someone drivin' it off. It's a small town. It ain't a concrete jungle."

Earl Wilkie's Spanish Harbor fishing camp-style home provided endless water views and quick access to both the Atlantic Ocean and the

Gulf via Bodie Channel. A rock shell road that meandered through the scrubby Keys foliage eventually reached a sun-bleached wooden structure that had survived hurricanes, brush fires, tornadoes and other natural disasters since 1936. The home was largely constructed with Dade County pine, a dense wood unique to South Florida, valued because it was highly resistant to decay and insect damage.

The camp's walls were soaked with legendary but eternally silent exploits of past decades. Its moldy natural tongue-and-groove ceiling and exposed beams characterized the dwelling as old Florida, as did the covered porch—the ideal place to marvel at a fiery green flash sunset, celestial delights or the approach of the cops or other unwanted visitors.

After an uneventful night at the Tiki Shak, the twins drove home to their Spanish Harbor residence at Big Pine. "What a waste of a night. We might as well have stayed home," said Belle between yawns.

"Yeah, boring," said her sister, known as Tinker by her friends.

The girls had driven up to the Tiki Shak in search of fresh meat—tourists from some foreign place like Milwaukee they could possibly bed and roll. Instead, it was the same old, same old—chatted up by undesirable fishing guides, captains and miscellaneous other low-spending, penny-pinching losers.

They were surprised to find their daddy, Earl Wilkie, on the porch with his older brother, their unbeloved uncle Sam. Despite the hour, the brothers were still up. A pair of flickering kerosene lamps emitted an acrid burned-fuel odor, discouraging incessant swarms of mosquitoes.

Sam's only child, their cousin Tiffani, was with them. Through a river of tears, "I ain't gonna get my Disney princess wedding?" she wailed. Her dad had promised her a no-limits fairy-tale affair. Now, he was ruining her life . . . again.

It was a tantrum worthy of precious Tiffani. Not getting the top-tier princess wedding at Disney, upgraded Package #1 complete with the Cinderella Pumpkin carriage, she sobbed. "It's so unfair." In unison, the twins rolled their eyes. Their spoiled princess cousin was putting on quite a show. Good grief, her daddy was buying it, all of it. So lame.

Uncle Sam was storming around the porch, waving his short, hairy arms. He would make a poor bobblehead doll. His head was connected directly to his body. There was barely enough neck for a tie, even if he ever wanted to wear one.

Younger brother Earl, sidekick and much taller lanky sibling who very closely resembled Abraham, a former neighbor, was eternally proud of not just his twins but even more so how he could make the mermaid on his right arm wiggle in just the right spots. It was a souvenir from his prospective Navy days. He had hoped the tattoo would impress the Navy recruiters when he was eighteen. His dreams of a life at sea dried up when he failed the required physical. The Navy had no interest in a recruit with such a bad stutter and a hand missing two fingers—a crabbing accident reminder from years earlier.

Uncle Sam, a leading denizen of Big Pine, now worked together with Earl at their family-owned business, the One-Eyed Pelican Fish and Bait House, under the watchful eye of their mama, Pearl.

Mama Pearl, the dominant family matriarch, descended from a long line of spongers and shrimpers who barely eked out a living. She had spent her entire life baking in the blazing Keys sun, without a drop of sunscreen. By the time she was in her early sixties, her skin was a match for dried beef jerky. It fit her reputation as being tougher than a $2 steak. If she felt the Wilkies were being screwed or slighted in any way, she didn't fool around—an eye for an eye. She was fearless and relentless. Methodical in her habits and behavior. Classic traits of her birth sign—Scorpio. Her stinger was always ready and positioned to strike, if threatened.

Throughout the day, she sipped on Old Milwaukee Light, always with a lit cigarette in her left hand, usually a Kool True Menthol.

Stubby Sam saw himself, mustache and all, as Tom Selleck of his favorite new TV show, *Magnum, P.I.* Others would quietly snicker. His facial hair resembled a shaky pencil drawing above his upper lip more than a movie star's thick and luscious mustache. Curiously, he had more hair on his body than his face. His short fire hydrant profile couldn't be disguised with his ubiquitous Hawaiian-style shirts à la Magnum. When out and about in the Keys, his shiny ruby-red Triumph TR7 was immediately recognizable. It was the sports car most closely resembling Magnum's red Ferrari that he could afford. All he needed was one big score to move up to the real thing.

The Wilkie brothers were new to the drug courier business. Over the years, they had made small amounts of money from quietly dealing on the side, but now they were moving up to the big leagues. Sam had watched diligently as friends and neighbors dipped their toes into the marijuana game with varying degrees of success. If they could do it, why couldn't he?

Sam had the brilliant idea to replace the "Cudjoe Key Cowboys" after they were busted by federal drug agents, leaving a huge void in the market and a dazzling opportunity for an ambitious wannabe. He was sure he knew how to avoid the stupid mistakes they had made.

Fast boats and police scanners were the trademarks of the Cudjoe Key Cowboys, a loose group of Lower Keys locals. They operated by land, sea and air. Low-flying planes and fishing boats hauled in loads from mother boats and U-Haul trailers running up US-1 to Miami.

The gang included an assortment of Key West's establishment, including the head of the Sears women's department, a local car dealer, a beer truck driver and a county commissioner's nephew. There were grandfathers, an electrician, a waterworks engineer and a local magistrate. In other words, ordinary nice people. Folks with families who loved hot dogs, drank beer and generally were fun to be around.

After the spectacular bust, the sheriff moaned, "Where the hell am I going to put them?" His already overcrowded jail became even more cramped when inmates destroyed Cell Block 3 during a Thursday night disturbance. "Howard Johnson's doesn't check as many people in and out a day as I do," he whined.

Their boats, generally docked at their houses, were fast and ready to zip into action when floating bales were dropped from the sky or delivered in some other manner. The Cowboys were experts in "night fishing." Planes flown in from Colombia on a full moon night with lights out were impossible to detect. At prearranged spots, the Colombians would drop their packages. Engines on idle in the dark, the Cudjoe Key boys would-be lying-in wait, sometimes for a guy who might have had only ten hours of flying lessons. That explained how some fishing holes had grown up around small planes permanently parked below the surface and now providing safe breeding grounds for fish, crabs and other aquatic creatures.

All in all, the Cowboys were cool. Their faster boats and knowledge of the local waters acquired since early childhood put the thinly staffed Coast Guard and local marine patrols at a huge disadvantage.

Sam was convinced the Wilkies could be the new cowboys in town. They knew the waters intimately. Every twist and turn. Every narrow channel and its tidal hazards. Every mangrove. But now he was getting a reality check. He was learning the game was more difficult than it seemed. And potentially a good deal more dangerous.

That was because there was a problem. A big problem. The family's trial run, which was to pay for the unforgettable Disney Princess wedding, had experienced an embarrassing and potentially expensive glitch. Overwhelmed by a disastrous case of panic, nervous Earl had fumbled, big-time.

"Sss … sss … Sam, I'm sorry, bro. I was sh …sure the cops had their eye on me."

Believing he had been spotted by the marine patrol, an adrenaline-fueled Earl had chucked the goods overboard wrapped in a large fishing net weighted down with an anchor for later retrieval. He couldn't believe how quick-thinking he was. The bales would be so easy to retrieve if they were wrapped up in netting like a neatly wrapped birthday present. He wasn't as stupid as his brother always told him he was.

Sadly, Earl hadn't counted on three things.

The packages, weighed down by the large net and anchor, had sunk deeper than anticipated. Jesus had grabbed his stuff, holding on firmly.

The incoming weather was making boating conditions less than desirable—making retrieval difficult.

In the distance, a solo dive boat was directly headed his way, bringing potential prying eyes.

He pulled away and motored towards some near-shore mangroves to wait out the tourist boat. When he returned, the load wrapped in the net was gone. How had the stuff managed to float away? For twenty minutes, he puttered all around the statue. No sign of the packages.

Not knowing what to do, he headed back to Big Pine.

Tiffani's sobs were getting louder. The veins in Sam's neck throbbed. "You dumbass! You ditched them in the best-known dive and snorkel spot in Key Largo, maybe the whole world. You had one job. Get the shipment safely from here to there. Mama is going to be really pissed."

But that wasn't the worst of it. With the Cudjoe Cowboys in the clink, Sam and Earl were being test-driven by their prospective new Colombian partners. But with four marijuana bales lost, they were off to the worst possible start.

"Now that asshole Colombian Rico is threatening me. He wants to know where his load is. If we don't get it to him within the week, we're fucking toast. How do I know you didn't take it for yourself? You little dipshit. If I get wind you double-crossed me, I'll kill you."

Spit sprayed out of his mouth as he yelled at his brother. Earl stared at him wild-eyed. How could Sam possibly believe his own brother would rip him off? Sometimes Sam could be a real asshole.

"Rico wants those packages," Sam moaned. "If we don't find his stuff, I'm on the hook for over a hundred grand plus interest."

And these were guys you really didn't want to fuck with.

The mention of the "state park" and "Key Largo" suddenly resonated with the twins. "Funny you should mention that," mumbled Belle as she reached into her pocketbook.

She held up a Captain Deep Dive's Snorkel and Dive Adventures matchbook with a guy's face on it. "Hey," she said, "this is the guy who bragged to us that he had picked up some bales at Pennekamp." Belle tossed the matchbook at Sam.

"Pennekamp?"

Loose lips sink ships.

10

BARRACUDA

~ Heart ~

After a sleepless night, the Wilkie brothers arrived at dawn at Islamorada's Paradise Isle. The one-hour drive had been filled with insulting language and threats. "He'll give us them packages or I'll kill that asshole," yelled Sam, his Hawaiian shirt flapping in the wind.

"Yeah," echoed Earl.

As they eased into the parking lot, all was quiet except for humming generators and a few idling diesel boat engines. A radio somewhere was softly playing elevator music.

The sun was gently but brilliantly creeping out of the Atlantic as Sam and Earl stepped out of the shiny red TR7 to stroll among the boats. Captains and mates were rummaging around, filling ice chests, checking bait wells and various kinds of gear, getting ready for their day on the water. The dew-damp docks were soaked with familiar smells of old fish guts and diesel fuel. A couple of brown pelicans and a large white heron flapped around looking for an early-morning handout. Some boats, where the captains lived, were running their air-conditioning units, cooling the otherwise stuffy interior cabins.

A couple of the larger boats featured TV sets. Weather forecasters were predicting bright sun and moderate-to-low wind at ten knots for

South Florida with temperatures in the high eighties. In other words, another chamber-of-commerce-perfect Keys day, the kind of day that brought visitors from all over the world for fishing, diving, snorkeling or, in this case, searching for missing square groupers.

"I . . . I . . . I see it."

"Quit pointing, dingdong." Stan slapped his brother's hand down.

Berthed at the very end of the dock was *The Reel Upside*. Deep Dive was readying air tanks and dive gear. As they approached the boat, Sam turned to Earl. "Go find a phone. Hurry up! Tell your girls to get their asses up and come pick up my car. And there better not be a scratch on it when I get home."

He moseyed around until Earl returned.

"Hey, we want to charter your boat," shouted Sam.

Deep Dive looked up. "Sorry, booked out."

"No, you don't understand," said Sam. At first glance, he looked like an ordinary touron in his Hawaiian shirt and Polaroid camera slung around his neck. "We're gonna charter your boat."

Deep Dive was mildly irritated. "C'mon, guy, I said I'm full."

Sam jumped onto the back of the boat next to Deep Dive. "I'll pay whatever you need to cover your bookings and then some."

"Can't do that. My customers are due here any minute now."

Sam flashed an obscene wad of cash. It represented a lot more than the day's charter would bring in, maybe even a week. "I'm gonna make it worth your while."

Already regretting the lost opportunity provided by the missing bales, Deep Dive hesitated. The sting from the lost bales would be a little less painful if he took what was being offered. After several more minutes of negotiation, he found himself holding an extremely generous payment. The indecision window had quickly snapped shut. "Okay, let's go," he said. Two private charters in a week. Cha-ching.

Deep Dive was feeling better. "Happy to have you. Hop on board, guys."

As they pulled away from the dock, the first half of his scheduled group, a family with four loud children, were bewildered to see the boat departing without them.

"Hey, hey! You forgot us!" the father yelled as he bounced his fussy toddler on his hip.

"Too bad, so sad," muttered Deep Dive as *The Reel Upside* slipped through the narrow access channel and out into the Atlantic. The upside in this case? He wouldn't have to deal with whining, screeching children. And even better–two adult customers had paid the fee upfront, in cash, plus some. The IRS wouldn't see a penny from this job. It was going to be a fine, fine day.

"Aye-aye, matey, Shep at your service," said a muscular figure emerging from the cabin.

The brothers hadn't counted on another person. "Who the hell is this guy?"

"Shep's my part-time mate. We're going to make sure you guys have an amazing snorkeling adventure today. The weather is perfect. Not a cloud in the sky!"

That, of course, was correct. The rain clouds had cleared from the day before. But as Deep Dive was about to find out, the adventure was not exactly what he was expecting.

Blinded by a fistful of money, Deep Dive hadn't considered that the two men were hardly dressed for a snorkeling or dive trip. In fact, they were an unlikely pair. The main guy in the Hawaiian shirt was short, stocky, almost Keys scruffy. His head was fixed directly onto his body. The other guy, tall and gangly, wearing Western-style jeans, with a hand that resembled a lobster claw, stuttered as he talked. The two were dressed like they would be just hanging out, not diving. Odd. Even odder, they had asked to go to Barracuda Reef on the outer edge of the reef clusters. How would a couple of tourists even know about it?

At Barracuda Reef, an obscure dive spot normally not frequented by out-of-towners, the mood changed. "Stop here," yelled Sam over the noise of the engine. Sam was no longer smiling. Deep Dive pulled the boat to a halt and threw his anchor into the water, oblivious to the damage to the coral below.

No, it wasn't just their dress or manners or the camera around the guy's neck. It wasn't just the tone of voice and the frowns that disturbed Deep Dive. It was the very menacing Smith & Wesson .38 Special revolver pointed at his stomach.

"Okay, where is it?" said Sam.

"What the fuck? Where is what?" said a truly surprised Deep Dive.

"You know what I'm talking about, asshole. I know you've got it."

Shep stepped backwards, away from the conversation. He had put on his best don't look at me, I got nothing to do with this crap face.

"I don't have nothin'. What in the hell are you talking about?" shouted Deep Dive. It was gradually dawning on him what this guy was about. But how could he possibly know? Nobody knew! Nobody.

Well, almost nobody.

"You know what I'm talking about. If you don't turn it over, you and your buddy here are going to end up in a chum bag."

Deep Dive was never known as a quick thinker. Clever at times, perhaps, but never quick. Who could he throw under the bus? Juan? Barry?

"I don't know what you're talking about," he said, trying to buy time.

"Looks like you're going to be fish bait," said Sam, waving the gun at Deep Dive. "This tub of yours will end up as reef material."

The Reel Upside was the closest thing Deep Dive had to something of value. He couldn't afford to lose it.

"Hey, hold on . . . you talkin' about a couple of packages in the water out here?"

Suspicion confirmed. "You fucking know I am."

That wasn't good. Somehow this goon knew about the packages. Right now, it didn't matter how. It only mattered what to do about it. The waving revolver was making him increasingly nervous.

"I, um, well, look, I did find a couple of packages out here a day ago. But last night, they disappeared from my boat. I've racked my brain. I have no clue where they are. Somebody took them off my boat. I swear to God."

Shep jumped in. "He's telling the truth, man. Somebody jacked them last night. I helped him look for 'em."

Sam clenched his fists and pounded the side of the boat. "That's bullshit! You guys have got 'em. They're mine. I want 'em. Now! Or you're out of business. Sunk. Permanently."

Deep Dive swallowed hard. He could kick himself. If only he had kept his drunken lips shut. A total doofus move. "I told ya, I don't have 'em. Somebody took 'em."

Earl emerged from the cabin where he had turned the place upside down. "I've looked all over. There's nothing here."

Sam threatened to sink *The Reel Upside*, but the boat was too valuable to plunge it to the bottom of the Atlantic.

Besides, he needed it to get home.

After a few more minutes of menacing intimidation, it became apparent to Sam that he was flogging a dead horse. Nevertheless, there was a steep price to pay for messing with the Wilkie family courier service. He thought of Mama Pearl's motto – an eye for an eye. It was only fair. If they wouldn't give him his bales back, he could sell the boat to cover his loss at least partially. Or he could use it at the fish and bait shop.

"Time for a swim," said Sam. "Clothes off. Chop-chop."

Deep Dive seemed to stop at his boxer shorts. "N . . . n . . . no, everything." Earl waved the revolver. "W . . . w . . . we're not, you know . . ." He demonstrated what he was trying to imply with a limp wrist motion.

Turning their backs to the boat pirates, Shep and Deep Dive stripped and with minimal further urging jumped off the boat. Both were bare except for Shep's sunglasses. Swimming through swarms of Portuguese man-o'-war jellyfish, getting stung with each stroke, Deep Dive and Shep paddled out to William Howard Taft Lighthouse, a rusty metal skeletal pyramidal tower decommissioned years earlier. Both men struggled as they climbed out of the water onto the platform. Despite the warm salty water and air, both men were shivering.

Sam raised his Polaroid camera to get a picture of the two bare-assed idiots hanging on. Taunting the naked men, Earl pulled the charter fee out of Deep Dive's wallet, waving the bills in the air, smiling ear to ear.

Sam couldn't make out the strange ink on Shep's dangling participle, a tattoo only visible when he had no pants on. It had been there since a very raucous party of tequila shots and quaaludes several years earlier. Whatever that thing was supposed to be, it cracked Earl up.

"You can't leave us out here!" Shep screamed.

"Oh yeah? You boys need some uninterrupted time to think your answers through. We'll be in touch. Real soon."

Sam and Earl pointed *The Reel Upside* back to Big Pine. Sam couldn't wait to add the Polaroid pic of the two blockheads clinging bare-ass naked to the tower to his prized Board of Shame.

Once the boat chugged out of earshot, Shep and Deep Dive summoned up enough courage to shout "Assholes!" at *The Reel Upside* as it gradually disappeared on the horizon.

Shep was, shall we say, less than happy to pay the price for Deep Dive's stupidity and loose tongue. The two men spent a very hot, sunbaked afternoon surrounded by huge barracudas, circling hungry sharks and other questionable ocean life, threatening them, taunting them. Nature's bait.

Just as the sun began to slip down into the ocean, a small boat emerged out of the distance, gradually heading their way. Hallelujah!

They could see it wasn't a typical Keys boat. As it drew closer, Deep Dive and Shep could see three scruffy men with straw hats puttering toward them. Slowly the craft approached. Deep Dive and Shep could barely speak, their throats parched after a painful day without water. They were saved.

"*Hola, amigos. ¿Key West?*"

Carlos Suarez was also relieved. He could see land only seven or eight miles ahead. Hopefully it was Key West, where his brother Jorge was waiting for him. He had reached America, ninety miles from their starting point two days before. He rubbed his tired, burning eyes. Now in front of them was an unusual sight. Two naked *americanos* clinging to the hot metal railings, holding on for dear life.

The Florida Keys Statue of Liberty?

In broken Spanish, Deep Dive and Shep convinced the salt-and-wind tattered Cubans to take them onto what was obviously a homemade boat powered by an ancient and noisy outboard motor. It was a sight for very sore—in fact, painfully swollen—eyes. They jumped into the water, paddling through more stinging jellyfish to crawl onto the rickety refugee craft that now barely held them all. The Cubans politely tipped their straw hats to welcome them on board praying their small boat would not capsize.

Deep Dive and Shep were sunburned on body parts that usually didn't see the light of day. Adding to their misery, they were blistered from various stings and bites. Shep recalled a useful Boy Scouts lesson; painful jellyfish stings were best eased with human urine. But the two of them were so dehydrated they had no urine left. Their bladders were as dry as an empty beer can. They suffered the stings. There was no way they were going to ask the Cubans to piss on them.

For a brief moment, Shep thought perhaps the swelling of his manhood might be a blessing—that was, until the pain returned. One of the Cubans had a small handheld radio. Carly Simon was singing— "You're So Vain."

Using hand signals and an elementary version of Spanglish, the overexposed sun-poisoned boys directed the Cubans back to Shep's house in Islamorada.

11

SMOKE TWO JOINTS
~ The Toyes ~

"You're an asshole."

"No, you're an asshole."

"Do you mind?"

"Mind what?"

"Quit tapping on the aquarium glass! You're upsetting Trixi." Shep's favorite new cutie, a vibrant green baby iguana, slid under a lettuce leaf, seeking shelter from the noise.

The bickering between Deep Dive and Shep confused the poor Cubans. They had just endured a nail-biting voyage from Havana to reach the promised land. They were tired, thirsty, hungry and not in the mood for these two Yankee imbéciles at a moment of relief and triumph.

If only Miguel had been on time, Carlos and his two cousins would have left with the larger group instead of risking the journey in a fragile single boat. It was a life-and-death gamble to head out solo into the Atlantic in a less-than-seaworthy craft. Nevertheless, they had made it to somewhere in the Keys, not the intended target of Key West where his brother Jorge and other recently arrived family members were waiting for them.

For the moment, they were stuck in Shep's smelly living room, surrounded by aquariums filled with iguanas and other scaly lizards. Across the room, wrapped around a table leg, was a very large and beady-eyed python.

"What the hell did you get me into?" Shep shouted. "Look at me! I look hideous! If any of this," he said, pointing to various body parts, "is permanent, I don't know what I'll do to you." Shep and Deep Dive were more consumed with themselves than being gracious hosts to the three refugees who had rescued them.

"I'm really sorry, man. How would I know this would happen? I'll make it up to you, dude."

"Yeah, sure."

Squatting on his grandmother's vintage velvet tuxedo-style sofa, a towel wrapped around his nakedness, Shep attempted to direct the cool draft from a floor fan up under his towel. He prayed the cooling sensation would give some relief to his uncomfortable burned and blistered bits.

Shep dug through the ashes of a shell ashtray to retrieve a half-smoked joint. He lit it, inhaled and attempted to pass it to the bewildered Cubans crammed next to him. Carlos and his companions waved their hands to decline.

"Agua," Carlos pleaded once more with hand motions toward his parched throat. They hadn't had much to drink for nearly a day.

"Ya, ya, sure, buddy," he said, finally acknowledging one of his rescuer's needs. Shep patted around underneath the couch. He scored an old forgotten can and handed Carlos the warm Pabst Blue Ribbon to share.

Josephine, Shep's beloved eleven-foot-long pet python, slithered by. It wasn't her suppertime yet, but the people in her room had made her restless. Shep gave her a loving stroke.

In horror, the Cubans swiftly raised their feet. Carlos grimaced. Had he risked his life on the open sea to get to America only to be dinner for a giant snake? Clearly, she was eyeing him. He didn't trust that devilish serpent one bit.

Cousin Miguel felt a trickle of warm moisture in his pants.

"C'mon buddy, show me some love." Deep Dive reached for the doobie in Shep's hand.

A still-peeved Shep unwillingly shared his joint. Deep Dive attempted to take a toke, but it went out. "Throw me those matches. This thing is dead."

Deep Dive caught the matchbook with his left hand and looked at it. There was an air of familiarity. He had seen it before. Where? Of course, the twins at the Tiki Shak. "How do you know Belle and Tinker?"

"Huh? What are you talking about?"

"You know, the twins from last night," said Deep Dive. "The ones who were really into me."

"Ha! You mean the ones that blew you off?" scoffed Shep.

"Shut the hell up. It's not like you scored last night." *And by the looks of your fucked-up face, you won't anytime soon*, Deep Dive thought.

"Where did you get them matches?"

"I lifted them from your boat last night, dummy. What's it to you, anyhow?" Shep asked.

A car motor sputtered outside. Micki, Hibiscus and Barry waltzed through the sliding glass doors to a sight they couldn't have imagined. A shirtless Shep, severely sunburned and swollen, was sitting on the couch with a towel around his waist next to three disheveled strangers wearing large straw hats and bewildered expressions. They looked very much out of place.

The girls giggled nervously, not sure how to process the scene in front of them. "Um . . . what the frick did we just walk into?" Micki suspiciously inquired.

"Like to introduce us to your friends?" chuckled Barry, barely stifling a laugh but unable to conceal a grin.

Shep recounted in detail the horror of the day, occasionally shooting Deep Dive the death stare. He described the two goons who paid for a special excursion and then forced them at gunpoint to strip and swim to Taft Lighthouse, where they baked in the scorching Florida sun until the Cubans showed up.

Gone was *The Reel Upside*. The jellyfish stings still hurt. Their faces were badly blistered. The only skin that remained untouched by the sun, thanks to his Ray-Bans, was the area around Shep's eyes. He now resembled a rabid raccoon.

The girls look stunned at the sideshow of misfits. Thoughts and questions ricocheted through their brains. Deep Dive had been truthful after all. So, who in the hell were these characters that stranded them in the Atlantic? Where was *The Reel Upside*?

"Wacky tobaccy to the right, please." Barry gently sucked in the smoke, allowing it to cool in his mouth slightly before inhaling it into his lungs. Always a thoughtful guy, he implemented the "one puff, two puff, pass" rule. Proper smoking etiquette. It was only right to make the communal experience fair to all.

"Holy cow, bro! Those were the dudes the weed belonged to? How the hell did they track your ass down?" Barry asked in between coughs.

"Beats me," Deep Dive replied sheepishly. His face turned an even redder shade.

Barry kept firing questions. "So, what did these guys look like? Have you seen them before?"

"Too many questions, man! Slow down. You're killing my buzz." Deep Dive took another toke.

"I dunno. One guy looked like a fat-ass troll in a stupid Hawaiian shirt. The other guy was tall and angular with a mermaid tattoo on his arm. He talked weird, too. Sort of like Laurel and Hardy, but a lot uglier."

"Yo, don't forget the tall guy was down two fingers," interjected Shep as he carefully smeared Vaseline on his blistered body parts.

Juan, on his day off from bartending at the Tiki Shak, opened the sliding glass door and entered, taking in the collection of crazy in front of him. "What is this? A Saturday Night Live skit?"

Shep and Deep Dive breathlessly recounted the story again, describing how the hotheaded no neck guy with the Hawaiian shirt and the gangly guy with the gun threatened to kill them over the missing bales, then stranding them on the scorching skeletal pyramidal tower lighthouse and taking off in Deep Dive's boat. The confused Cubans on the couch had somehow been left out of the retelling of the day's events.

Juan's palms started to sweat. These people sounded dangerous. He patted his upper lip with his sleeve.

A shaky, tired voice from the couch jolted him back to the moment.

"*¿Hablas español?*"

"*Sí,*" Juan replied.

Carlos filled Juan in on his version of the day's events, including their unnerving ocean voyage from Havana. The now-stoned, non-Spanish speakers in the room were able to make out a few words, "¿Dónde estamos?, Cabrón, loco . . ."

Micki was watching her old high school flame, Juan. He was acting weirdly. Why was he not more inquisitive about the situation? He seemed nervous. And sweaty.

Fist raised, Barry started shouting, distracting Micki from her thoughts. "Let's find those fuckers!" A *Norma Rae* moment.

"Really, Barry? How are we going to do that? You gonna ask your Magic Eight Ball for directions?" Hibiscus jeered.

"Very funny. C'mon, let's figure this out. Let's go over it again. What actually happened last night?"

Deep Dive recounted the hazy evening at the Tiki Shak, admitting he had told Micki and Hibiscus about the goodies on his boat. All eyes turned toward the girls.

"Don't look at us! Deep Dive told us. But . . . but we had nothing to do with this," said Micki. "Puh-leeze."

Hibiscus nodded aggressively in agreement.

Juan, feeling a sudden urge to take a leak, removed himself from the conversation. He headed toward the bathroom before wandering into the kitchen for Doritos and water for his new Spanish-speaking friends. Juan's self-removal did not go unnoticed by Micki.

"What's with him?"

Hibiscus shrugged her shoulders.

When he returned, Barry was still grilling Shep and Deep Dive. Shep brought up the twins, throwing the matches at Barry. "Hey, the chicks that Deep Dive was slobbering over gave him these matches."

"Well, did you mention anything to them?"

"Maybe...?"

"What the hell, maybe? You either did or didn't. Fess up, man!"

Deep Dive's look said it all. Shep, Barry and the girls groaned. This guy would never learn.

"You think Deep Dive's twins have a connection with Laurel and Hardy?" Hibiscus asked.

For Micki, a bit of fresh clarity. "How else would they know Deep Dive had their square groupers? The twins must have told them."

Hibiscus appeared confused. "So did the twins take the bales?" One puff, two puff, three puff, pass. She handed what was left of the joint to Juan.

Barry observed Hibiscus's extra puff. Rudeness noted.

"Good question. A definite possibility. Only one thing is for certain– someone took the bales and did not return them to their owners."

"I think we need to pay the One-Eyed Pelican a visit. Can't hurt to see if the boat's there. Juan, girls, you in? Deep Dive, you want *The Reel Upside* back?" Adrenaline coursed through Barry's body, fueling his rash decision.

Humiliated by the day's events, Deep Dive nervously ran his fingers through his sandy-blond hair. He had to get his boat back.

Juan swallowed hard. Maybe it hadn't been his best idea to poach Deep Dive's find. At this point, his only option was to save his own ass. Wasn't it best to keep harmony within his friend circle? There was no need to divulge the reality that he had snuck away from the bar after the whiny New Yorker left, grabbed the prize from *The Reel Upside* and hidden the bales in his car.

Playing along with Barry's plan made the most sense. Divert suspicion. Unless . . . he wanted to man up and tell them he was the asshole who triggered the whole mess. Nah, that didn't sound appealing or smart. "*Remain calm, remain calm,*" he kept repeating to himself.

"Big Pine it is!" Barry declared.

Juan replied with a half-hearted thumbs-up.

Shep and Deep Dive thought it best to lay low. They didn't want another run-in with Laurel and Hardy and their shiny Smith and Wesson.

Carlos had his own agenda. "¿Teléfono?"

12

EVERYBODY WANTS TO RULE THE WORLD

~ Tears for Fears ~

The truck cab was boiling. Four clammy friends, crammed into the front of Barry's father's 1960s sewage pumper truck, felt as comfortable as hot-tubbing in a pot of simmering swiss cheese fondue as they bumped along the narrow two-lane US-1. Their drive took them south over many of the forty-two bridges that linked the Keys, including the world-famous Seven Mile Bridge. Their damp cotton shirts clung to them like plastic wrap. Without rain, there would be no cooling. With no air conditioning, it was a rolling sauna. As the girls would say, a really bad hair day.

Over the ocean, the sky was dark with occasional flashes of lightning. Even with a breeze blowing through the rolled-down windows, the oppressive humidity was unbearable. The smell from the cracked leather seats, tobacco residue, sweaty bodies and a tank nearly full of poop was one degree short of nauseating. The truck bounced over potholes, sloshing its load. The passengers bounced on squeaky seat springs.

Barry just wanted to find *The Reel Upside* and the two goons who'd stolen it. Now he was having second thoughts about going to Big Pine. Had he been too gung-ho last night? Did he really want to get mixed up in the Deep Dive drama?

Squeezed against Barry, Hibiscus squirmed. "Move your slimy, sweaty leg over. Gross. I can't take much more of this."

"Relax, we're almost there," Barry replied as they rolled over the North Pine Channel bridge.

With each mile, a prickly Hibiscus was enjoying the ride less. "Barry, this was a stupid idea."

Micki attempted to lighten the mood. "Hey, remember the soft serve sprinkle fiasco? It's as sticky in here as it was in Barry's dad's car our sophomore year. We were so baked, the ice cream melted all over us. Roo had to hose off the inside of the car and us. Barry, I don't think I ever saw your sister so mad."

The friends chuckled at the memory, just one of many shared by this tight group of four.

Crammed on the outside door next to Micki, Juan had no complaints about sitting next to his ex. It was physically the closest he'd been to her since they broke up. Sweat and all, she still smelled good. There was something about her wavy brown hair, her very presence. So close once again, but still so far. Micki shifted in her seat, trying to get comfortable. Somehow her hand touched Juan's leg. He grinned.

Micki peered out the open window, feeling the salty sea air on her skin. On the left side of the bridge was the gusty but gorgeous Atlantic decorated like a cake with scattered whitecaps against a dark sky. On the right, the Gulf of Mexico was more tranquil. A bonefish guide with a client on a flats boat was casting with the wind, a living portrait of the two-ocean view uniquely associated with the bridges and enthusiastically highlighted in vacation ads and articles about the Keys.

On Big Pine, nothing characterized old Florida more than the One-Eyed Pelican Fish and Bait House. Originally, a small conch house selling bait, cigarettes, beer and Mason canning jars just off the Overseas Highway, the place had grown over the years into a full-fledged trading post or general store, selling groceries, ice cream, chewing tobacco, fishing tackle, T-shirts, aspirin, bathing suits, sunscreen, condoms and other essential provisions. And if you knew what to ask for, a bit of weed.

Locals tied their boats up at the dock out back to buy provisions and fuel. Mama Pearl was happy to make bologna and mustard sandwiches and provide them with ice for a day out on the water. If she was feeling chatty or liked you, she would share her special recipe to keep mold off your paper currency.

It was common practice to store newfound, undocumented money in Mason jars and bury them in the backyard. Unfortunately, due to the humid environment, there were serious downsides to underground banking. Mold quickly grew on paper, and the distinct damp smell of buried bills was recognizable. Entrepreneur Pearl had come up with a foolproof recipe to keep the bills fresh and clean as a whistle. Before too long, Pearl's mold-free money method was highly popular. There was, therefore, an ongoing demand for Mason jars in the Keys.

"Here we go. Destination straight ahead." Barry slowed the truck.

"Okay, Juan and I will go in and shovel up some BS. Full distraction action. Tell 'em the Septic Baron got a call for a septic tank problem. Micki, and Hibiscus, check out the dock. See if *The Reel Upside* is there. That's all we want. Nothing more. Just confirm the boat is there. Let's not make a scene. Play it cool, you know."

Wearing the Septic Baron's bright yellow company shirts with the company slogan on the back, Barry and Juan entered the building. Greeting them at the cash register was a tall, gangly man. A mermaid tattoo peeked out from under his sleeve. More noticeable was the man's oddly shaped hand missing two fingers.

"Www . . . www . . . what can I do you for?" stammered Earl. "Bait? Gas?"

"Hi. We received an emergency call that your septic tank is full. It needs to be checked, immediately. You'd hate for that thing to blow."

"Shooot. That don't sound good." Earl called out to his mother, Pearl, who was filling up a chum bag between sips of Old Milwaukee. "Hey, Mama, d . . . d . . . do ya know anything aaa . . . aaa . . . about this?"

"Boy, what the hell ya talkin' about? Ask Sam," she shouted.

"Hold up, bbb . . . bbb . . . boys. Let me fff . . . fff . . . find my brother." Earl went looking for Sam. Why hadn't Sam mentioned this? It must have slipped his mind.

Barry nudged Juan. "Psst, did you see his arm? The guys got a mermaid tattoo in American traditional style. Classy. A real clean job, I might add."

Barry had not yet reached that level of tattooing. It was on his to-do list. But first things first.

Outside, Micki and Hibiscus casually strolled down to the dock. The boat was sitting there. But something had changed. "*Reelly*" changed! The pirates had crudely spray-painted over the word "Upside." Deep Dive's beloved boat was now *The Reel Downside*.

Ouch. That was going to sting. Captain Deep Dive would not be happy.

"Shh, follow me," said Micki. She and Hibiscus walked to the back of the building. They paused at the rear door, listening for voices. Silence. The door squeaked as Micki slowly opened it. No one was there. Pulling Hibiscus with her, she quietly tip-toed in.

The small office reeked of tobacco smoke and stale beer. In one corner, papers were strewn over a cluttered desk holding an ashtray, several empty Old Milwaukee cans and a half-eaten bologna sandwich. The ashtray had not been emptied in a very long time. A spider had created a small web on the window's upper edge. A multicolored crochet blanket hung over a chair. Most interesting was a row of Mason jars lined up on a shelf, crammed with bills and an odd powdery substance. In several of the jars, they could make out $100 designations.

Hibiscus pointed at the jars. "Crapola! You see what's in those jars?"

"Don't even think about it," Micki whispered.

Pictures covered a large cork board above the desk. A yellow Post-it note read, "Rico called. Where you at?" Two large dollar signs followed the question. Above, a handmade wooden plaque read, "Deuteronomy 19:21 Thus you shall not show pity: life for life, eye for eye, tooth for tooth, hand for hand, foot for foot."

Peering at the photos, it was immediately evident they weren't about happy family moments. Rather, most of them showed people in questionable, compromising and even uncomfortable positions.

"Creepy . . .," said Micki. "And . . ." She stopped, surprised by what she saw. Two very familiar faces.

Front and center on the cork board, hanging on to William Howard Taft Lighthouse, stood a very naked Shep and Deep Dive. It was definitely them. Their looks defined distraught. What caught Micki's attention, however, was something else.

She zeroed in on the Polaroid picture. What in the world? What was that? A worm tattoo? Happily, Micki was not familiar with that "thing."

If Barry was responsible for that monstrosity, he needed to rethink his dream of becoming a tattoo artist. The wonky dolphin on her foot and Shep's questionable slithering creature were not something Barry should showcase in his tattoo portfolio. Barry needed to stay in the poop business.

A topless plastic hula girl was also on the desk. Unmistakable. Hibiscus had given it to Deep Dive the year before. Attached was Deep Dive's key to his dive boat. Impulsively, she grabbed it. Hearing a large commotion, she reached for Micki's hand. "Let's go!" The girls took off running towards *The Reel Downside*.

Sam had been located, a colorful presence in his Hawaiian-style shirt. A stormy moment followed. "What the hell you talkin' about? It might blow? Our septic system is fine! What is this? Who called ya?" His face turned a darker maroon with each question.

Were these two guys in yellow shirts undercover government/DEA agents? Was he going down like the Cudjoe Cowboys? Maybe these punks were just looking for a quick buck. Or were they just full of shit? Sam didn't like the feel of this.

"Sorry, mister. We must have read our paperwork wrong. Is this the Salty Dog Fish and Bait House?" Barry and Juan backed out the door without waiting for an answer.

Sam followed them out. "What are you two clowns talking about? There's no place 'round here called—"

Before Sam could finish his sentence, the sound of a revving boat engine distracted him from his tirade. Looking around the building, he could see his new possession, *The Reel Downside*, sliding away from the dock. Two attractive but unfamiliar women were heading out to sea with his newly captured boat.

Pearl stopped filling the chum bags for a minute to light a cigarette and take a sip of her fifth Old Milwaukee of the day. Uncharacteristically quiet, she took in the scene. She dropped a half-filled chum bag in a bucket and mumbled Deuteronomy 19:21 quietly to herself: "Thus you shall not show pity."

Barry and Juan stood in shocked silence. They hadn't anticipated Micki and Hibiscus doing something as ballsy as taking the boat. That wasn't part of the original plan.

With Sam distracted, the boys panicked. They jumped into the truck, hastily cranked it up and, without looking, backed into Sam's beloved ruby-red Triumph TR7. Sam was now shouting incoherently. His arms swung wildly like Grape Ape's. This was no longer about just a couple of missing square groupers.

The boys sped north on US-1 as fast as the heavy poop-filled truck could go, bouncing, rattling and making other disturbing noises.

13

DIRTY DEEDS DONE DIRT CHEAP
~ AC/DC ~

Juan and Barry's adrenaline levels were bubbling like hot water on a stove as they rumbled north on US-1, constantly checking the rearview mirrors. The truck was straining at close to its top speed of forty-five miles an hour. Passing through Islamorada and finally reaching Tavernier, there was still no sign of the red Triumph. They high-fived. Relieved. They had escaped immediate danger.

Freed from their pursuers, Juan called for a quick pit stop at Peter, Dick and Willy's before returning the truck. As luck would have it, the weekly Manic Monday Happy Hour was an all-day affair. Owner Chuck Feelers had often wondered why bars would limit "happy" to an hour.

The boys deserved a beer or two and, yes, something to eat while winding down, listening to a recording of the house band, the Bushwhackers, who would play later in the evening. After lunch, they would return the truck. No big deal. They didn't have far to go. The Septic Baron's office was pretty much across the street.

Nevertheless, their nerves remained on edge. "I wonder if it was such a good idea to take the company truck?" Second-guessing can be a troublesome disease, corrupting positive feelings and optimism about the immediate future.

"Whaddya mean?" asked Juan.

"Dude, we screwed this up. We drove down in one of my dad's trucks. We announced ourselves in company shirts. And unless they're deaf, dumb and blind . . . crap, what have we done? Think about it. We dinged his car and the girls took off with the boat. Who the hell knows where Hibiscus and Micki are or what they're up to? Didn't I tell them to stick with the plan? Maybe we should have taken your pickup."

"We dinged? Ah, first of all, I'd call that more than a ding. Secondly, only one of us was driving."

"This is not the time to get technical," Barry replied curtly.

They pulled into the parking lot. Two beers. Tops. And a juicy burger.

They parked the truck on the side of the bar, partially concealing it behind a row of mangroves, difficult to see from the highway. Just in case the little red car showed up. A blackboard next to the door spelled out Peter, Dick and Willy's special. "Soup of the day, draft beer." As they entered the bar, familiar rowdy calls greeted them.

"Cheers," Barry shouted. It always felt great to waltz into a bar where everybody knew your name.

※ ※ ※

Finding the Triumph's fuel gauge close to empty, an irate Sam was forced to drive south to Big Pine's only gas station and wait in line for a precious fifteen minutes for two cars ahead of him to fill up, thereby losing valuable time before he could double back and head north.

"Dammit, Earl, can't you ever follow directions? I told you last night— the car needed gas." He had conveniently forgotten that he discouraged anyone else from driving his prized roadster.

The septic guys were long gone. Those assholes had crossed the line. Frustration bubbling over, Sam was barely in control of himself.

"Fuuuuck!"

Earl nodded obediently as the Triumph roared up the highway, its exhaust pipes crackling. Sam blew past other cars and trucks on the narrow two-lane road, frequently crisscrossing the double yellow line, bouncing over periodic potholes. Somewhere in Lower Matacumbe, the twisted right fender rattled violently before ripping off and flying to the side of the road. It would be a miraculous find for anyone looking for a spare TR7 body part, particularly a red one.

A fuming Sam did not slow down. His mind swirled with questions. His thoughts—foggy at best. Revenge had taken a huge bite and then swallowed his judgment. He would settle it.

Sam and Earl rolled into town as Juan and Barry were sipping their second beer, waiting for their cheeseburgers in paradise. The septic truck was nowhere in sight. But, holy crap, look! The billboard—right there on the road.

"The Septic Baron Tanks and Service. *A Great Day Starts with a Good Dump*!" God was looking out for them after all. A large truck designed for emptying septic tanks was parked in the driveway. Alas, it was not the one they were looking for.

The Wilkie boys sauntered into the office, heavy with the scent of Lysol. Barry's sister Roo looked up from behind the counter. She wasn't expecting the two grumpy strangers. Roo knew most of the company's customers, who mainly came in to pay their bills or discuss some specific service need. Very seldom did strangers drop by unless they had just moved into town and wanted to register for service.

"Can I help you?" she asked.

"We're looking for two of your employees." The rough-looking older guy with no neck and the Hawaiian shirt described Juan and Barry.

Roo rolled her eyes. Whatever mess Barry had gotten himself into, he was on his own. She was not bailing him out.

She wasn't particularly fond of her younger brother, Barry Jr.. He was lazy. He had no work ethic. He had no interest in or vision for the

$ea Weed | 67

business. He was more of a good-time boy, ready at any moment to get the party started.

That was why it drove her crazy that her father was determined to make him heir to the family business. She was older. Far more qualified. More mature. She was proud of her associate degree in accounting from Miami Dade Community College, which made her the first person in her family to ever go to college. Clearly, she was a better fit for running the business than her asshole brother who'd barely graduated high school.

Roo was concerned, rightly so, that Barry would inevitably destroy what her family had proudly built over three generations. The Septic Baron was a respectable company. It was highly regarded in the community. Her father was a former president of the Moose Club. He supported several local charities and Coral Shores High School sports programs.

She had dreams, big dreams, to expand the business. To create a septic tank empire—without her brother. Rebrand the company. The Septic Baroness had a nice ring to it. Meanwhile, her no-good baby brother mainly dreamed of poking people with an ink-filled needle—that was, when he wasn't drinking, smoking pot and poking women with a different kind of needle.

Roo didn't move from behind the counter. She nonchalantly pointed her finger at the bar across the street. The probability was high that the boys would be there. It was Manic Monday Happy Hour after all. The men didn't say what they wanted to talk to the boys about. She didn't care.

"Check over there," she said.

Sam couldn't help himself. Walking out, he rudely blurted, "That Lysol don't hide nothin'. Your place still smells like shit." He slammed the glass door shut behind him, rattling it.

What a peckerhead, she thought.

Peter, Dick and Willy's. He knew that place. His mama used to go there a lot. Sam crossed the road. Sure enough, parked behind some mangrove bushes was the truck.

Amateurs. Idiots, he thought. He whistled to his brother.

Earl stepped out of the Triumph with a stick of musty old dynamite, which the Wilkies kept hidden in their shed. Mama Pearl insisted on always having a few on hand.

In the past, the family had routinely used explosives to carve out or deepen boat channels in shallow areas. It was common practice in parts of the Keys, primarily on New Year's Eve or during July Fourth celebrations, where the illegal explosions would be masked by fireworks.

Sam opened the cover of the gas tank, gently placed the lower tip of the stick in and quickly moved away, leaving his brother standing there.

"Hurry up, Earl. What's taking you so long? Light it up."

Earl lit the fuse and the brothers ran back to the car. Earl was already in short supply of fingers.

In anticipation, Sam raised the Polaroid camera to his face.

"BOOM!"

Two thousand gallons of prime raw sewage and pieces of metal rained down, creating an enormous, unforgettable shitstorm.

Just out of range, Sam and Earl shook their heads to clear the ringing in their ears. They smiled broadly.

Sam had promised himself something was going to blow. He was, after all, a man of his word. "Click" went the Polaroid camera.

14

ONE WAY OR ANOTHER
~ Blondie ~

Their mouths full of half-chewed cheeseburger, Barry and Juan instinctively ducked down as the walls of Peter, Dick and Willy's shook with a monstrous explosion. Customers froze. Dead silence. In a nanosecond, Barry's father's truck had become a smoldering pile of gooey crap.

The combined stench of rotten eggs, week-old garbage, 3 a.m. vomit and an overflowing sunbaked porta-potty drifted in through the air conditioning vents. On its most horrible day, hell could not smell more putrid.

Immediately, the bar emptied out onto the street. Motorcycles and vehicles were covered in disgusting odorous poopy goop. Looking at the carnage, the shocked customers, wearing shorts and Keys standard flip-flops, were overwhelmed by the stench as well as the sight of the poop-drenched wreckage. They pulled up their shirts to cover their noses, revealing hairy beer bellies, tanned stomachs, various scars and boobage. At this moment, the women didn't care who saw what. The stench overwhelmed any thoughts of modesty.

"Gross!"

"Holy crap!"

"What is this? Shit?"

"My Harley!"

"My fucking truck!"

The boys stared blankly at the mess, trying to comprehend what had happened. Barry's sewage truck had strangely exploded.

Glancing across US-1, they spotted the mangled bright red Triumph with a missing fender. Two Big Pine assholes were grinning at them. No-Neck in his bright Hawaiian shirt greeted them with a one-finger salute. The gangly guy with the mermaid tattoo made a slicing gesture across his throat.

Suddenly, Barry was afraid. Deathly afraid. No, not about the rat bastards from Big Pine. Afraid of his dad. Afraid the Septic Baron's wrath would be swift and powerful. Disappointed once again in his intended heir.

Off-duty bartender Juan was equally fearful, for a different reason. He had the goods, but he no longer wanted them. Was it worth being done in by these Florida crackers? No way! For chickenshit Juan, the stress was too much. He began to sweat profusely.

Like a couple of peacocks in full feather, Earl and Sam eased themselves back into the Triumph. They had outdone themselves. They never thought that blowing up shit could be considered a work of art. But that's what it was. A masterpiece!

Sam raised his trusty Polaroid for another snap to add to the corkboard. Their work was too beautiful to be immortalized with just one picture.

"Mama will be proud, don't ya think?"

"I th . . . I th . . . I think so," stammered Earl. "Da . . . da . . . damn. Just like Dirty Harry! Them Cudjoe Cowboys got n . . . n . . . nothin' on us. We're the new c . . . c . . . cowboys in town." He positioned the fingers on his good hand, to look like a pistol as he fired a few imaginary shots at Barry and Juan.

"All right, cowboy, simmer down," said Sam. "We gotta get out of here before the po-po show up." He turned the rattling Triumph south and headed back towards Big Pine. Wailing sirens were drawing closer.

For Juan, the generous present from the Jesus statue was now the curse of the devil. It was an unwanted gift that kept on giving – anxiety and a growing headache. He needed to dispose of the threat quickly without his friends realizing he was to blame for the increasingly threatening chain of events. He was in deep. Too deep. Water was virtually up to his nose. He wanted out of the pool, to be drained of all this craziness.

If he didn't fix things immediately, his dream to bartend on the open seas, on some fancy-ass cruise ship, was hanging on a thread. At least "it" was stashed in a safe place—his parents' house.

※ ※ ※

At the Zamora house, Juan's dad, Enrique, had decided to surprise his wife, Carmen, and clean her highly decorated yard. Lavishly dotted with large statues and some of the world's tackiest figurines, the yard was Carmen's pride and joy. She loved all her statues, but she was particularly fond of her squatting bare-bum garden gnome, the gazing fairy with wings, Bashful the Bigfoot statue, the quiet little Buddha, a guitar-playing frog and, as any sophisticated art lover would appreciate, a large pink flamingo.

The yard was also dotted with a generous selection of rustic metal agave plants topped off with an especially cute stone octopus flipping five birds. That was Carmen's snarky nod to her nosy neighbor Tabby, who for some reason did not appreciate great art and the finer things in life.

Enrique was a gentle soul, viewed by others as a tad boring, always eager to please his wife. And thanks to a nice inheritance, he still had the means to do so. Still, his friends wondered how he'd ever landed such a hottie. Carmen was a serious looker with a striking resemblance to Sophia

Loren or Raquel Welch. Even at fifty-three, she turned heads when she walked into a room.

Pulling weeds from the blindingly white pea rock, seventy-four-year-old Enrique tripped over one of Carmen's gnome figures, stumbling into his wife's beloved oversized granite Neptune, which responded by falling over on him.

"Ayee, Enrique, what's that?" No response. Hurrying to the garden, she was shocked to see Enrique face-planted into the pea rock, the heavy cracked Neptune on top. "What happened? Enrique, you hear me?" Panicked, she ran inside to call 911.

For the emergency dispatchers, the past couple of days had been unusual. In a quiet community where nothing ever seemed to happen beyond occasional boating accidents, a fender bender or dive boat customers with the bends, they had found themselves dealing with a strange tourist death at Seas of Wonder, a sewage truck explosion and now a man trapped under a statue of Neptune.

Out of the ambulance emerged a muscular EMT pushing the rolling stretcher. His puffy sunburned raccoon face was badly blistered. Preoccupied with her husband lying unconscious on the pea rock, Carmen initially didn't recognize him.

You see, this was not Shep's first rushed visit. The previous visit also had been a matter of urgency, but a different kind. Carmen had an itch that badly needed to be scratched. Her beloved Enrique was a good and generous man, bless his heart, but he was as boring as a day of fishing with no catches. She was too young to accept that this part of her life was over. Juan's friend Shep was a strangely appealing young man. It wasn't just his well-developed body. There were lots of young studs around. But this one radiated an electrical charge that pulled her in like a magnet.

Shep at first tried to stay at arm's length. After all, she was his best friend's mom. Carmen, however, was far too experienced and determined not to get what she wanted. She knew how to arouse a naturally horny twenty-four-year-old. His poorly tattooed johnson proved to be the spice she sought, despite the fact that it resembled more worm than snake. For Carmen, the "worm" wiggled just right. For her, the term "emergency" in emergency medical technician had its own definition.

🌿 🌿 🌿

Still shaking and anxious to get away from the exploded poop truck, Juan spotted a purple ten-speed bicycle parked on the side of the building away from the blast. He had to hurry. Barry had his problems. Juan had his own.

As fast as he could pedal, Juan booked it down the highway breathlessly, turning into his neighborhood to find Shep just as he was loading his dad into the back of the ambulance. Closing the ambulance's back doors, Shep yelled "Don't worry, dude. He'll be okay. Your dad's in good hands. Your mom too." Shep gave his buddy a reassuring thumbs-up and shut the back doors of the ambulance.

Inside the compartment, Shep winked at Carmen, then leaned forward for an attempted quick kiss as he started to unzip his pants. "Hey, hot stuff," he said under his breath.

"Shush," she said, quickly looking to see if Enrique had regained consciousness.

Getting his "snake" back into the cage after letting it escape was not easy. Lying on the stretcher, poor unconscious Enrique was oblivious. He had no idea Shep's "worm" was entertaining his wife.

The short reassuring greeting from Shep did little to ease Juan's fears. Not yet knowing what exactly had happened to his dad, Juan wondered if the Big Pine boys had sent another clear message. But how had they tracked him down so quickly? He was sweating profusely from sheer panic.

Juan rushed to his room in the house. Stored in two heavy-duty jumbo black garbage bags shoved into the back of his large closet, the square groupers had been safe from inquiring eyes. Now he had to get rid of them. One at a time, slinging the bags over his shoulder, he hurried down to the dock, where his small skiff, the *NNB Snapper*, was tied. Dumping the bags into the boat, he started the motor and headed toward the Dubicki house on the bay side just a few canals over. It was the only logical place Hibiscus could have taken *The Reel Upside*. He'd try there first.

Now he was going to put this smoking hot potato right back where he'd found it—on *The Reel Upside*. That would take the heat off him and hopefully cool things down.

15

YOU BETTER RUN
~ Pat Benatar ~

News of the explosion at Peter, Dick and Willy's began to circulate. Micki's dad, Michael Wilson, arrived on the scene, ready to investigate the most unusual septic tanker explosion for the local paper. A freak accident? Or something more sinister?

Septic tanker truck explosions were as rare as elephants in pink tutus in a community that billed itself as the dive capital of the world. Of course, occasional propane tank explosions were not unheard of. But a sewage truck? What kind of malfunction could that be? As far as he knew, poop wasn't explosive. Otherwise, every bathroom in the universe would be fitted with a warning sign— "Danger Zone."

There also was the issue of motive. Who could possibly benefit from blowing up one of straitlaced Barry Baron, Sr.'s work trucks? A disgruntled homeowner? An unhappy employee? A jealous Moose Lodge brother? Most of the employees were family members. It didn't make sense.

With a lack of manpower and funds, the case would probably never be fully resolved by the local cops. After many years of reporting on the wonderful and strange goings-on in the Florida Keys, Michael Wilson knew one thing: not every question had an answer.

⚜ ⚜ ⚜

Back in Big Pine at the One-Eyed Pelican, Mama Pearl was tapping her foot to country music on US 1 Radio when the station interrupted with a news flash.

"*This is a US 1 Action News Alert with a pretty, ahem, dirty story. Reports are just coming in of a truck explosion in the parking lot of Peter, Dick and Willy's in Tavernier. Initial police reports are still murky, but it appears a septic tank truck with a full load of sewage exploded in the bar's parking lot. There are no immediate reports of casualties, but vehicles in the parking lot are now said to be covered with number two.*"

The professional newscaster could not control a chuckle and then, his voice cracking, he lost it with a loud, uncontrolled belly laugh.

Laughter is contagious. Mama Pearl roared. She rubbed her hands together. The incident sounded like a Wilkie special. Her boys had delivered a helluva message.

But quickly, little but mighty Mama Pearl began having second thoughts. Her numbskull sons might be drawing too much attention to themselves. Born and raised in the Keys, she had been around the block long enough to know that in implementing vengeance, discretion was the much preferred, and safer, path.

Payback was sweetest when it couldn't be directly linked to the payer. A harmless favorite was the time Pearl had stuffed her neighbor Angie's hollow curtain rod with shrimp heads after she complained about noise made by young Earl and Sam. The hidden rotting crustacean pieces stank up the house so badly the family considered burning the place down before the smell finally dissipated after a few months. To this day, the origins of the mysterious odor still mystified Angie.

It wouldn't be the first time Mama Pearl had had to pull her boys out of a jam. When the boys were caught robbing Skimpy Simpson's stone crab traps, they were threatened with police and even worse. That situation was successfully settled with some cash, a Mason jar of Daddy

Wilkie's moonshine and some weed. But this new mess Sam and Earl had created might not be so easy to scrub clean or bribe their way out of.

Pearl's connections, built up over sixty-plus years, spanned from Key Largo to Key West. If her boys were ever associated with the case, her contacts would be helpful.

She was proud of the Wilkie family name and of her boys for taking action. But for two obvious reasons, pride and prison, Pearl did not want their name associated with the explosion. Already, the explosion was creating an increasing and uneasy amount of attention with bad jokes and lamebrained remarks now being broadcast on the radio. People were making fun of the Wilkie masterpiece. It was distasteful.

"Have you seen the latest Disney movie playing in Tavernier, Shitty Shitty Bang Bang?"

"What did the turd say at Peter, Dick and Willy's? Let's get this potty started!"

"Knock, knock. Who's there? Woody. Woody who? Woody like to hear another poop joke?"

Enough was enough. She had heard enough about the parking lot being covered with "the finest shit" in the Keys. The explosion was meant as a serious threat, not amusement at the Wilkie's expense. Laughing at her family's handiwork was not acceptable. For goodness' sake, who would ever take the Wilkie family seriously again?

For Pearl, however, the more pressing and less visible issue was the asshole Colombians. They wanted their goods in a few short days. Her boys had slashed a hornet's nest with their sloppiness. If the bales weren't returned, the Wilkies owed the Colombians more than what they would have been paid for the job. Far from an ideal situation.

A cigarette perched in the right corner of her mouth; Pearl left a trail of ashes as she ambled into the office. She stood in front of the corkboard, staring at the strange collection of photos.

The Wall of Shame, a reminder of the folks who thought they had one-upped the Wilkies, was a constant source of satisfaction. There was the newspaper clipping of Bum Farto, the former Key West fire chief, a greedy pain in the ass if ever there was one, smirking in his red jumpsuit, unaware Pearl had smeared bird crap all over the back of his pants. That asshole was long gone, though, wasn't he? Pearl smiled at the thought.

Then there was V.C. Matthews, who was caught lightening the One-Eyed Pelican's cash register during the five months she worked there. V.C. was posted on the board in her underwear, drinking like a dog from a dirty toilet bowl.

Mama Pearl's favorite image was a damn Yankee perched like a heron, his ankles and feet encased in wet concrete. What possessed him to think he could start a general store business within spitting distance of the One-Eyed Pelican? That guy was now a state senator back in Delaware.

Tucked under Mr. Delaware's photo was one of their tall, gangly old neighbor Abraham, embracing a poisonwood tree without any pants on. Mama Pearl had never explained why. That picture had been taken by Daddy Wilkie before he died. RIP.

She focused heavily on one picture in particular, the new Polaroid of Shep and Deep Dive, totally naked, hanging on for dear life to the timeworn metal lighthouse. The moment had come to introduce herself to these two asswipes. They had major explaining to do. It was entirely their fault the Wilkies were in such a pickle.

Pearl wanted to know—had those nitwits actually told her boys the truth? Was it possible the square groupers had been lifted off the captain's boat by somebody else? How did the septic guys fit into the picture? Who were the gals who'd driven off with *The Reel Downside*? Where was it now? There were too many unanswered questions for her liking.

She grabbed the Polaroid and slipped it into her baby-blue Members Only jacket pocket. The commercial said, "When you put it on, something happens." Pearl could guarantee something *was* going to happen.

Somebody owed them four stolen bales. She was collecting. The Wilkies weren't going down in flames over a couple of missing square groupers. The Polaroids told the story.

Pearl called her longtime friend Pam, who worked at the Paradise Isle motel. No, *The Reel Upside* had not returned to its dock.

"Okay, if it's not there, where did you doofuses stash it?" As far as she was concerned, they were on the hook until the Colombian debt was cleared up.

There was one person in the Upper Keys she trusted more than anyone, someone she knew would know the two guys in the photo—Bum Farto's former friend and her old drinking and bed buddy, her occasional partner in crime, the mouth of the Keys, Chuck Feelers.

16

THE GAMBLER
~ Kenny Rogers ~

Rico Valentine had been keenly watching the goings on at the One-Eyed Pelican. He was not sure what to make of the septic tank truck that backed into the TR7 earlier in the day. The incident perplexed and concerned him. What were those Big Pine hombres up to? Was the commotion a ruse to trick him? Rico had a lot to think about.

One thing was certain. It had interfered with collections. Sam had driven out of the parking lot like the Tasmanian Devil and had not returned. Rico was in no mood to wait. He was getting restless sitting in the hot van. Perhaps it was time to go inside the Wilkie establishment and say hello to the family.

He glanced at his face in the rearview mirror, noticing some long, unruly eyebrow hairs that had somehow escaped being trimmed. Rico opened the glove box and retrieved a leather nail kit. He unzipped it and took out a small pair of scissors. Very carefully, he cut the longer hairs to match the size and shape of his manicured black eyebrows. Much better. While he was at it, he slightly snipped his manly, thick mustache. It was facial hair Sam could only dream of.

Being well-groomed was important to Rico. When you looked good, you felt good. He liked what he saw. *¡Madre mía! Call la policía. Dju chould be locked up for looking so handsome!* Officer Frank Poncherello, from the popular TV show CHiPs, had nothing on him. Well, maybe one thing. Perfect picture-book teeth.

Rico's smile, an unfortunate flaw, was offset by his major feature—two oversized mismatched Bugs Bunny front teeth. A large gap between them showcased shoddy dental work, necessitated by a slight mishap during an initiation ritual.

The cartel had destroyed his God-given pearly whites.

A Colombian who had relocated to Miami, Rico was a resident of the Carlita Hotel near Government Cut on South Beach. His boss, cartel *jefe* Felize Mendoza, enjoyed putting new recruits through the wringer to see what they were made of. At headquarters in Medellín, his favorite game was Bolos Humanos, a.k.a. Human Bowling, sometimes called Bolos Por Pesos—earning money for each person knocked down.

The rules were simple. Five human pins would kneel at the bottom of a hill. At the top of the hill, a human ball would have to curl up and launch himself down the hill to hit the pins. A hit won a prize, which could be money, or, more seriously in some cases, a pardon from a death sentence. In Rico's case he had played for a job in the organization.

Besides the amusement factor, the game kept Manny, Señor Mendoza's pimply little weasel of a son, busy. When he was thirteen, a potential business idea blossomed. He noticed many of his father's "players" were missing teeth. Why not charge Papa's friends for new teeth, some of which he found on the ground following the bowling games?

As the son of the boss with life-and-death control over his organization, he had the market cornered. A guaranteed business with guaranteed profits. What could be better?

Mendoza was proud of his son's initiative and entrepreneurial spirit. With Papa's backing, Manny's business grew. As they say, practice makes perfect. Except when it doesn't.

Teenager Manny put his classmates' dental retainers at the top of his list of must-haves. The inventory proved useful with the found teeth superglued onto them. Unfortunately for young Manny's patients, they did not experience perfection. Many members of the cartel sported crooked, mismatched smiles just like Rico's.

Señor Mendoza's "import-export" business, as he called it, was doing well. When President Jimmy Carter promised the 1980 Mariel Cubans they would be welcomed "with open arms" in the United States, Señor Mendoza accepted the offer. He obtained fake Cuban identity papers for Rico. The Mariel boatlift was the perfect cover to enter the US without too much fuss and unnecessary paperwork. Rico was sent to Miami to start hustling, networking and getting things started.

On Rico's arrival, he headed to the south end of Miami Beach. Known for its collection of once-beautiful art deco buildings, the area was largely populated with older Jewish immigrants from Eastern Europe along with criminals, drug users and unemployed Mariel refugees who eked out a living peddling flowers or oranges at traffic intersections.

Increased crime on the south end of Miami Beach kept many Miamians from appreciating the beautiful white sandy beaches and the clear blue-green Atlantic—or from interfering in Rico's work. Surrounded by water, it was the perfect location to receive shipments and sell drugs. Rico made it his home base, distant from much of his primary operating territory that extended all the way down to Key West. In Miami and the Keys, he did his best to blend in and not draw uninvited attention to himself. Rico was a good soldier. He did as he was told.

Following the bust of the Cudjoe Key Cowboys gang, Sam met Rico in Key West through an introduction provided by a cousin of one of the cowboys who had avoided being snagged. They had previously met briefly during some small buys Sam made for a select group of Big Pine locals. After a missed meeting at Sloppy Joe's, Sam and Rico finally connected at Captain Tony's. Rico offered him a chance for a trial run that could set him up as a major player. Sam was in.

He recruited his brother, Earl, who would be responsible for picking up an air-dropped shipment and taking it to a Miami Beach delivery point. The fee was $20,000, paid in cash after successful delivery. A very healthy paycheck for a day's worth of work considering the median annual income in the US was $16,354. If all went well, there would be another, larger shipment. And then more. Perhaps a lot more.

Sam loved the deal. So did Mama Pearl and Earl. It was like a Christmas present that just had to be unwrapped. Pick up some packages and deliver them. The boys had spent their lives on these waters; they knew every reef, every inch all the way to Miami. They could do it blindfolded. A mini-FedEx on the water. What could possibly go wrong?

The 2 a.m. drop from Medellín went more or less smoothly. Sam and Earl had taken both their boats, Sam acting as lookout and signaler to the small plane. Earl was the mule. Initially, a minor mix-up about the lights confused them. A couple of shrimpers were working in the area. Seeing their lights, the pilot almost mistook them for the drop zone.

Sam and Earl frantically waved their flashlights, ultimately getting the pilot's attention. The four packages in the net splashed down out of the sky off Cudjoe Key, where the boys were waiting. It was easy and safe. It was now up to Earl to deliver them to Rico's South Beach contact through the patrolled waters leading to Miami.

Upon completing the successful drop, Mendoza informed Rico by phone that the shipment had been dropped by the pilot. Sam acknowledged receipt, but the load never made it to Miami. Now it was Rico's job not only to find out why but to get it back. The boss man breathing down your neck was not nice.

El jefe Mendoza did not tolerate lost packages or unreliable partners. He most certainly did not have time for peons and collection issues. In the boss's eyes, the responsibility for the loss fell solely on Rico—who, unfortunately, would take the hit if it wasn't rectified. There were plenty of other worker bees ready to step in and claim Rico's position in South Florida.

Rico desperately wanted to make a name for himself, to be a standout and move up the ranks of the organization. He would need to make good on the lost bales.

Obviously, Sam Wilkie was a crook who couldn't be trusted. Rico was in no mood to play games. Actually, he had one in mind. He just had to find Sam.

He adjusted the mirror to get a better angle and tilted his nose up to make sure there were no bats in the cave. A few fast-growing nose hairs poked out. Scissors were not the solution. He reached back into the glovebox, feeling around for tweezers.

Out of the corner of his eye, he detected movement outside the One-Eyed Pelican. Old lady Wilkie was on the move. He dropped the tweezers and slammed the glove compartment shut. She seemed to be in a rush. He cranked up his van. Would she lead him to Sam?

17

SLIP AWAY
~ Clarence Carter ~

Pearl climbed into her rusty gold 1967 Chevrolet El Camino. The truck sputtered, coughed and lunged forward as she shifted into gear. She took another drag on her cigarette before flicking the butt out the window. She dusted the stray ash off her sleeve.

Her natural impulse was to put the pedal to the metal but after her boys' stunt at Peter, Dick and Willy's, she thought it best to obey the speed limit and not draw unnecessary attention to herself. Pearl kept one hand firmly on the steering wheel, using her other hand to lift a can of Old Milwaukee to her lips, pulling the aluminum tab open with her teeth. She took a long sip and belched.

As she headed out for Tavernier, deeply focused on learning more about the boys in the Polaroid and their connection to the boat thieves, she failed to notice the shabby white Ford van parked across the street from the One-Eyed Pelican. The turquoise word "Sears," faintly visible on the back door under a thin coat of cheap white paint, provided no clues to its real identity or purpose.

Rico pulled out behind her. He was happy to have the breeze of the open road circling around him, opposed to the humid stagnant air of a parked vehicle. He kept his eyes firmly focused on his prey. Even though the "Sam *problema*" was a real nuisance, Rico needed a break from a certain somebody in South Beach.

His neighbor at the Carlita, Marty the Diaper Man, was getting on his nerves. Marty was part of Castro's Mariel flotilla of more than a hundred thousand Cubans sent to Miami in 1980, including those released from jails and mental institutions.

Marty had a horrible habit of wearing a cloth baby diaper and running up and down the beach sucking his thumb and proclaiming in a British baby voice, "I make a stinky." Rico's future plans included a creative way to eradicate the annoying diaper man.

In the meantime, he thought, *Focus. Collect djurself, man. Dju got a job to do. Boss man wants what's his.* Rico prided himself on being thorough and efficient. If Señor Mendoza was unhappy, Rico would feel it. Life was easier when the boss was in a good mood.

Oblivious to Rico trailing her, Pearl pulled into Peter, Dick and Willy's. Part of the area was blocked off with yellow police tape. She reflexively sniffed. The vile stench from the septic tank explosion permeated the air. Pickups, motorcycles and other casualties of the carnage were still covered in various degrees of sewage. Firemen were busy diluting the sludge by hosing it off the wreckage into the mangroves.

Pearl got out of her truck, evaluated ground conditions and decided to remove her new Reebok tennis shoes. She could hose her feet down later.

Entering the bar, Pearl passed Barry Baron, Sr. ripping his son to shreds for taking the truck without asking. She'd seen a happier version earlier that morning. Pearl chuckled to herself. She would deal with the little twerp later—when he wasn't so preoccupied.

"Pearl, you gawgeous woman! It's been ages." Chuck smiled at the unexpected arrival of the beast of Big Pine, little Mama Pearl. He had known her since she was a desirous woman with a loose approach to life. They had done a number of interesting things together.

Light streaming in through the open door caught his gold eyetooth, giving it a twinkly flash that enhanced his smile.

In Boston, Charles "The Janitor" O'Feelers had run a successful "consultancy" business. If Mickey Spillane or any of the other top Irish mob leaders needed to be rid of a troublemaker, Charles would be called in for a consultation and elimination of the problem. He was regarded as efficient and reliable. He rarely needed more than two 9 mm rounds to get a job quietly handled. His added value as a proven cleanup specialist, never leaving behind any mess or solid clues for crime investigators, made him additionally valuable. Knowledgeable observers estimated that he was responsible for close to a dozen unsolved deaths in the Massachusetts underworld.

One day, however, he found himself on the target list of Anthony "Fat Tony" Salerno, who was very unhappy after figuring out that Charles O'Feelers had taken out one of his leading capos, Shookie "Wild Man" Scalercio. Opting on the side of caution, Charles fled to the isolated Florida Keys where, under his new name, Chuck Feelers, he had remained successfully obscure.

Chuck arrived with enough cash to open the bar now known as Peter, Dick and Willy's—an homage to his first three successful "consultations."

His timing was virtually perfect. The 1960s had been lean years in the Keys. But with the '70s, business began to thrive with an uptick in visitors along with new products from Columbia. Uncoincidentally, new businesses also popped up with a single purpose—laundering money. He quickly had more than enough customers with lots of coins in their jeans. Bills too. Lovely twenties and more delectable hundreds.

An early customer of the bar was Joseph "Bum" Farto. It didn't take them long to recognize each other for what they were. Farto provided regular "nonalcoholic" provisions to Chuck that were silently sold under the counter. The culture was such that selling drugs wasn't really seen in a seriously negative way. Among many folks, it was seen as more or less the equivalent of shrimping. Farto was often seen hanging out on a bench outside the fire station in Key West, quietly making small deals without any worries about being caught.

In addition, Chuck's well-honed discretion served him well. He was sophisticated enough to remain positioned safely above the law. Moreover, his support of the local hospital charity and as an active member of the Moose Club along with Barry Baron, Sr. scored him civic points and positive recognition. Hosting and judging the Tiki Shak bikini contests was an additional perk of being an upstanding member of the community.

As an escapee from the Northeast, he also savored the warm climate that was so friendly to his aging bones. There was never snow to shovel or leaves to be raked. When it got deadly hot, he would say, "One good thing about Florida heat is no one is ever waiting in your backseat to take you out."

Fit and feisty, Pearl had made spare money as a casual runner for Farto. When it suited her, she made deliveries for Farto at Peter, Dick and Willy's. While Daddy Wilkie was away on fishing excursions, Pearl would occasionally overnight at Chuck's upstairs apartment. Love was never in the air, but both greatly enjoyed a friendly, uninhibited roll in the proverbial hay.

When Farto was arrested and convicted, Chuck and Pearl initially feared their connection to Farto would become public. Their flashy and prominent Key West acquaintance sealed his fate when he threatened to take them down if they didn't contribute generously to his defense fund. Pearl never took kindly to demands or threats. It wasn't in her wheelhouse. Chuck had no intention of getting bopped in his retirement years.

When Farto was released on bail prior to sentencing, they invited him for a friendly, "we got your back," drink to discuss the matter. Within hours, he was fish food.

They took his car to the Miami Airport parking lot. It would appear he had fled to South America. His body was never found. After all, without a body, there can be no murder charges, right?

"Quit trying to flatter me, you old fart." Pearl laughed. "You gotta real mess out there."

"That I do, dahlin'. That crap"—he laughed— "is bad for business. The soonah it's cleaned up, the bettah. Thank God they'ah hosin' it down as quickly as they ah." You could take the boy out of Boston, but you could never take Boston out of the boy.

"So, what the hell happened?" Pearl asked. It never occurred to Chuck that Pearl more than knew the answer. Her boys had done it.

"Wicked pissah. Who the heck knows?" said Chuck. "That shittah truck from Baron exploded, right in my driveway. Some sawta freak thing."

"Baron, huh?" she asked.

"Yup, the septic business across the street. Good people. Nobody knows how it happened. I mean, whoevah heard of shit exploding? At least no one was hurt."

"Oh, I can't imagine . . ." Her bottom twisted on the barstool as she struggled to suppress a smile.

They chatted for a few moments. Pearl, finally having enough of the small talk, slipped the Polaroid photo out of her jacket pocket and laid it on the bar. "These dipsticks look familiar to you?" she asked in her raspy smoker's voice.

Chuck glanced at the picture. The hair on the back of his neck stood up. This didn't feel right. His friends Shep and Deep Dive were somehow in some deep doo-doo.

The Wilkie matriarch's tough reputation had been appropriately earned over many years. His old buddy Farto had learned that the hard way.

18

867-5309 (JENNY)
~ Tommy Tutone ~

Pearl retrieved a pack of Kool True Menthols from her jacket and tapped it on the worn bar ledge, loosening the contents. She lifted a cigarette to her puckered lips. As Chuck lit it with his turquoise Miami Dolphins lighter, his head was spinning.

Why in God's creation did she have a picture of Shep and Deep Dive in the buff hanging on a deteriorating metal lighthouse tower in the Atlantic? Had those guys lost some sort of bet? No. It had to be more serious than that. An uneasy feeling crept over him. Were the Polaroid picture and the truck explosion related in some way? Those guys were all close friends. So, what was it?

Nonchalantly, Chuck responded. "Yup, I've seen 'em around." Naturally cautious about how much to share, Chuck didn't like giving out too much too soon. This was particularly true with his old drinking friend who in the distant past had provided some very sweet benefits. They had always remained on friendly terms. Nevertheless, his inner caution light was always on when they were together. The light was blinking brightly.

"Hey, Tom, an Old Milwaukee for milady." Some things were never forgotten. It had been her brand for as long as he had known her. Chuck turned back to Pearl. "Um, I think theyah regulahs at the Tiki Shak."

As they were chatting, a fit dark-haired man with a bold mustache swaggered in. Chuck looked up and gave him a warm smile, pleasantly surprised that with all the hoopla and disgusting stench outside he had a new customer. He was relieved to break away for a moment from his conversation with Pearl.

"Welcome. Sorry about the mess out theah. We had a bit of a mishap. First beeah is on the house. Tom, a draft for this fine gentleman."

Chuck didn't recognize the guy. He certainly wasn't a local. Maybe a foreign tourist. Chuck didn't care. Fresh thirst with money in the bar was always good for business.

"*Gracias.*" Rico nodded, flashing an awkward-looking smile as he climbed onto a barstool just down from Chuck and Pearl.

Whoa, buddy, Chuck thought. *Those ah some ugly gnashahs.*

Pearl's own radar had switched into alert mode. Something seemed familiar about him. Quietly, she asked, "Know him?"

Chuck shook his head. "So, wheah were we, my deah?"

Pearl tapped on the Polaroid sitting on the counter.

Chuck knew Pearl all too well. She was on a mission. It was in his best interest to be truthful. "Ahh, yes. Captain David Deep Dive Rogers and his mate Shep Smith. Why the need to know? Some sawta joke?"

"The dive captain and me have a lil' unfinished business." With that, Pearl stubbed out her cigarette and walked out the door, taking one last look at the stranger gobbling peanuts from the small bowl on the bar.

Chuck turned his attention to the new face with the flowing mustache and the strangest, most ill-fitting set of teeth he had ever seen. It looked like this guy's dentist had glued fake teeth to a kid's retainer. "You new to these pahts? Visiting?"

"Sí, djour Keys are very beautiful. I come from eh, Spain. I look to go diving. Dju know a place?" He stroked his mustache as though he was petting a long-haired chihuahua.

Chuck couldn't help but zero in on the peanut lodged in the gap between the man's two oversized mismatched front teeth. He fantasized about jamming a straw into the guy's mouth to knock out the peanut in the same way he would put an eight ball into a corner pocket. Unable to stop staring at Rico's jacked-up teeth, Chuck responded, "I have just the guy faw yah."

Feeling guilty for giving up Deep Dive to Pearl, Chuck thought it only right to throw him some business. "Ask for Captain Deep Dive at Paradise Isle. He runs *The Reel Upside*. Tell him I sent you. He knows these watahs bettah than anyone. He's yahr man." Rico acknowledged Chuck's recommendation with a generous smile.

Unable to let the guy leave with something stuck in his teeth, Chuck tapped on his own front teeth as a friendly heads-up.

Another quick *"gracias"* and Rico got up and left, leaving a half-full beer on the bar. Chuck shook his head. You never knew what tourists from Spain were going to do. In any case, a good beer should never be wasted. He picked it up and chugged the rest down.

A downtrodden Barry wandered in, depleted after the dressing-down for taking his father's now-demolished truck without permission. Fortunately, Barry Sr. still hadn't connected the explosion itself to his son's actions. "Where's Juan?"

"Beats me. He took off on a bike just aftah the big boom," Chuck replied. "Probably gone to work."

"Freakin' fuck-tacular . . ." Barry turned his attention to the bartender. "Tommy Boy, a double shot of tequila over here." The glass emptied quickly. He couldn't believe his best friend would ditch him and get out of Dodge without him. Barry put five dollars on the bar and headed to the pay phone on the wall to call Deep Dive at home.

Waiting for Deep Dive to pick up, Barry scanned the raunchy sketches and messages left by previous callers on the wall next to the phone. "For a good time, call Jenny at 867-5309 or, if you prefer, her husband Henry at 788-6342."

There was caution in Deep Dive's voice as he answered. "Hello?"

"Dude, what took you so long to pick up?" Barry looked around to see if anyone was listening.

"Your assholes blew up my dad's truck! I'm royally screwed. Senior ripped me a new one for taking it out without asking. I've never seen him so pissed. Said he'll throw me out of the house if he ever finds out I had anything to do with the truck getting cremated. We're in deep, dude. Deep! I'm like freaking the fuck out. I'm telling you, man. Like, I'm out! Finito!"

"You jerking my chain about the truck?"

"Does it sound like I am?"

"Shit. Um ... do the others know?" Deep Dive's nervous stomach was not happy. His innards were imitating the large washing machine at the coin laundry with a full load.

"Juan does. I dunno about Shep, Hibiscus and Micki." Barry continued to fill his friend in on the day's events, starting with the trip to Big Pine.

On the other end of the line, Deep Dive, lost for words, turned white as a shark's underbelly.

"You better give 'em a heads-up!" Barry demanded.

"You do it."

"What? Me? The hell I will!" Barry couldn't believe Deep Dive's audacity.

"Actually ... come to think of it, I'll do it." Deep Dive didn't need his friends running scared, and he most certainly didn't want to tango solo with the Big Pine crazies. He needed time to think about how he could work the situation in his favor.

His stomach cramps could no longer be ignored. "Uh-oh. My belly is killing me. See ya." He hung up and dashed to the bathroom. Dammit, his urgent gut issues hadn't given him time to inquire about his pride and joy.

Barry stared at the black handset. Hadn't he just told that asshole he was out? He smashed it down on the cradle hook, drawing a few curious glances his way.

19

EMOTIONAL RESCUE
~ The Rolling Stones ~

The Dubicki house was located on a side canal on the bay side of US-1. A classic stilt Florida Keys concrete home, it was specifically built to withstand the inevitable hurricanes that regularly blasted through the Keys. Three bedrooms, two bathrooms and the kitchen and living area were situated over the sheltered parking and storage area. There were excellent views of the dock and swimming pool from the kitchen. Using his seasoned woodworking skills, Stan had crafted rich trim throughout the house from broken branches of gumbo-limbo, black ironwood and lignum vitae trees collected after tropical storms and hurricanes.

Outside her circle, Hibiscus Dubicki qualified as a sometimes airhead. This was reinforced not so much by her California blonde Barbie look but more by her occasional naive reactions to life. Her blue eyes were bright and friendly. At times they seemed to sparkle, giving her a vulnerable Marilyn Monroe aura that men found compelling. Indeed, Hibiscus had never been known for her ability to think through ideas. But for once, with a little guidance from her best friend Micki, she was confident she had made the right move.

The Reel Upside could not return to its home dock at Paradise Isle. That would be far too visible. It made even less sense to consider taking the boat to Micki's place on the Atlantic. There might be awkward questions from her inquisitive father, who was always on the prowl for the next big story for the local paper. Until they could figure out the next move, the only logical hiding place was the Dubickis' house on the bay side.

Conveniently tucked away from the main highway, the house was out of sight from boats skimming the shoreline. A perfect hiding spot for Deep Dive's rechristened boat until things cooled down. For the time being, Hibiscus would safely shelter the boat in the remote location, shielding it from prying eyes.

After running through a brief rain squall, *The Reel Upside* with the two young women aboard pulled up to the Dubicki dock. High fives celebrated their return.

"Micki, let's call Deep Dive, pronto. He's going to be one happy bastard when he sees the surprise we have for him," Hibiscus said.

It didn't take Deep Dive long to get there. He couldn't believe his eyes. It wasn't Stan's naked backside as he hosed down the family car. That he had seen before. It was the sheer delight of his beautiful boat. He teared up.

The joy of the reunion lasted only momentarily until, to his horror, he saw it. A desecration. A violation of his pride and joy. Those Big Pine assholes had used white spray paint to cover up the word *Upside*, which had been replaced with the word *Downside* in gaudy red paint. Those fucking pirates had a special place in hell waiting for them.

His stomach kept churning, creating something a lot nastier than butter. He didn't know what his next step should be. How much did the girls know about the explosion? What should he divulge that would best suit his interests?

The basic problem was still unresolved. Deep Dive had a worried, nagging feeling that the no-neck Hawaiian shirt guy and his goofy gangly brother would hunt him down again, still demanding the boat as payment for the missing square groupers. The problem was far from over.

For this reason, he thought it best to keep to himself one little bit of info he had just learned – the explosion at Peter, Dick, and Willy's.

Hibiscus and Micki hadn't mentioned anything. The less they knew, the better.

Why spook them unnecessarily? From his experience, chicks could be so overly dramatic. He was sure Hibiscus and Micki would get their panties in a wad and make him move his boat away from safety, potentially putting *The Reel Upside* in harm's way. He had no other place to keep her. Above all, he had to protect his beloved primary asset.

There was one other hiccup—cash flow. If his boat was out of business, Deep Dive would need a job. Rent for his apartment was due in a week. Even more urgent, the all-important dock rent at Paradise Isle was due in two weeks. No way in hell could he let some other dive or fishing boat come in and take over his highly coveted prime dock space.

"Do you think your dad could hook me up at the Pink Flamingo until things get straightened out?" asked Deep Dive.

Hibiscus shrugged her shoulders. "I don't see why not. Meet me there at eight a.m. tomorrow. I'll hook you up."

Working at the Pink Flamingo would not be ideal, but if he had to sell tacky Keys tchotchke crap to dumbass tourons, so be it. It would buy him time until his grand return with *The Reel Upside*. For now, he had to lay low and let things cool off. In addition, *The Reel Upside* couldn't return to prime time without a new paint job. The graffiti on her side made her look like a hoochie.

Maybe it was time to rethink his life and get out of the dive/snorkel business. Just do fishing charters. For one thing, there was far less responsibility and liability. He wouldn't have to worry about customers not resurfacing. Or drifting off where they couldn't be found. That was probably why dive insurance was way more expensive. Besides, fishing was more fun, more exciting. The big rollers always tipped well after a great catch.

Or, maybe he could get into treasure-hunting. A guy named Mel Fisher in Key West was said to be recruiting a crew to look for a seventeenth-century Spanish galleon loaded with gold and jewels. That would be quite sexy with the ladies. Deep Dive was already imagining how a new cover for his matchbook would look. His gorgeous face with a pirate hat on top of his head, a winning look indeed. Yes, and an added mysterious black eyepatch would be a lady catcher.

Micki interrupted his thoughts. "Hey, can you drop me off at home? I've got to go to work."

"I wish I did." Deep Dive sighed morosely as he walked toward his car.

"You forgot your boat key!" Hibiscus yelled.

"She's parked here. You hold on to it. I'll get it later." Micki and Deep Dive drove off.

By then Hibiscus's mother, Patricia, had joined her husband in washing the car. The ultimate pair of free spirits, they were holdover hippies from the 1960s. Patricia's long and straight braided gray hair almost covered her sagging buttocks. There was no cover for the sagging front parts.

Stan had his own sagging issues. His horseshoe-pattern baldness and handlebar mustache were a full Pittsburgh. The two Steelers fans had migrated south to the Keys during the 1967 Summer of Love—bringing along their daughter, Hibiscus, and their love of free expression. Translation—they were nudists. Well, recovering nudists.

The initial Keys venture for Stan and Patricia was a nudist trailer park. Due to their timing and location choice, their au naturel concept was not warmly embraced by the locals. Only earthy German tourists seemed to love being *unbekleidet* in front of strangers.

The traditional fishing and diving community of the Upper Keys was open to living life free from constraints and conventions *if* the lifestyle choices fit in the confines of acceptable Keys values and unwritten rules.

A "rustic" yard or a brightly painted home was embraced, as it contributed to the Keys' eclectic feel. It was a way to put your own stamp on things, leaving little room for the boring white backgrounds seen in suburbs north of Key Largo. HOA was a dirty word.

Running pot discreetly was okay. Sleeping with a neighbor's wife, wink, wink, was generally overlooked, often with a sly smile or even a giggle. Public drunkenness along with loutish and outlandish behavior generated good fellowship along with hearty laughter, snickers and guffaws.

But a trailer park full of *sober* middle-aged nudies? That was just too much. Getting the monetary meaning of the message, Stan and Patricia shut down their nudist trailer park and opened the Pink Flamingo with a colorful sign proclaiming, "Flamingos and a helluva lot more."

Within a year, the shop had developed into a destination store with a growing must-see reputation. Tourists went out of their way to make sure they could tell the folks at home they had visited the Pink Flamingo. The store proudly sold over one hundred different varieties of flamingo merchandise ranging from garden decorations to mailboxes, branded candy bars, matchbooks, wall art and images on shirts and jackets.

The store offered plenty of other kinds of T-shirts, sweatshirts, hoodies, flip-flops, beach towels, hats, trinkets, sunscreen, crappy artwork, souvenirs and autographed photos of local fishing guides, the true Florida Keys celebrities. The more famous of them had fished with presidents like Harry Truman or sports stars like Ted Williams.

Over the years, as the business became more prosperous, the recovering nudists matured. One could say the Dubickis sort of grew up, trying their best to be respectable, fully-clothed Keys citizens. An occasional relapse could occur on weekends, especially if the car needed washing. It was so hot the clothes would soak through from sweat. Didn't it make more sense to put on clothes afterwards? A more natural order to things. Their property was more or less sheltered from the neighbors by gumbo-limbo trees and mangroves anyhow, so who cared?

Silently pulling up alongside *The Reel Upside*, Juan was practically hyperventilating. Over the other side of the boat, he caught a glimpse of naked Stan and Patricia in the driveway washing their vintage light blue Beetle artistically decorated with puffy white clouds, a Pittsburgh Steelers decal and bright pink flamingo stickers on the hood and the back window.

As quietly as possible, he shoved the two sixty-pound black bags, one at a time, over the railing of his skiff onto *The Reel Upside*. Then, without creating any more wake than a manatee or a trolling snook, he slipped away without being noticed. A successful drop and run. An enormous sense of relief flowed over him. Now he had to hurry. He was going to be late for work at the Tiki Shak. It had been quite a day and he hadn't even been to work yet.

Looking out the kitchen window while washing dishes, Hibiscus thought she saw a strange movement. Was that a garbage bag being pushed onto the boat? What was that about? She dried her hands and headed out of the kitchen and down the steps. In the driveway, her naked parents were bent over polishing the tire rims. They stood up and waved as they noticed her heading for the dock.

"Gag me with a spoon. Really? Hello . . . clothes, please," said Hibiscus.

Pointing to his white crew-length socks and whiter-than-white tennis shoes, Stan laughed. "Do these count?" He was amused. When had his bikini contestant daughter become such a prude?

Ignoring his comment, Hibiscus avoided any more eye contact with their personal bits and pieces and headed to the boat. Even though she'd been exposed to their junk since she could remember, it still grossed her out.

What the hell? Two large black garbage bags were now on the boat's deck. She jumped onto the boat and cautiously prodded the first bag with her foot. Nothing moving. No unusual whiff. Carefully, she untied it.

"No way!" The gift from Jesus! Two bags' worth. She looked around to see if anyone was watching.

20

PASS THE KOUCHIE
~ The Mighty Diamonds ~

"Well, lookie here! How did this get here?" Hibiscus, flushed with excitement and now in possession of the square groupers, needed a moment to figure out what had happened. She was still blissfully unaware the Big Pine cowboys had blown up the Septic Baron tanker truck she had ridden to Big Pine in that morning.

"Take a deep breath," she told herself, waving her hands at her face to cool off. She was giddy with the thought of selling the pot and making some easy cash. Finally, she could afford some quality bikini photos instead of the cheap shit Drooling Fred took at Glamour Photos next to K-Mart. And find an agent. Her dream of modeling could come true.

Hibiscus carefully opened one of the black garbage bags and pulled out a bale. It was heavier than she'd expected. A lot of weed professionally compressed into a single tightly wrapped package.

She needed something sharp to open it. A screwdriver would do. One on the console was a bit rusty but usable. Hitting the bale a few times, she poked a hole in it.

She stretched the opening wide enough to extract some of the contents, inhaling the familiar odor. Not bad. Not bad at all. "That's some good-ass *sea weed*," she proclaimed, giggling at her own cleverness.

She needed to sample a bit. Plucking out a handful of green for a few generous bong bowls, Hibiscus walked up to the house in keen anticipation of a nice relaxing hit. The kitchen bong was in its normal place of prominence on the shelf above the toaster. She excitedly made her way back down the stairs to the pool. She would be able to think much more clearly after testing the merchandise.

With the glass bong and lighter in hand, Hibiscus was ready to rip. Light. Her. Up. The beautiful, pleasing smoke drifted upwards. She inhaled deeply. The taste and smell were somewhat tropical. The feeling was magnificent. A delightful high.

It was the richest and best weed she could remember.

For Stan and Patricia, the enticing smell was even more than familiar.

"Fee-fi-fo-fum. I smell Colombian Gold and want some." Stan tried his best to imitate the giant's voice from Jack and the Beanstalk. His attempt at humor. Hibiscus cringed.

"Sweetie, don't you want to share with your poor ol' folks?" asked Stan as he wandered over with Patricia, ready to float into orbital bliss.

Over the years, Stan and Patricia had become serious ganja connoisseurs. They knew, without blinking, that Hibiscus's stash was a major step up from some of the musty-smelling brownish weed provided locally by the high school kids. These golden spotted buds were fluffy and airy with very few tiny, spotted seeds.

"Ahhh . . . weed nirvana," sighed Patricia. The taste was spot-on. Amazing, sweet notes with hints of lemon and pineapple. Very mellow indeed.

Three very stoned Dubickis melted into the lounge chairs by the pool. Two naked, one fully clothed. Their bodies felt as firm as day-old Jell-O. Hibiscus wasn't scolding her parents now for being naked. Everything was copacetic. Wonderfully relaxed.

"You know what would be really good right now?" asked Patricia. "Key lime pie."

A brilliant suggestion. Hibiscus peeled herself off the sun lounger to climb the stairs to the kitchen. The pie was waiting on the kitchen counter. Tasting a fingerful before carrying the pie and three forks down to her parents, Hibiscus was overcome with a culinary epiphany. Next time, she could add a little weed to the Key lime pie crust. A guaranteed winner!

They enjoyed the pie along with a few extra hits. Hibiscus took another long draw, the rich smoke creating a satisfying feeling in her lungs and a light, flighty feeling in her head. Together with the sugar rush from the pie, the feeling was just too good. Waiting until her parents had drifted off, a certainty when they got too high, Hibiscus waltzed upstairs to call Micki.

Grabbing the handset from the wall, she placed it next to her ear as she twisted the curly cord in her other hand. "Is the dial tone always this loud?" she wondered. She loved the idea of a pink phone with a stretchy cord. Only a genius could have created that.

She dropped the cord and dialed. After a weed-induced eternity waiting for her friend to answer, Micki was on the line. "You need to come right back over," gushed Hibiscus. "You're not going to believe what I got!"

Micki arrived with Sherman, the family bloodhound and recent K-9 school dropout they had adopted. Bloodhounds were known for their strong sense of smell. With the uptick in drugs being run through Florida, it had been assumed Sherman would be a star on the police force. He had a great nose for food, dog pee, dog poo and female dogs in heat but, sadly, not for drugs. As it was, Sherman had no complaints about not being in service. He was a happily relaxed pooch, living a life of leisure with the Wilsons.

Asleep on a pool lounger, a naked Stan lay on his side—butt exposed to the world and Patricia. Occasionally his rear end emitted little tooting noises. Fluffs. The consumed Key lime pie enhanced with some strong weed left a lingering odorous presence around Stan's air space.

Sherman had little interest in the bong next to the loungers. There was something more appealing in the air—remnants of dessert and Stan.

Before searching for crumbs on the ground, the bloodhound sniffed Stan's butt, a friendly dog greeting. Micki grimaced and pulled him away so as not to wake the sleeping Stan and Patricia.

Hibiscus headed to the boat with Micki and Sherman. On board, Hibiscus showed Micki the black plastic bags.

"Whoa...where the heck did *that* come from? You think that's Deep Dive's missing stuff?"

"I'm thinking, yes." Hibiscus smiled broadly. "I'm not sure how. But who's complaining?"

Hibiscus knew what she wanted. Turning it over to the cops was not on her to-do list. She explained to Micki her idea of making baked goods infused with marijuana. Perfect for under-the-counter sales at Conch on the Bay or the Pink Flamingo.

Micki briefly pondered Hibiscus's idea. "Why not? If you can add it to brownie mix, why not Key lime pie?"

"It would be like the dish of the century! I dunno...maybe too much work. Dime bags might be an easier way to go."

Micki's head spun. Yes, snap money. Selling pot could get her closer to her dream of owning her own restaurant. They'd have no problem finding interested buyers.

Hibiscus hugged Micki. "We could be business partners!"

Could she confidently go into business with her flaky, fun-loving friend? A tempting proposition, but trusting Hibiscus to keep her mouth shut would be a gamble. Maybe a big one. One wrong move or conversation could be extremely problematic. Was it worth the obvious perils?

On the other hand, finding jetsam, pot in this case, cast overboard deliberately by the person being pursued, could dramatically and quickly fatten up a bank account. Life would be substantially improved, assuming, of course, the dealers didn't come back to claim what was theirs.

Or a friend found out you double-crossed them.

Micki remembered her dad's stories about former Key West Fire Chief Joseph "Bum" Farto. She recalled briefly meeting him as a little girl.

Larger than life, he was known for his fire-engine-red clothes, his flashy lime-green Ford and his rose-colored glasses.

Chief Farto mysteriously disappeared in 1976 while awaiting sentencing for a drug trafficking conviction. Operation Conch, a sting operation, had found the fire chief selling cocaine and weed out of his fire station. Bum's mysterious disappearance turned him into a Keys legend—the Jimmy Hoffa of Key West. Local T-shirt shops sold shirts emblazoned with the question, "Where is Bum Farto?" Another best seller: "Bum Farto is alive and well in Costa Rica."

The Keys rumor mill was still swirling about Bum's fate. Micki had no interest in being the next Bum Farto.

What to do, what to do? Take the risk and sell it? If her by-the-book journalist dad got wind, he'd have her on the first plane to boring old Aunt Kathy in Iowa. Unsettling thought number two.

Or was the wisest move just to do the right thing? Return the stolen bales to Deep Dive so he could settle with the Big Piners?

The One-Eyed Pelican folk wouldn't let up easily. It wouldn't be long before those assholes would be back sniffing around like a couple of bloodhounds nosing Stan's behind. They weren't going to just walk away from this much money.

21

ANOTHER ONE BITES THE DUST

~ Queen ~

Whistling his favorite tune, "Escape (The Piña Colada Song)," Rico drove to Paradise Isle. The summer sun was sliding toward the sea but had not yet set. The blue-green water glistened behind the resort with a distinctive postcard quality. The parking lot was busy for an early Monday evening. Rico scanned the cars, noticing many out-of-state plates. A caca-brown wood-paneled Pontiac station wagon with a Las Vegas sticker pasted on the back had a Nevada plate. Sí, Vegas would be fun. Those topless showgirls at the Tropicana were said to be the most beautiful girls in the world. Yes, he could operate with a setup like that. He tugged on his mustache, a habitual move that soothed him, just the way women seemed to be constantly reassured by brushing back their hair.

He was on the hunt for a Monroe County, Florida license plate screwed onto a well-worn gold Chevrolet El Camino truck.

There it was. Taking up two handicapped parking spots.

Stepping out of his van, Rico was greeted by a swarm of mosquitoes. He swatted them away as he entered the Tiki Shak. If Sam's *madre* was looking for this dive man, it was probably in his best interest to follow.

Rico spotted Pearl, with her volumized permed short hair and oversized Diane Von Furstenberg fashion glasses, sitting on a barstool. Her feet dangled above the foot rails. She was engrossed in conversation with a young bartender. He was too far away to hear their chitchat. The bartender, however, appeared to be extremely uncomfortable. There was a trace of moisture on his forehead suggesting he didn't like what he was hearing.

In fact, Juan was apprehensive as Pearl took the last drag on her cigarette. He was perplexed by her ability to smoke a cigarette down to a nub so small that it almost certainly burned her tobacco-stained fingers. The nicotine discoloration repulsed him. It reminded him of the orangey-yellow fungus on an unwashed Tiki Juice blender.

"So what happened to Captain Deep Dive?" she asked. "On vacation? His boat's not in the usual slip."

Juan swallowed hard. Uh-oh. Who was this old woman? She looked vaguely familiar. What was it he didn't like about this?

"Um, ma'am, I don't know anything about that. I'm just a bartender here."

"You guys aren't buddies? I woulda thunk you'd know all the captains that dock here." Pearl loved how uneasy he looked. She was the cat eyeing an uncomfortable mouse caught in a trap. "You ever been to Big Pine?"

"Yo, yo, Juanster! Where's my Tiki Juice?" a familiar voice boomed from across the way. It made Juan jump.

Crap! It was Shep, sun blisters and all. The now off-duty EMT was the last person he wanted to see at this moment. Didn't he understand the concept of lying low? Did he think wearing sunglasses at night made him less noticeable?

Now Juan was sure. The crusty old lady sitting across from him was most definitely the same old bat he had seen filling chum bags at the One-Eyed Pelican in Big Pine. And here she was asking awkward questions. He didn't want her putting the puzzle together and connecting him to Shep and Deep Dive. At this point, he'd be happy to cough up some cash to pay for the damage to the red car, but he didn't want to be connected to the weed in any shape or form.

He had already seen firsthand what these Big Pine assholes were capable of. The thought of being crushed under a Neptune statue like his dad or something worse shook him. His dad's accident appeared to be another warning shot, no doubt. They could be capable of much worse.

Juan had been wise to "return to sender" the bales. He was in the clear. Clean as a whistle. It was now up to Hibiscus to decide the next move. She was the new owner. Juan was pleased with his quick thinking. He had successfully dug himself out of a very deep hole.

Pearl turned to see who was talking. Well, well . . . if it wasn't one of the Polaroid numbnuts newly featured on the Wilkie Board of Shame. What spectacular timing. She was happy he would join her at the bar with the other spaz who had some serious 'splaining to do. A two-for-one special.

"Juanster, I just heard about Barry's truck! That was weird, huh? Oh, and sorry about your dad, too. He lucked out, man—only two broken legs, three cracked ribs and a head injury. It could have been much worse. They say he'll wake up soon. But, damn, your mom looked sizzlin'."

Sizzlin'? My mom? What the hell was wrong with this guy talking about his mother like that?

Juan coughed, tilting his head toward Pearl, trying to signal Shep, praying he would shut his mouth. Reading the room was not Shep's strong suit. His mouth continued to run. Hoping Shep would pick up on his hint to clam up, Juan spoke to him as coldly and formally as possible. "Nice to see you again. Was that a Tiki Juice you'd like?"

Mama Pearl was having none of the theater. Hell hath no fury like a mad Pearl Wilkie.

"Okay, assholes. Cut the crap. No more games. You barf bags have been a real headache. Where's the head turd?" She lit another cigarette, blowing the smoke into Shep's face.

Meanwhile Rico, disappointed that Deep Dive was nowhere to be seen, headed toward the bar, positioning himself so that he couldn't easily be seen by Pearl. The animated conversation was apparently not going well.

$ea Weed | 113

"Look, lady, I don't know who you are. What are you talking about?" It took a second for Shep's lightbulb to turn on. "Oh . . . that."

"You dumbass. My boys were out with you Sunday morning. As far as I'm concerned, they were far too friendly. Where's that captain friend of yours? Does he have my stuff or does one of you?"

Shep held up his hand, making the Boy Scout honor sign. "Listen, we told the God's honest truth. He doesn't have it. We don't have it. Deep Dive found it and someone hijacked the shit off his boat. Scout's honor."

Juan nodded his head in an exaggerated up-and-down motion, his eyes bugging out of his head. He was too afraid to speak. Sweat dripped into his eyes.

"Stick your scout's honor up your ass. I want what's due me. Gimme back the bales. I'm not playing. Pass the message along or someone is gonna disappear faster than a toupee in a hurricane."

Stunned by the sharpness of Pearl's words, the men stood there with their mouths wide open like hooked groupers, unable to respond.

Pearl clicked her tongue. "Don't think I've forgotten about the boat. Your posse came on my turf and took my partial repayment—*The Reel Downside*. It belongs to me now. You and your amigos think I'm going to stand by and not do somethin'? Well, then . . . your brains are scrambled mush. Ya dumb scat scum."

With a steely gaze, Pearl focused on Juan. "You and your Shit Baron guy also owe my son for his car. He don't take kindly to having his car messed up. The whole lotta ya better git crackin' on clearing up your mishmash of stupidity. I ain't gonna ask again so nicely."

Before hopping off the barstool, Pearl turned to Juan and tapped his tip jar with her leathery, bony finger. "Here's your tip, sonny." She stubbed her lit cigarette out on Shep's peeling sunburned hand, "Don't put your nose where it don't belong. Most importantly, don't touch what don't belong to ya."

Shep screamed in real pain. Pearl grabbed his face. In a low, husky voice smelling of beer and menthol cigarettes, she whispered, "I hope you're paying attention, barnacle brain. Toodle-oo. See you boys soon."

Adding insult to injury, as she dismounted, she slapped Shep upside the head. Walking away, she pulled the Polaroid picture out of her jacket pocket. With her back still turned to them, she lifted the picture in the air and shouted, "P.S., nice worm."

Juan looked at Shep. "Huh?"

Shep shrugged. "I dunno. You got some ice?"

22

DESTINATION UNKNOWN
~ Missing Persons ~

Rico emerged from the shadows and plunked down on the barstool vacated by Pearl. It was still warm from the heat she generated. He looked at the badly blotched hombre sitting to his left. Didn't this guy know about Bain de Soleil? His sunburned face with the raccoon eyes was almost too painful to look at. Rico needed information.

Juan handed Shep a Tiki Juice-stained bar towel filled with ice.

"What happen?" Rico asked Shep.

Shep pointed to his blistered red face. It was a question.

"Ah, no." Rico pointed down to Shep's hand.

"Um, that . . . some lady dropped her cigarette on my hand."

"Owie, that hurt, huh?" Rico winced. He didn't really care what happened. But deep down he felt a little sorry for this guy. He obviously had enough going on all over his body. Adding a cigarette burn on his already red and blistered hand was some bad shit.

"Bartender, give him what he wants. I have the same. I buy."

"Hey, that's mighty nice of you. Thanks." Shep patted Rico on the back.

Rico forced a smile. He didn't want that disgusting hand touching him. Who knew where it had been?

"No hay problema."

Juan passed Rico and Shep two Tiki Juices. Instead of adding the rum floater finishing touch to the drinks, he poured the Bacardi 151 down his own throat. His nerves needed serious calming.

From experience, Rico knew it was best not to bombard folks with questions. Be still. Be a fly on the wall. Quietly, quietly catchee monkey. People speak more freely when no one is listening or cares. With the straw firmly planted between his two front teeth, he sipped his drink cautiously. Not too fast. No brain freeze needed.

Positioning himself with his back to the bar, he watched a couple of sloppy drunks from Miami Palmetto High School whooping it up on the dance floor. The music and their shrieks made it difficult to hear everything the men were saying. Frustrating.

At a whisper, Juan murmured the words, "God help us. We're dead meat. What now? That crazy bitch means business."

"Yeah, how did we get sucked into this? We didn't take the stuff. It's not our problem," Shep said.

"You're right, man," Juan agreed.

The blame game was on.

"I mean, I kinda see why they might be pissed at you. You drove down there with Barry. Right? But me? I didn't crash into their car. I didn't take the boat. I don't have the weed. I was just in the wrong place at the wrong time. And what do I get for that? I've been turned into a fucking human punching bag!"

Juan couldn't disagree. If one got down to the nuts and bolts of the matter, the pecking order of blame when it came to Juan was hazy. To the naked eye, Juan would place second to last behind Shep. The ranking got trickier when it came to Barry, Hibiscus, and Micki. It was a chicken and egg scenario. Which was a worse offense? Smashing into the red car or taking off with a boat that didn't technically belong to the Big Pine crowd?

One thing everyone could agree on—Deep Dive was the head turd. Unless, of course, someone figured out it was Juan who had stolen the square groupers from *The Reel Upside*.

Shep's voice began to falter. "Dude, my hands are clean. Damn, it's been a rough couple of days. Top it all off, I got fired today."

"What? Why?" Juan asked.

Shep thought it best that Juan didn't become privy to the intricate details behind his termination considering that Juan's mother was partly responsible for him getting the boot. Turned out the ambulance company frowned upon fraternizing with patients' wives. He was busted for becoming a member of the Sea Level Club, the EMT version of the Mile High Club. The siren-screaming ride to the hospital provided just enough time for a quickie as Juan's unconscious dad lay beside them. If the driver had just minded his own beeswax, kept his eyes on the road and not reported what had happened, he'd still be employed.

Juan and Shep sighed. Both were guarding secrets that could not be shared—under any circumstances.

"I kinda broke some sorta ambulance rule. Maybe it was meant to be. Anyhow... I've been thinking about starting a new business. Hairy critter removal and extermination. Whadda ya think?"

He plucked a cute bright green baby iguana from his front shirt pocket and placed it gently on the bar. It was from the latest litter of one of his favorite pet females, Bertha. It was fun to watch the little ones run around. He called her Trixi. She was as cute as could be. He had just begun training her to beg for food.

"Sure, sure. Sounds great." Juan was only partially listening. His mind was racing.

Rico smiled. He didn't need to rough up these two gringos to milk information. He just sat back. The conversation flowed freely. Naive and inexperienced—they had a lot to learn, including not to talk business in a crowded bar.

Rico reached for his drink. A repulsive swamp creature had taken a dump next to his cup. Reacting in disgust, he smashed Trixi with his fist, killing her instantly. He flicked the limp remains of the baby iguana off the bar and wiped his hand on a paper napkin.

Stunned, Shep screamed. "What the hell did you just do, man?" The fucker had killed Trixi.

"No worries. Back in my country I feed it to the *gatos.*"

An enraged Shep picked up the squished iguana, giving it a loving stroke. Tears welled in his eyes. "You'll burn in hell for this," he shouted as he stormed off. He couldn't believe the guy who'd nicely bought him a drink could end up being such a heartless asshole.

Juan chose to remain silent. The last thing he wanted was a brawl in the bar. It was always disruptive, usually expensive and sometimes even bloody. That meant more cleanup.

Rico never gave Shep's reaction a second thought. What was the big deal? It was just a scrawny lizard. Anyhow, it was time to head south for a heart-to-heart with his dear friend Sam. But first, the music was just getting good. He'd head south in the morning.

As the evening slipped by and the drinks flowed, patrons got louder and wilder. Rico was enjoying the show of beautiful drunk distractions all around. Tipsy beauties were his specialty. It was time to turn on his best Latin charm. It was going to be a good night. He fluffed up his mustache and breathed into his cupped hands, checking that his breath was free from any offensive odor. Rico sat back for a few more songs, waiting to pounce. The drunker the ladies got, the better looking he would be.

Rico spotted his target. "Ay, ay, ay. I like. Bartender, wish me luck." Rico boogied his way over to two girls dancing. They looked like twins. The "Sam *problema*" could wait until morning.

23

I LOVE ROCK 'N' ROLL
~ Arrows ~

What a night! Well, maybe for Rico. For the twins, not so much. They regretted it the moment they woke up and stared at a snoring and hyper-salivating Rico. His oddly configured retainer thingamajiggy lay on the pillow next to him. Belle looked at her sister and stuck her finger in her mouth, a universal sign. "Really gross. Makes me want to barf."

Latin lover, their ass. Before sneaking out the door, Tinker helped herself to some bills and a partial roll of mint Certs on the nightstand. The night didn't need to be a total bust. Good to have some additional real upside in the transaction and fresh breath.

The motel room door slammed shut. Rico rolled over. His arm flopped across the bed, feeling for his booty from the night before.

Gone.

Disappointing. He had been hoping for a breakfast round. Never mind. Time to get going anyway. There was stuff to do. Time was running out for Señor Sam. Rico entered the hot, steamy shower with an extra bit of pep. His shower voice broke into song. Not remembering all the words for "I'm All Out of Love," he hummed the rest.

It was 9 a.m. before Rico reached Big Pine. No complaints about the commute. Zero traffic with spectacular sea views of the Atlantic and the Gulf as he drove across the Seven Mile Bridge. Boats were out on both sides. The water sparkled with the bright morning sun. Not a cloud in the sky. It was a brilliant summer day. The Tourism Council was loving it. There was nothing to exaggerate.

It was a normal Tuesday morning at the One-Eyed Pelican. Guides had been coming in to purchase gas, chum, beer, and other items needed for a successful day of fishing. Tourons traveling to Key West from New York and Boston loved the quaint feel and smells of a 1950s-era general store, tobacco, fish, a hint of mold and more often than not a faint whiff of weed. The display with the green "You Are Here" T-shirts featuring the state of Florida with a big arrow pointing to Big Pine had run out of mediums.

Out in the parking lot, Sam was tinkering with his once-pristine red TR7, which was going to need serious restoration. The loss of the fender and other collateral damage made him sick with anger. He was calculating the cost when Rico rolled up in the white van.

"Psst, psst, Sam the man." Sam looked over. To his dismay, it was Rico summoning him over. Slow as molasses, he walked to the van, buying as much time as possible before he had to face the music.

Rico stepped out of the van, walked to the back and opened the rear door. "Please, into my office." The knife in Rico's hand made it clear. It was not a suggestion.

A large metal dog cage dominated the back of the van. "Dju like jukeboxes?"

Sam winced. He didn't like anything about Rico. In particular, he didn't like where this was going. Rico opened the cage. Sam also didn't like the idea of what could happen with the highly threatening serrated knife.

"*Amigo*, we going to play a leetle game. Come. Climb in." There was nothing friendly about Rico's crazed, gap-toothed smile. Prodded by the not-so-gentle sharp point of the blade, Sam squeezed himself into the cage. His buttocks pressed firmly against the metal. *Clink*. What would otherwise have been a quiet locking sound hit his ears like the closing snap of a casket lock.

"Dju know ... my boss, he not happy with dju."

Sam tried to speak. Rico put his fingers to his lips. *"Silencio.* Listen carefully. Dju will answer me. Dju don't answer correctly, dju will have to sing a song."

"Sing a song?" Sam's face twisted into a question mark.

"Shush ... let's practice." Rico had a handful of coins. He set the coins next to the cage. With the tip of the knife, he pushed Sam's Hawaiian shirt up and pulled the back of his pants down, exposing his butt crack.

A horrified Sam yelped as the air hit his skin and the cool knife blade rubbed against it. "Please, Rico, no. I beg you! I'll pay up."

"Now? Dju have it for me now?" asked Rico

"Well, not-no, not exactly. Give me a couple more days. I promise. I'll have it!"

"Cha-cha-cha. Sorry, not so good. Time for jukebox." Rico grabbed a quarter and slipped it through a gap in the metal dog cage into Sam's butt crack.

"Sing, chico, sing."

The first song that came to Sam's mind was "She'll Be Coming 'Round the Mountain."

"Aye, I don' like dat one." Rico grabbed another quarter and shoved it where the sun don't shine. "Peek someting betta. I like, 'I'm All Out of Love.'"

With proctologist-level discomfort, Sam was getting the message. The Colombians wanted to be paid, like yesterday.

Earl wandered out of the store to the parking lot looking for his brother. Mama wanted to talk to him. Sam's tools were on the ground next to the TR7. The Polaroid camera was perched on the convertible top. "That's odd," murmured Earl. "He never goes anywhere without his camera."

The old white van parked under a coconut tree was the source of odd noises. It almost sounded like his brother singing.

Spotting Earl, Rico pushed the cage with Sam in it out the back. It crashed down with a painful thud. Stray coins that had dropped to the bottom of the cage tinkled to the pavement.

What an opportunity! Gangly Earl grabbed the Polaroid and pointed it at the Sam-stuffed cage. The shutter clicked. As soon as the camera's rollers ejected the photo, he pulled it and shook it. Oh boy, he was saving this goody for another day. A snicker escaped Earl's lips. He couldn't help himself.

"Earl, you asshole. Get me out of here!"

"Ho . . . ho . . . hold up, br . . . br . . . bro." Sticking the photograph in his back pocket for safekeeping, he trotted over to his brother. Sam's bare ass mooned him through the cage bars.

As Rico sped off, the twins arrived to start work—two hours late. They watched as their father, Earl, opened the crate to release their raging bull of an uncle.

"Weirdos," they said in unison. "Jinx." And with that, they walked into the One-Eyed Pelican. Tinker blew a large bubble with a double piece of Bazooka bubble gum, not thinking twice about why their uncle might be in a dog crate with his pants half pulled down.

Old people did some crazy shit when they were wasted.

"What the bl . . . bl . . . blazes is goin' on, Sam? Colombians?" Earl asked his brother as he dusted him off. "You okay?"

"Who else would it be, jerkoff? Get off me." Sam reached into his pants, easing the pain as he pulled out a quarter. He sniffed it and put it into his pocket.

Earl shouted, "You better t . . . t . . . tell Mama."

Sam wasn't going to tell his mama shit. He didn't appreciate being made to look like a fool. He'd handle it. That asshole Rico would get a taste of a Wilkie payback.

24

ANOTHER TRICKY DAY

~ The Who ~

While Rico and Sam were playing silly games in the back of a van, Captain Deep Dive had begun his first day working retail. He was reconsidering his complaints about dive customers on his boat. Tourons, shopping tourists on land, were worse, much worse.

Stan Dubicki had finished giving Deep Dive a tour of the store when a family of four with strong Midwestern accents walked in. Dad looked bored. Mom was eager to check out the kitschy merchandise. The two children took off, playing a wild game of chase. Deep Dive was exhausted. He had a hellish headache and had barely slept since hearing about the truck and Juan and Shep's visitor. His stomach was still gurgling.

A glass flamingo fell to the floor. A freckled boy of about nine with a brilliantly white zinc-oxidized nose ran past the front counter and stuck his tongue out at Deep Dive. The boy studied Deep Dive's face.

"Hey, mister, why are you so ugly?"

"Huh? What did you say?"

I said . . . why—are—you—so—ugly? The boy reached for a foot-long Maui-punch-flavored Pixy Stix next to the counter and stuck it into a blister on Deep Dive's face that had begun to crust over.

Deep Dive swatted it away. "You little . . ." A voice from the back of the store stopped him from letting the boy know how he really felt.

"Robby, where are you? Come look at this nice alligator head pencil sharpener."

Robby ran off laughing – the foot-long powdered candy Pixy Stix in hand. Little shit. Deep Dive's dislike for children significantly deepened.

Hibiscus strolled over with a dustpan in her hand. "Well, ya think you can handle this gig?

"No choice, is there?" Deep Dive felt burdened by a heavy air of doom surrounding him. It wouldn't be long before the Big Piners called in their chits. The clock was ticking. And the way things were going—it didn't look too good for him.

"Them bastards made it clear. They want their weed. My boat, too. I'm so hosed. Where am I gonna get that kinda bread?"

"Yeah, you'll have to butter someone up. You're in a real jam." She giggled. "Get it? Bread, butter, jam?" Hibiscus thought she could provoke a laugh. The grumbler needed one.

Deep Dive was in no mood for humor, of any kind. Realizing he was not amused, she half-heartedly, with a generic smile, acknowledged his predicament. "Yeah, right now, it sucks being you."

But maybe not for me, Hibiscus thought.

In her mind, the Big Piners hadn't been too aggressive in their collection tactics. What was he bellyaching about? He had plenty of time to figure out a solution to his self-inflicted problematic situation. He needed to lighten up. She needed time to ponder the pros and cons of four bales of premium quality *sea weed*.

The idea of Deep Dive taking one for the team was very much to her benefit. After all, she wasn't the one who had been so careless in sharing details of the find with the trampy twins from the Tiki Shak. It kinda was his own damn fault. Why should her dreams be put on hold for his stupid moves?

With a large chunk of seed money, Hibiscus was one step closer to a career like her idol, Cheryl Tiegs, whose iconic "Pink Bikini" poster was on bedroom walls across America. Hibiscus already had a white bikini picked out for when she would be the next "it" girl. It was incredibly exciting to think about. She didn't want her dream spoiled.

"Considering everything that is going on, you're in an awfully good mood today," Deep Dive said.

"Am I?" She needed to play it a little cooler. "Oh no, man. I'm feeling your pain."

Deep Dive wasn't buying it. She was far too chipper for his misery. He wanted her to reflect his suffering.

"You know, you're kinda in this mess with me . . . maybe worse." Deep Dive thought about how much information he wanted to share with her.

"What do you mean?"

"Isn't my boat at your house? If they get wind about it . . . those Big Piners won't take kindly to that. Hey, listen . . . I'm just saying . . ."

Hibiscus hadn't thought of that. Troubling.

"Look, if that wrinkled-up prune went to see the boys, how long before she or her cronies pay you and Micki a visit?"

The lady from the bait shop paid the boys a visit? Doubly troubling.

Barry walked in, interrupting the conversation.

"Barry, do you ever work?" Deep Dive asked.

"Suck a fart out of my butt, dude. Listen, my dad's not too thrilled with me right now. I thought I'd give him a couple of days to cool off. You know, get out of Dodge."

Nine-year-old Robby ran past them. Deep Dive stuck his foot out, sending the little brat sprawling. Pixy Stix spilled onto the floor.

Deep Dive picked him up by his armpits and whispered in his ear. "You seen the movie *Friday the 13th*? I'm Jason's brother. Why do you think I look like this? I'm going to find you when you're sleeping and gut you like a pig, you lil' piece of crap."

Robby looked at Deep Dive in horror. "Ma, I wanna go! That man . . ."

Deep Dive glared at him, putting his finger to his lips. The family departed and the store quieted down a few decibels.

In a low voice, Barry shared a tidbit "I have more info on the folks from the One-Eyed Pelican."

Deep Dive's curiosity was piqued. "What?"

"Tom, the bartender at Peter, Dick and Willy's, knows them. It's the Wilkie family. Sam, Earl and their mom, Pearl. An old well-known Big Pine family. A rough bunch."

"That don't sound good." Deep Dive's stomach began to rumble.

"Tom said the old lady came into the bar askin' a whole lot of questions."

"About me?" Deep Dive asked nervously.

"Yup and then some. I don't know if you've talked to Shep and Juan yet, but she paid them a real unfriendly visit last night. She made it clear she wants money for the car as well as everything else."

Barry shot a look at Hibiscus. "Don't go thinking you and Micki are off the hook. The hag's looking for y'all, too. She made sure to mention some girls stole their boat."

The new information was not sitting well.

"And guess what, blabbermouth?" Barry turned and faced Deep Dive. "The twins are also Wilkies. That's what started this whole mess."

"The family is running shit on the side. Crap, we messed with the wrong folks." Deep Dive paused. "What next?"

"We?" Barry was not enjoying the fact that the situation had become a "we" one.

"Don't you think over time they'll forget about all this?" Hibiscus asked.

"Dream on," said Barry. "Not on your life. If they could blow up my truck, imagine what else they're capable of. We really . . . oh, hi, Mr. Dubicki."

"What are you kids talking about? Anything exciting?"

"Nothing much. Ya know, same ol' stuff." Barry flashed Stan a large grin.

"Groovy." Stan wandered back through the store.

What nice friends Hibiscus has, Stan thought. He was pleased to help out Deep Dive while his boat was getting repainted. The young lad seemed to catch on quickly and was doing a fine job. The extra help was nice.

Life was swell for Stan Dubicki. His business was booming. Not only that, he was looking forward to enjoying more of Hibiscus's remarkable stash after work. He trotted off in search of his beloved Patricia.

The horror reflected on Hibiscus's face was real. "Back up, Barry. What did you say? Your truck was blown up? By the Wilkies? What the fuck! When were you guys going to tell me?"

"You haven't heard? Deep Dive didn't tell you?" Barry asked. "I told him to!"

Hibiscus turned with a death stare for Deep Dive. "He most certainly did not. That detail seemed to have slipped his pea brain when he was over yesterday, checking out his boat and acting all nice and grateful. You are such an asshole. Did you tell Micki?"

"Calm down, girl. It's no big deal. Don't make too much of it. I didn't mention it because I didn't want to scare you gals. I was looking out for ya."

"My ass. You were looking out for yourself, as usual."

At that moment, Hibiscus couldn't stomach Deep Dive. What a piece of garbage for keeping menacing secrets from her. If she was inclined, Hibiscus could very easily resolve the Wilkie issue. All she had to do was hand over the bales. Any quandary about relinquishing anything, to save Deep Dive, had just been resolved. Hell no. She needed to talk to Micki ASAP.

"Guys, we need to be on the same page." Barry looked at Hibiscus. "Since you and Micki are working at The Conch this afternoon, why don't we all meet there?" Barry suggested. "We need to hash this out—face-to-face. I'll call the guys. We have a lot to figure out."

Barry had read Hibiscus's mind. "We sure as hell do," she said.

"One for all, all for one!" Barry proclaimed, trying to unify his friends.

Musketeer this, thought Hibiscus. *I know what I want.*

Deep Dive was relieved. His friends were also feeling the heat. Which potentially could work in his favor. He pulled some Tums out of his pocket and shoved two in his mouth. *Just in case*, he thought.

Hibiscus regretted offering Deep Dive the job at the Pink Flamingo. He had intentionally put her in danger by not divulging the truck explosion. Maybe these Wilkie people weren't as harmless as she had hoped. She just wanted to run home before her shift at The Conch. Have a nap. And, of course, a dabble of the Columbian Gold might help her relax and forget about what she had just learned.

25

LAVA

~ B-52's ~

Mama Pearl had good reason to be grumpy. Like magma coursing through a volcano, the pressure was building. It was 3 p.m. *General Hospital*, the daily soap opera that had captured the nation's attention, was starting. Wouldn't you know it, the damn office TV was acting up. She twisted the fucking rabbit ears again.

She had missed yesterday's episode because of the boys' crappy septic tank stunt and their stupidness with Deep Dive and his band of dumbass misfits. Now today's show was threatened with bad TV reception. Could it be any more irritating?

Pearl thrived on routine. Her 3 p.m. *General Hospital*, smoke, drink and crochet sessions were sacred. The phone in the office would be off the hook. Her boys and granddaughters knew the rules. From 3 to 4 p.m., Monday through Friday, the office was a no-go zone unless they sat like frozen statues. No chitchat until 4:01 p.m. The thought of missing another episode of her beloved soap really cooked her grits.

The storyline was intense. Nurse Bobbie Spencer was now romantically involved with studly Noah Drake, who was easy on the eyes. If only Noah had told Bobbie he loved her, she wouldn't have had to fake blindness for his love and attention. Pearl wondered what Bobbie would scheme up next. Would she leave Noah and Port Charles? And on top of Bobbie's shenanigans, her brother, Luke, finally asked Laura to marry him. But she had to place an ad in the Mexican newspapers so she could find her ex-husband, Scotty, to obtain a divorce. As usual, self-absorbed Luke was of no help. He was more focused on finding the missing Ice Princess diamond than helping his fiancée. So typical.

"Earl!" she shrieked. "Git your ass in here! The TV is on the blink."

Yes, Mama. C . . . c . . . comin' right now." Earl walked into the smoky office. His mom was pounding the top of the TV with her fist. She held a crochet needle tightly in her other hand. Uh, oh. He looked up at the bright yellow Squirt Soda clock. *General Hospital* time. Nothing but fuzz on the screen.

"Damn you, boy! Why is this blasted thing not working?"

Deflect immediately. Turn the heat elsewhere. Self-preservation at all costs. He whipped the Polaroid of Sam in the cage out of his back pocket. "Mama, you need . . . need to see this."

Like a possessed demon, Pearl flung her head around and, with a murderous glare aimed at her son, croaked, "What?"

She grabbed the Polaroid. Her eyes widened. "What the frick is this? What's your brother playing at?" Pearl was bug-eyed seeing her eldest son crammed in a dog cage with his bare rear end sticking through the gaps. It looked like he had a quarter crammed in his ass.

"Rico was here. He wants money if we don't get him the bales."

"Why the hell was I not told about this?" She slapped the TV harder like it was that guy Rico. "Git your brother, now!"

Earl booked it out of the office to look for Sam. On the dock, the twins were holding homemade aluminum foil sun reflectors to their faces, working for an ever-deeper tan. They were wearing their skimpiest bikinis to maximize exposure. It never occurred to them to relate that exposure to Nanny Pearl's leathery prune face. Tinker reached over for another Virginia Slim.

"Where's Sam?"

The girls pointed toward the shed.

"Girls, get inside and man the c . . . c . . . c . . . cash register." The girls glanced at him, insolently ignoring their father's request, taking another drag on their cigarettes. "Nanny Pearl said so." At that, the girls were quickly upright and skedaddled into the building. No one ignored Pearl.

Sam hadn't recovered from his humiliating session with Rico. He was throwing things around the shed.

"Whatcha doin'?" asked Earl. "Mama wa . . . wa . . . wa . . . wants you."

"What for? Isn't it three o'clock?"

"Ddd . . . ddd . . . don't be mad. Mama knows about Rico."

Sam stared at his brother. "And how does she know that, you idiot? You opened your big trap?" Sam grabbed the first thing he could reach and slashed his brother with a rope.

A raspy voice shouted, "Boys, now!"

Sam dropped the rope. They hustled to the office. This was not going to be good.

"I've had it up to here with you two! I should've cast you no-goods adrift on a leaky burning raft years ago!"

"Mama. Please. Calm down. I've got a plan."

Sam had no such thing. But he had to come up with something quickly. Out front, the twins were now chatting up a customer, giggling and laughing as they teased him to buy another six-pack of beer and a box of Trojans.

Sam scrambled. The girls. Of course. Use the twins as bait.

I'll sic the twins on him. Rico won't be able to resist. Of course, Sam would never consider using his precious Tiffani, now planning her marriage. His perfect angel was off-limits. In any case, she was far too classy for a job like that. Not swamp trash like his nieces.

A more objective observer might have thought Tiffani couldn't catch the most desperate man on a deserted island. She couldn't even attract a hungry hammerhead.

"I'm all ears." Pearl looked at the clock. Still time to catch the end of *General Hospital* if her boys would quickly explain the plan. And get the TV working.

"Mama, I'll call Rico tomorrow morning. I'll tell him to meet me. Let's make those assholes in Colombia believe they were double-crossed by Rico, not by us."

Mama Pearl's head jerked upward. Did her stumpy, dumbass son actually have a good idea? "What does this Rico look like?"

Sam filled her in.

"Mustache? Funny teeth? You don't say..."

Asshole, she thought to herself. She looked at the wooden plaque above the Wall of Shame. Bad thoughts were racing through her mind.

Bum Farto had disappeared. That was easy enough to do. It was a big ocean out there. If Bum Farto could disappear, why not Rico, too?

26

STUCK IN THE MIDDLE WITH YOU

~ Stealer's Wheel ~

Conch on the Bay restaurant was another prominent Keys landmark along US-1, also known as the Overseas Highway. A large plastic pink-and-white conch shell recently erected on an oversized rectangle slab of coral rock was impossible to miss along the two-lane road, the only road from Key Largo to Key West. An oddly shaped conch stuck out from the shell, holding a large sign welcoming guests.

Attached to the sign was a large gray tarpon with a bright silly smile, waving to tourists, luring them in for food, a vacation photo op and a chance to feed the fish. The place had it all.

It was premium Keys tacky, but the gimmick was brilliant and effective. The restaurant was a hit with visiting families and locals alike, not only for its conch fritters, grouper sandwiches, fried shrimp, Key lime pie and spectacular sunsets over the bay, but for the beloved tarpon feeding attraction. Locals regularly brought their out-of-town guests for the fun, particularly the kids. It was a winning concept. A goldmine of touristy goodness.

Most folks north of Jacksonville had never fished for or interacted with the magnificent tarpon. These sport fish played a big role in supporting the fishing guide community. They were highly prized by both visiting anglers and the expensive guides who took their well-heeled customers to secret fishing holes to challenge the rugged tarpon's strength, determined fight and fifty-mile-an-hour speed.

For those who didn't fish, Conch on the Bay had created one of the most popular tourist attractions in the Keys. Cleverly, the restaurant sold food to feed the scores of tarpon that hung around the dock. For a quarter, a visitor was given a feed bucket filled with small pinfish, squid or scraps from the kitchen. The tarpon certainly weren't picky. They devoured anything that could fit into their mouths. There was always plenty of food, most of it paid for by the tourists. Adding to the excitement, greedy brown pelicans tried to muscle in on the action, creating minor moments of chaos by aggressively flapping their wings in an effort to steal their share of the feed. It was a perfect gimmick. A brilliant business model. And of course, the tarpon were protected, not just at the dock. The entire cove was a no-fishing zone.

So, it wasn't surprising that many of The Conch's fat and happy tarpon grew to be huge, some reaching up to eight feet or more and weighing up to two hundred pounds. For a tourist or a child, a big tarpon was extremely intimidating, particularly when a wide and gaping hungry mouth flashed its pointy, needlelike teeth. The massive ones seemed like they could swallow a toddler if the parents weren't paying close attention.

The "Feed at Your Own Risk" sign reminded folks to use common sense when dropping food into the water. A weather-beaten laminated cartoon illustration demonstrated the proper feeding technique. Drop and release—don't hold on to food—a person could be pulled into the water. The Conch would not accept responsibility for missing watches, wedding rings, other jewelry, fingers or toes. No swimming was allowed.

Micki and Hibiscus walked out from the kitchen on a break waiting for their friends to arrive. Micki strolled over to the dock and tossed a few stale french fries to Scarface, The Conch's largest tarpon, rumored to be almost forty years old. A quick splash. Poof! The fries vanished.

"Micki, I don't trust Deep Dive anymore. If he kept the explosion from us, what else could he have left out? The only person he's protecting is himself. As usual. I have no sympathy for him."

"I get it. Listen, we both know what a shyster he can be. Geez, think about all the crap we've seen him do. But are we as slimy as him for letting him take the rap for the missing weed?"

Chef Mel opened the back door and yelled at the girls. "You've got half an hour, no more!"

"Yeah, Mel. We hear you." Micki looked at her watch.

Hibiscus nudged Micki. "Shush. Here comes Shep."

Shep arrived first. Then Deep Dive, Barry and Juan. They stood around looking at each other, waiting for someone to show a card. An awkward moment for old friends indeed.

Juan broke the silence. "Um . . . what now?"

Barry piped up. "I don't know what y'all know or don't know, but here's the gist. Listen up and then we gotta decide how to play this." He filled everyone in on what he had heard from Tom the bartender.

"Shep? Juan? Care to chime in?"

Shep touched his cigarette-burned hand as he gave Deep Dive the stink eye. Deep Dive closely studied the girls for any reaction. Micki and Hibiscus exchanged noncommittal looks. They didn't flinch. Juan glanced at Hibiscus, wondering why she wasn't fessing up to the square groupers he had secretly put on the boat. Was it possible she hadn't seen them?

"What the hell am I going to do?" moaned Deep Dive, breaking the lull in conversation. "They want my boat. And the bales I don't have. I'm running out of time before those nut bags come to collect. I don't want to end up as chum fed to the tarpon." He pointed to the dock, where a few tourons were teasing the big fish with small pinfish before heading off for drinks and a fried shrimp basket.

"Just give them your boat. It's better than nothing and anyhow, it's old. You can find a new one," Hibiscus offered nonchalantly. "I want it off my dock sooner rather than later. I don't want my parents involved." She was too annoyed with him to take pity or admit to what was sitting in her closet. Emotions had a way of overriding common sense.

"Sheesh . . . easy for you to say. It's not your boat. Or your source of income."

"Do you even have a choice? Don't those Big Piners want it? Plus, you have a new job at the Pink Flamingo. So what's the big deal?"

"Are you fucking stoned?"

Indeed she was. On Deep Dive's Columbian Gold.

"You call working at your parents' shop my new job? You got a screw loose."

Hibiscus was offended. "I don't think it's safe to have the boat at my house anymore."

There was some concern for her folks. But the sooner *The Reel Upside* was gone, the less likely someone would connect her to the missing weed stashed in her closet next to her shoes.

"C'mon, Hibiscus. *The Reel Upside* is safe there. Let her stay a little longer." She could really be selfish.

"So you're not worried about my parents? Hello . . ."

Juan was sweating more than usual. He was thinking about his dad's mysterious accident with the Neptune statue. Hibiscus wasn't wrong to worry.

"Hibiscus, don't be such an ass. Like I want something to happen to Stan and Patricia? Really?"

"Just saying," Hibiscus retorted.

"Maybe we should go to the cops," Juan suggested. All heads turned toward Deep Dive, waiting to see his reaction.

"I don't know about that . . ." If only it was that simple. Deep Dive didn't want the police sniffing around his past. There would be lots of questions about how a young guy, with no signs of any financial resources, had afforded a dive boat.

Juan scolded himself. Why in the hell had he even suggested such a thing? If the police came into the picture, the truth would be uncovered and he most certainly would lose his friends and become a Keys pariah.

"Yeah, maybe not such a good idea." Barry didn't want his dad to find out he was responsible for the loss of one of the Septic Baron's work trucks.

Micki nodded her head slowly in agreement. She too was worried. How would it look if she was featured on the front page of her father's newspaper?

Shep no longer cared what anyone decided to do. He was bitter and confused. Why was he feeling the pain for others' bad choices? He had nothing to do with any of it.

Hibiscus nodded her head in agreement. She didn't want to go to the cops either. For the love of everything good, she had the pot and didn't need to be charged for possession. No modeling agency would touch her if she had a rap sheet. Sheesh, Cheryl Tiegs probably never had to worry about four bales in her closet.

Deep Dive couldn't shake an uneasy feeling. Something wasn't right about Hibiscus. She was off. Combative, almost. She wasn't her easy-breezy, bubbly, airheaded self. Hibiscus and Micki *were* the first ones he'd told about his find . . .

Micki had had her fill. The conversation was going nowhere.

"Enough already! I'm done with all of this," she said. "Y'all are getting on my damn nerves."

Micki exhaled and plopped down on a sun-ravaged plastic chair before continuing.

"Deep Dive, go home. Call the One-Eyed Pelican. Plead your case. Beg for mercy. I don't know . . . what else can you do? Maybe, with luck, those shitheads will budge on your boat. And the other stuff."

Deep Dive winced. "I don't have the four bales or cash to offset their loss. Don't take this the wrong way, but you're light in the head if you think they're not going to want my boat or restitution for the missing bales. They don't exactly come across as forgiving folk."

"I dunno . . . maybe a miracle will happen." Micki shot Hibiscus a quick pleading look, hoping her friend would come to her senses.

"Barry and Juan, you better be prepared to come up with some cash for the car damage. Let's end this. The faster the better."

Juan was a little annoyed. He had been the passenger, not the driver who had hit Sam's car. Why was he on the hook? On the other hand, he had triggered the whole thing. Silence was his only play.

"Okay." Deep Dive cleared his throat. "I'll call the crackers if Hibiscus promises to keep the boat until a deal has been reached. I don't want *The Reel Upside* back at Paradise Isle. Please."

Deep Dive clasped his hands together in a prayerful manner. *The Reel Upside* needed to stay hidden. He needed time to figure out his options. He didn't want the Wilkies to get his baby. Ever.

With a strange tinge of guilt, Hibiscus reluctantly agreed. "Fine. Not a day longer." *What a butt-wipe*, she thought.

"What about them paying for my dad's blown-up septic truck?" injected Barry.

"You want to go there with the Wilkie family? Barry, you're crazy. I suggest making nice as quickly as possible." Micki shook her head in disbelief.

Deep Dive leaned against the dock railing, nervously picking at his cuticles. "I wish I never found that shit."

"No kidding," Micki agreed. "C'mon, let's get this mess cleaned up and behind us."

She looked at each of her friends. Her glance rested on Hibiscus the longest. Micki wished she had the ability to will Hibiscus to do the right thing. A dejected and suspicious Deep Dive noticed her lingering gaze.

Micki walked toward the kitchen door. A wharf rat ran over her foot. "Dammit! I'm sick of these nasty critters and their raisin poop everywhere. Yuck, so grody." It would be an awkward time for a visit by the health inspector.

"Micki, I got you covered," said Shep. "I'll get rid of the rats." This was the perfect opportunity to launch his new hairy critter removal and extermination business. Conch on the Bay would be his first client. "I'll swing by Wednesday night. I have the perfect solution." Shep was excited. His future was looking brighter.

"Sure, whatever." Micki was stressed and testy. She didn't have time for this idiotic weed drama or a rat infestation. The Conchy Tonk festival kicked off on Friday and she had once again entered her conch fritters in the Best Conch Fritter category. The fritter recipe needed to be perfect, but her recipe was still a work in progress, causing conch fritter anxiety. It was missing something. She couldn't quite figure out what. Maybe more habanero? This was the year her recipe needed to finally win. Always the bridesmaid, never the bride really sucked.

A young woman in pink heels and a sundress accompanied by an academic-looking man strolled into the restaurant like a queen bee. It was happy hour, featuring early dinner at lower prices.

Micki immediately recognized the side pony with a beaded ribbon band. She was not someone Micki wanted to see. Ever.

Could her day get any worse? What was that skank doing here? It was Kimbo the Bimbo, her former high school best friend. Since marrying Gerald Pratt, the Key Largo Elementary School principal, Kimbo had become even more insufferable.

Micki imagined massaging her face with a cheese grater. She had never forgiven Kimbo for kissing Juan at the prom, a moment that had led to Micki breaking up with him. Micki was convinced Kimbo orchestrated the disastrous game of Truth or Dare that night. She had a reputation for taking what wasn't hers, especially if it was connected to Micki. The saying was true. Once an asshole, always an asshole.

"Yoo-hoo! Micki. How fantastic to see you. Have you met my husband, Gerald?" Kim offered him up like a prized Pekinese at the kennel club.

"Yes, Kim. Every time you come in here."

Kim giggled. "Ah, my memory. We're still in our honeymoon bubble. Right, schmoopy?"

Like a lost puppy on a leash, Gerald stood quietly. He was still in early husband training. His previous wife had divorced him when Kim barged into the picture. He was already beginning to think his old boss was a better deal.

"Two grouper sandwiches. No onions and two Tabs. Oh, and an order of conch fritters. Please hurry. We have an important event we need to get to." Kim shooed Micki away with a casual wave of her hand.

Sure you do. An event, my ass, thought Micki.

"Oh, wait! Micki, come back. I forgot to tell you. Guess what? I'm a judge in the Best Conch Fritter category. Isn't that just fab? I saw your entry form. Maybe this will be your year," Kim proclaimed with a shit-eating grin. "Good luck. Gerald, sit." Kim pointed her husband to a table and chairs in a corner by a window overlooking the bay. Table Number 6, served by Hibiscus.

"Zip-a-Dee-Doo-Dah . . ." Micki turned and walked toward the kitchen. "Worst day ever," she muttered.

Micki couldn't stand the sight of Kimbo, the sound of her irritating voice, the smell of her old lady perfume, her better-than-you attitude. There was nothing redeemable about the bitch.

She dug into the fridge, looking for the two worst pieces of old grouper she could find. She battered them and plonked them into the fryer. As she fried up the grouper filets, she eyed a bottle of eye drops tucked away on the counter corner. Hadn't Betsy told her Visine could cause uncontrollable diarrhea if ingested? She didn't know if it was true or not, but it was an appealing thought to try it out on Kimbo. The worst thing that could happen—she'd croak. Gerald could start shopping for wife number three.

Her hand reached for the eye drops, but she thought better of it. She spat into both Tabs and stirred the drinks with a straw. Unfortunately, poor Gerald was going to be a casualty. She couldn't take the chance Kimbo would get a loogie-free soda. To make herself feel even better, she dropped some cooked fries on the grimy kitchen floor, gently kicked them around a bit, picked them up and added them to the plates. She made sure to sprinkle pepper and Old Bay Seasoning on them to hide any peculiarities.

Betsy, a friend and coworker of Hibiscus and Micki, couldn't stand Kimbo either. She opened the buns, spat in the mayo and closed the sandwiches back up. Betsy and Micki gave each other an understanding look. With a smile, Micki placed the plated food under the heat lamp and shouted, "Hibiscus, order for table six is ready."

27

YOU DROPPED A BOMB ON ME

~ The Gap Band ~

Rico was pleased. It had been a busy and productive morning. Sam understood the message. He would deliver on time. That would bring him back into the good graces of Señor Mendoza. Before rushing back to the Carlita to feed his cats, Rico treated himself to a few extra hours at Paradise Isle relaxing by the pool.

He savored the moment, quietly grading the various bikini-clad women. These ladies were a definite improvement over those wearing more modest bathing attire around South Beach. The meat here was fresher and leaner. Even the young mothers chasing their tots in the kiddie pool seemed special. Lots of desirable 7s and 8s. Even an occasional blockbuster 8.5. He rarely awarded a 9 or 10. That called for not only a really special body and a great face but also that extra special something. In any case, his cats could wait. He had left them plenty of food and made sure to leave the toilet seat up for fresh drinking water.

Rico lathered himself with Bain de Soleil Orange Gelée SPF 4, for a promised St. Tropez tan. Before getting too comfortable, he sauntered over to the Tiki Shak for his new favorite drink, Tiki Juice, and a small order of conch fritters. Walking back to the pool, he surveyed the scene. Definitely a feel-good situation. The Florida Keys were growing on him.

Not just the girls. The gorgeous pristine clear water filled with fish and beautiful coral. The food–not just the fresh fish but the locally caught stone crabs and lobsters. The never icy weather and warm, comforting sunshine. The opportunity itself. Maybe he could eventually go out on his own. Set up shop in the Keys.

After a couple of hours tanning, he forced himself up and off the chaise. He went to his room to pack and head north. He'd be back soon enough for collection day. Feeling a little itchy, he wanted a shower. Perhaps too much sun.

Rolling north, Rico spotted a large conch shell statue on the left-hand side of US-1, delivering a message. The best conch fritters in the Keys! Maybe in the world. He'd be the judge of that. Why not? The ones at the Tiki Shak he found rather bland, and he was already hungry again.

Rico parked the van, got out, stretched, scratched his crotch and walked toward the tarpon. Time to see if the conch fritters were as good as they claimed. Nearing the dock, he spotted two familiar faces.

Juan and Shep were leaving. A tall guy wearing a "Dive Deep off The Reel Upside" t-shirt was with them. Could that be the elusive Deep Dive?

Rico threw old Life Saver wrappers and other scraps from his pocket to the tarpon before heading into the restaurant. A woman was complaining to her companion.

"Schmoopy, these are just revolting, right? How does that tart expect to win anything? Garbage out of a dumpster would be better than this." Gerald nodded in agreement—the expected and permitted answer. Kim smiled. Training was going well.

Truthfully, Gerald didn't think they tasted bad. In fact, the fritters were quite tasty. He planned to sneak back and order them again when his wife was busy elsewhere.

Rico shrugged. The conch fritters at Paradise Isle had tasted okay. But he was ready for something more. The food here couldn't be as bad as the woman said. A lovely waitress in shorty-short cut-off jeans and a pink tube top sauntered over to the table.

"Welcome to Conch on the Bay." In a mildly bored voice, she introduced herself as she had hundreds of times before. "Hi. My name is Hibiscus. I'm your waitress today. May I take your order?" She was too exhausted to be at work today, especially after her exchange with the boys and smoking the extra bong bowl at home. The nap had not helped. Man, oh man, that stuff was strong. She probably should have waited until she got off her shift.

Without looking up from the menu, Rico asked, "What dju recommend?"

"Our conch fritters are the best. I also have a nice grouper sandwich that people love. Naturally, you must have a slice of our world-famous Key lime pie." It was Hibiscus's go-to spiel. It was easier to offer up what she knew than the special of the day, which she could never remember.

"*Sí*, I take those conch fritters and the grouper sandwich. Also, a Coke. You know, the drink," he snickered. He looked up, more than delighted to be served by the perfect Barbie girl. He liked what he saw. Hibiscus smiled her best leave-me-a-nice-tip smile. "Comin' right up."

Rico watched her bottom swish back and forth as she headed toward the kitchen. A definite nine. Possibly a ten. He was immediately in deep lust.

Hibiscus returned with Rico's soda. He attempted to chat her up. But Hibiscus wasn't feeling it. Rico was convinced she was simply shy. Playing it cool.

"Hey, mister, I'll get your food now."

"Señorita, please call me Rico. Dju is beautiful." He tapped her gently on the butt. It was not the first time that had happened to Hibiscus. Some men were just like that. She would ignore the gesture unless he left a crappy tip.

When the food arrived, Rico was pleasantly surprised. The conch fritters were *excelente*. Crispy golden on the outside and soft on the inside with a generous portion of conch, not breading. So much better than the dry, stale ones at Paradise Isle. These conch fritters were the product of Micki's latest recipe, a perfect combination of sweet and savory. Her recipe required fresh conch, nothing canned. She had tenderized the meat to highlight its natural sweetness. Her beer batter was enhanced by onions, bell peppers, garlic, cayenne pepper and a touch of habanero. Micki served the fritters with a slice of lime and a tangy tomato-based dipping sauce on the side. No doubt, these were the best he had ever tasted.

Hibiscus returned with his check. "My compliments to the chef," he said. He opened his wallet, flashing a large collection of bills. Hibiscus perked up. She giggled, flashing Rico her widest, brightest Marilyn Monroe come-hither smile. Rico was suddenly more interesting and attractive.

"I hope to see you again sometime. My name's Hibiscus."

"Beautiful flower, dju will." He tapped her on the butt once more. For the $8 meal, he left a $100 tip.

Rico had met his dream girl, at least for the month. The entire ride home to the Carlita, he fantasized about her movie star smile and her ripe apple-shaped bottom. Arriving at the hotel, he felt the nagging itch getting worse. He found himself incessantly scratching his balls.

Rocky, Cedar, Gus, Alex, Dash, Daisy, Annie, Denver and Mia greeted Rico as he opened the door. After being cooped in the hotel room for five days, Charon, the once-feral cat, was too miffed to greet him. He slunk to the closet and pooped in Rico's favorite shoe. The litter box was too full for Charon's liking.

28

HIT ME WITH YOUR BEST SHOT
~ Pat Benatar ~

A ringing phone woke a groggy Rico. He had not slept well. The constant itching was too much. The ringing phone next to his head was not only annoying, but it also didn't soothe the itch.

"What dju want?"

"Um, Rico. It's, uh ... Sam Wilkie."

"*Sí*. Well?"

"Everything is under control. I have your"—he coughed twice— "items."

"Ah, *amigo*. Good. I don't like naughty boys."

"Do you know Conch on the Bay restaurant?"

Rico's eyes lit up. Did he know it? For the moment, it was his favorite place on the planet. But his mother had warned him. Be cautious with snakes. Keep things close to your chest. The Wilkies were a family of vipers who needed to be trapped, if not exterminated.

"I find. No problem," he said.

"Thursday, eleven p.m." Sam hung up before Rico could reply.

The itch in his groin was becoming unbearable. He rolled out of bed and went to the bedroom window. He opened the curtains to let the morning light shine in. Marty was standing outside, holding a baby bottle. He waved to Rico. "I make a stinky," he proudly proclaimed.

"*Oh, por favor . . .*"

Rico jerked the curtains shut and headed into the black-and-white-tiled bathroom, avoiding the cracked tiles where he had stubbed his toes multiple times. Lines of black mold ran along the edges. Rico had other things to worry about. He needed a better look at his very itchy situation. He pulled down the front of his shorts and leaned down to survey things. It was not good.

"*¡Ay, caramba!*" What was this? Angry bright red bumps dotted his crotch area, reminding him of a lit-up Christmas display. Scratch. Scratch. What the hell? Looking closer, he spotted movement. Live crabs! Something had to be done. Pronto!

But how? Where had they come from? There was Mitzie, his aging once-a-week fling at the Carlita. Or, now that he thought about it, his evening with the twins. "*¡Esto no es bueno!*" Scratch. Scratch.

※ ※ ※

In Big Pine, Sam hung up the phone. He was pleased with himself. That asshole Rico. He had him right where he wanted him. It was payback time. The Polaroid camera was standing by. He wouldn't need a cage.

Warmed by a unique moment of pride, Pearl glanced at her eldest son. Sam had come up with a brilliant solution—frame Rico for the whole fiasco. It was a Hallmark moment, Wilkie style.

The night before, Sam had received an unexpected call from Deep Dive pleading his case. The sob story of stolen square groupers wasn't enough to have Sam reaching for a box of Kleenex. Sam made it perfectly clear. No bales meant he was owed $120,000. Cash. Or else. The boat was part of the deal. Period. Finally, at Deep Dive's suggestion, they would meet at The Conch. Thursday at 11 p.m. after closing.

No cops, or else. Yes, things were coming together.

Now they would make the Colombians believe they were double-crossed by Rico. They would pocket the $120,000 in restitution from

Deep Dive plus his boat. They'd tell the Colombians they'd delivered the bales to Rico. Rico had crossed them. As a gesture of good faith, they wouldn't accept the $20,000 payment for a completed job because of Rico's treachery. A show of both penitence and good faith in the hope of maintaining the Colombian relationship.

There was, however, one nagging problem. Sam had no idea who Rico worked for.

At this point, he had no intention of divulging that to Mama Pearl. He was confident he could wrangle the contact info out of Rico before he disappeared. Potentially, if all went well, it could mean more lucrative deals with the Colombians.

They just had to get the twins to follow the script. Anything involving the unpredictable twins was always tricky.

Nevertheless, the stars were aligning. Two birds, one stone. Sam was happy Deep Dive had finally come to his senses.

"Okay, boys, let's go over this one more time. Y'all screw it up and we're all dead meat. Understand?" Pearl glared at her sons. Earl sat patiently in the corner, spinning the cylinder of Daddy Wilkie's old revolver.

"You payin' attention, donkey brain?" Mama Pearl was getting annoyed. She opened the office door and whistled at the twins. They were goofing around in the store, unaware they were about to be the baited cheese placed in a rodent trap. "What the hell do y'all think you're doing? Cut the shit and git to work."

Sam spelled it out one more time. "We're gonna get the boat and cash from that asshole captain. We'll cut out his tongue or perhaps something a little lower if he doesn't cooperate. When Rico arrives, the twins will be in the parking lot, pretending their car broke down. They'll ask Rico for help. All they need to do is to distract him. For best effectiveness, show him some skin. How hard could that be? Earl will sneak up and immobilize him. We'll get Rico to the boat and head toward the Ten Thousand Islands. Tie his body to some weights and dump his ass into the ocean.

If anyone sees anything, Deep Dive takes the rap. After all, it's his boat, right? If we have to give it up, so be it."

Droning on, Sam had no clue. Rico and the twins were already acquainted.

"Sam, you sure about everything?" Pearl asked.

"Mama, I promise. I've got it all figured out. It's under control. You just sit back, relax and look pretty." Behind his back, the fingers on his left hand were crossed.

※ ※ ※

Meanwhile, at the Wilson house, Hibiscus and Micki were sunning themselves on pool floats when Micki's dad appeared. He was heading off to work as editor of the Keys' leading newspaper.

"Have a great day, girls. I'm outta here. Not sure what today holds. The last few days have been nuts. I mean, whoever heard of an exploding poop truck? Now that was news. It's the kind of crap that sells newspapers." He chuckled at his own cleverness. "This week delivered. Bad news sells papers."

"Bye, Dad. Have a nice day. Hope it's not too exciting."

Micki got out of the pool and dried herself off. "What the hell are you going to do?" she asked Hibiscus. "It's decision time. Deep Dive's meeting Sam tomorrow."

"I vote to keep it," said Hibiscus. "Let Deep Dive fend for himself. He created the mess, not me or you. Just think about how much we can make selling the shit."

"Hibiscus, please! Think for a second … someone knows you have the weed—not me, you. That person put it on the boat that was tied to your dock. Look at the big picture. Your hands aren't clean for two reasons. You and only you have the square groupers and the boat. You takin' that risk?"

Hibiscus couldn't ignore it. The Big Piners were looking for two female boat thieves. Only one of them had it parked at their house. It wouldn't take the Wilkies long to find her. Then what?

Hmm, maybe there was a better, but slower and safer, option to fund her modeling career. Score a rich dude. The traditional foolproof road to wealth.

Hibiscus hated feeling rushed into a decision. She needed more time to noodle things over. Micki needed to step back and let her think.

In the meantime, Hibiscus was hopeful big tipper Rico would pay her another visit.

※ ※ ※

The more he thought about it, the more convinced Deep Dive became. It was obvious. One of the girls had the weed. It had to be Hibiscus. A cute sheep in wolf's clothing. How could he ever have trusted her? The signals were there. Nevertheless, he was still second-guessing himself. On the other hand, maybe it was Micki.

His suspicions were now flowing totally out of control. At the same time, he didn't want to consider the potential disaster if he didn't deliver the boat to the Wilkies as promised. Why in hell had he trusted Micki when she'd suggested the call to the Wilkies? Terrible advice. He was more and more upset. And then it became clear. The girls had set him up. They'd set him up for failure, as the fall guy.

Well, he had his own ideas. Maybe Sam and the Wilkies wouldn't get his boat after all. He would show those conniving chicks who the clever one was. He wasn't going to be fucked. Let the girls get stuck with the cleanup. It would serve them right. An old story, wasn't it? Play with fire. Get burned.

※ ※ ※

"Josephine, you are such a good girl. Daddy loves you. You got your first job tonight." Shep hadn't fed her in a few days. He wanted to make sure she was extra hungry for those wharf rats. She was going to be a busy girl.

"What do you think of the new company shirts?" he asked Josephine. He modeled the white T-shirt on which he had carefully painted the company name *Hairy Critter-B-Gone*. He just wanted to look professional and presentable. Things were really looking up.

Carmen rolled over and patted the empty spot on the bed next to her. "Am I a good girl too?"

※ ※ ※

Juan and Barry zipped along on Juan's skiff, beers in hand. "Cheeseburger in Paradise" blared from the radio speaker. They sang along without missing a beat. Jimmy Buffett was their man.

Wednesday was looking up for the boys. Barry Sr. had finally calmed down. He was no longer yelling at his son. A tentative truce had been reached in the Baron house.

Juan was feeling more relaxed after consuming a few cold ones. He put his worry aside. Micki would fix things. She always did. Maybe he'd fess up. A big maybe. But first a pit stop at Shep's. It had been a while since the three of them had spent the day together fishing. Shep deserved a nice surprise.

Juan pulled up to the dock and jumped out. "I'll be right back with knucklehead."

From outside, he could hear Shep's voice. "Where's the beef?"

A female squealed with delight.

Juan slid the glass doors open.

Most moments in life are just fly specks, something done and quickly or ultimately forgotten. But some moments are explosions, imprinted on the brain or the heart. They are there eternally.

It was a scene that would be imprinted on his brain until the day he died.

His mom and Shep were playing naked Twister.

29

I SAW THE LIGHT
~ Todd Rundgren ~

What had started as a great day lurched into the shitter before lunch. One of his best buddies had punched him and was no longer speaking to him. And the love of his life, Carmen, had now pulled the plug on their afternoon delights. Shep was devastated at the loss of her acrobatic skills.

But after Carmen left, when his life had totally caved in on him, came a knock on the door. A swarthy heavyset man with a Spanish accent stood there carrying a suitcase. He handed it to Shep. "Please, get your *chooze*." He did as he was told and slipped on his flip-flops.

Initially, Shep was startled but not surprised. He knew the drill, which was well known and widely accepted among many locals. In fact, he had been half-expecting it.

Several months earlier, at the Tiki Shak, an out-of-towner had struck up a conversation over a Coors. After learning that Shep had a house on a deepwater canal, the man asked Shep if he might be willing to "rent" his house for a week. For the right price, of course.

As a security measure, the drug cartels routinely changed locations where they could safely offload drug shipments before transporting them by land to Miami and other points north on the mainland. The tactic was quite simple. A waterfront home with deepwater access and at least partially sheltered or remote would be selected. After minimal vetting, the targeted resident would be bribed to vacate the house for a long weekend or week, in any case long enough for the smugglers to bring in a shipment by boat and take it north on the highway before moving on to the next virgin location to handle a shipment. Keep moving, always a step ahead of the feds.

Proper protocol was to take the suitcase, put on your "chooze," gather the kids, pets, whatever and go visit the Mouse in Orlando. Even those who instinctively wanted to decline with a polite "No, thank you," usually concluded that wasn't the best decision.

Upon returning home, it was important to glance cautiously, to look for yellow crime scene tape or a notice posted on the door. If the feds had busted the smugglers using the house as an unloading point, then the Department of Justice owned the property. But at least there would be the consolation cash-filled suitcase. There was another even brighter upside. If the operation wasn't busted, then the owner had both his house and the suitcase. It was the Keys' version of hitting the lottery. It was an opportunity to open a small business selling T-shirts on US-1 or to find some other way to launder the cash. The lovely part was it was almost like money from the sky. In some cases, it fell on you whether you wanted it or not. And who didn't want money like that?

Shep plopped the suitcase filled with banknotes from the "chooze man" on the passenger side of the bench seat. He then packed his reptiles and a few belongings in the back of his Chevy truck. One way or another, he was flush, a good deal wealthier than he had been twenty-four hours earlier. He headed for The Conch.

At least he still had his hairless pets and his sweetie and business partner, Josephine. She would never do him wrong. He knew she loved him. The heavy suitcase also slightly soothed his tattered emotions.

After a busy night, Conch on the Bay had closed. The last party of seven had just pushed away from their messy table, satisfied with the delicious house specials from Mel and Micki's kitchen. The coconut pineapple fried shrimps were praised. The blackened snapper mango salad had delighted. But above all, the conch fritters, cooked exactly to Micki's latest secret recipe, had drawn noisy compliments. Inevitably all washed down with multiple rounds and joyous clinks of bottles and glasses filled with Pabst Blue Ribbon.

"Night, Micki. I'm beat. See you tomorrow." Hibiscus unlocked the door and stepped out into the parking lot. Poor Hibiscus had no idea what was waiting at home.

She got in her car and backed out, waving to Shep as the two vehicles passed each other. His face looked odder than it had earlier in the day.

A brokenhearted Shep approached the restaurant door. He was rubbing his jaw. It ached from a devastating left hook from his former friend Juan, enraged at Shep's involvement with his mother. His nose was no longer bleeding, but it was badly swollen. A large piece of Kleenex jutted out of his right nostril.

He was hoping his bashed-up face wasn't too noticeable. Before leaving his house, Carmen had done her best to cover Shep's growing number of imperfections with her CoverGirl Oil Control Translucent Powder. The product promised a natural look. Somehow the promise didn't work on a man with drying sun blisters and a badly bruised face. The powder clung to his beard stubble, peeling skin and healing blisters, accentuating the crusting edges. As for the bloody nose—much tougher to hide.

The bell-shaped door chime ting-a-linged announcing his arrival into the restaurant. He sat down on a chair still deep in his thoughts.

"Hello ... Shep? Anyone there?" Micki snapped her fingers in his face. Shep's mind had drifted elsewhere. "What the hell happened to you?"

"You don't want to know," Shep responded, still pondering his run-in with Juan and the loss of Carmen. It was one of the worst days of his life but, paradoxically, the most lucrative.

Shep was right. With all the stress in her life, Micki didn't want to know. She couldn't pile any more aggravation on her plate. If his injuries weren't Wilkie-related, she could wait until after the conch contest for the sordid details.

"Wilkies?" she asked.

"Nope."

"That's a relief. Good. Let's get started. Where's your exterminating stuff?"

"Hold up. Let me go get it." He took off toward his truck. Shep returned with Josephine wrapped around his shoulders.

"Your snake? You gotta be kidding me."

"Hardly! I swear you won't regret it. Josephine knows what to do. It's her business. She's good for the environment. No harsh or poisonous chemicals. It's the future of rodent control."

"Mel's going to kill me . . ."

"Don't worry. We won't leave a trace. We'll be gone before sunrise. I'll watch her the whole time."

Shep started singing a tune he made up. "Now you see it. Now you don't." Pretty catchy! A perfect slogan for his new business.

Micki threw Shep the keys. "Be sure to lock up when you're done. Put the keys in my mailbox."

"Aye-aye, boss. Will do."

"I left some conch fritters on the counter for you. My latest recipe. I think I nailed it. Let me know what you think." Micki walked out the back and headed home. She was wiped out. She liked her job. She loved making conch fritters. But on any given day, enough was enough.

Shep took Josephine off his shoulders and gently laid her on the sticky floor. "Josie, Josie, it's time to get to work. Make Daddy proud." Josephine was hungry and cross. Her human had cut back her food supply. She wasn't used to that. She slithered slowly across the floor and headed toward the refrigerator. She had already detected the pitter-patter of little feet.

Shep grabbed a conch fritter and started munching away. "Damn, these are good." He considered sharing one with Josephine but didn't want to spoil her appetite. He wrapped one fritter up in a paper napkin and put it in his pocket for her as a little snack for later.

Quickly bored, Shep wandered around looking for something to do. Spotting pens, markers and empty cardboard boxes in the kitchen, he decided to make some company signs for his truck. Free advertising. Why not? In big bold letters, he wrote HAIRY CRITTER-B-GONE. Underneath the company name, he wrote his new jingle, "Now you see it, now you don't." He was proud of himself. Snooping through Mel's desk, he scored some tape.

Sneaking out the front door so as not to alarm Josephine, he taped the cardboard sign to the side of his truck. Ta-da! It looked great. One detail was missing—his contact info. It would have been helpful to add that. Ah, later.

Back inside, he found a thumbed-through Cosmopolitan magazine. Relaxing in the dining area, he flipped through top-notch articles such as "Outrageously Odd Couples—Why Opposites Attract." He took the "How much do you feel guilty about?" quiz, scoring a "not much" ranking.

Before long, his eyes got heavy. He dozed off, unaware that Josephine had made her way into the air shaft, where she was swallowing a family of rats. Her belly was getting full.

As Shep enjoyed his siesta, a group of fraternity brothers from the University of Miami were on a road trip with several inebriated, blindfolded pledges wearing nothing but their tighty whities. A rite of passage in Greek life, hazing was part of the initiation process. The tarpon attraction was too good to pass up. It was a popular destination for many fraternities in the Miami area.

Seeing lights on in the restaurant, the pledges were instructed not to make a sound. Any noise out of the wannabe brothers would result in a swift paddle across the backside.

Brother Steve lined up the blindfolded stooges and led them to the dock. One by one, pushed into the dark water, they were swarmed by hungry tarpon ready for a midnight snack. The pledges thrashed around, quickly deciding they preferred the paddle to bites by very large mysterious sea creatures. Scared out of their minds, the pledges tore off their blindfolds to see the gleeful smiles of their so-called friends and future fraternity brothers, paddles in hand, laughing and waiting to play whack-a-mole as they climbed back up onto the dock. They didn't hear Shep's snoring.

Steve had one more trick up his sleeve. He had spotted Shep's truck with the glass aquariums in the back. The light from the restaurant drew attention to movement in the truck bed. He found a family of iguanas, two savannah monitors, four bearded dragons, three crested geckos and Shep's most valuable creature, a two-foot Argentine black-and-white tegu.

"Who's ready to make some new friends?" Steve asked the soaked pledges who had finally been allowed back on land. Crammed like sardines into the trunk of his Oldsmobile Cutlass, the pledges would have plenty of time to acquaint themselves with their new scaly-skinned buddies on the ride back to Miami. It was the cherry on top of a very productive Hell Week. One for the books.

Crybabies would be left on the side of the road.

30

BOYS DON'T CRY
~ The Cure ~

Edward Lambert IV, known as Eddie to family and friends, sheepishly tapped on the glass entrance door to The Conch. Shep was jolted awake. He had been soundly sleeping on a dining room lounge chair, dreaming of a naked dancing Carmen.

A Howdy-Doody doppelgänger of about eighteen peered through the door. In soiled white briefs, he looked like he had just crawled out of a rotating cement mixer. His eyes were even redder than his hair.

Startled at first, Shep stood up, stretched his arms above his head and yawned. Stiffly, he walked to the door and opened it.

"Excuse me, sir. Can I use your phone?"

Shep motioned the wet and shivering teen through the door. "You okay?"

"Yes, sir." Eddie sniffled. "I need to use your phone."

Stuffed into the hot, crowded trunk of the Cutlass with the other frightened pledges and the god-awful lizards with a deadly odor, Eddie had lost it. The iguanas were like fearsome baby dinosaurs. But it was finally too much for him when the two-foot-long tegu crawled over him and flicked its tongue in his face. Its breath smelled like day-old puke. That was when he started screaming. For Brother Steve and the other frat boys, the shrieking was too much.

Branded a crybaby, Eddie was dumped out of the Cutlass onto the side of the road. He hiked back to The Conch, barefoot and dressed only in his Hanes white classic briefs. The other pledges had no complaints. More room to breathe.

"Follow me." Shep led him into Mel's small office and pointed to the phone. "All yours."

Shep thought it best not to pry. He didn't want to get pulled into any other shit. "Hungry?" He pulled the conch fritter he had saved out of his pocket and placed it next to the phone. Quietly he walked out of the office and shut the door.

Eddie dialed a number. After a few rings, someone picked up. "Mom? It's Eddie. I've had a really bad night. The guys . . ."

The floodgates opened. He cried a river. Choking back his sobs, he said, "You need to come and get me. I'm in the Keys. I know it's almost morning. Mom, calm down. I'm okay. I . . . I . . . I promise."

He could hear his hysterical mother on the other end of the line yelling, "Oh my Gawd! Ed, wake up! Something's happened to your son. I told you this would happen! You never listen to me."

Eddie leaned over and threw up in the wastebasket. Getting hazed, particularly with lizards in a cramped, dark, threatening space, was just not his thing.

Edward Lambert III sighed and rolled his weary eyes. That son of his. What was Eddie crying about now? He got up and dressed. This was not how he had envisioned early retirement on Star Island. He'd gotten more sleep when he was a marketing executive with Pepsi.

Shep looked at his watch. He hadn't seen Josephine in a few hours. It was best to check on her. He started looking. She was probably napping somewhere. No trace. That was the thing about pythons. They were very adept at hiding when they didn't want to be disturbed.

Shep started to panic. He needed to hightail it out of there before Mel arrived. If only he hadn't fallen asleep. He didn't want Micki to know he had broken his promise to be alert and out of there by the time Mel showed up.

Was it possible Josephine had escaped and headed back to the truck? He hoped so. Anywhere but the docks. The tarpon feeding machine frenzy could be vicious. He couldn't stomach the thought of the aftermath.

"Josephine, Josie! Josie! Come to Daddy!" There was no movement or acknowledgment of any kind. That was another thing about pythons. Unlike golden retrievers, they didn't come when called. No python in history had ever chased a ball and returned it.

Above him, Josephine was curled up in the very comfy attic with a full belly, dreaming her own dreams of finding another nest of rats. Josephine had done her job well. Now she wasn't going anywhere. Or showing up when summoned.

As Shep approached his truck, something else was troubling. Aquarium lids were strewn all over the ground. "What the fuck!" Shep ran as fast as he could to the back of his truck.

The aquariums were empty. His supply of hairless pets was gone. His gorgeous lizards. The priceless black-and-white tegu named Suzy. She was close to being housebroken. He slumped to the ground. With his head in his hands, Shep watched his teardrops hitting the ground. What else could possibly go wrong?

The ting-a-ling of the rusty entry bell alerted Shep to Eddie's departure. Eddie was wearing Mel's apron to protect his modesty. Chewing on the conch fritter, he walked toward Shep. He ran his fingers through his wavy red hair. The call with his mom had calmed him.

"Thanks for letting me use your phone. My dad's coming to get me. This is really good," he said, holding up the remainder of the conch fritter. "This your truck?" He pointed to the Hairy Critter-B-Gone sign.

Shep nodded.

"Um, did you catch all those things that were in there? Well, you're in luck, dude. Those assholes did you a favor. Those lizards are on their way to Miami. They'll get rid of them for you."

It was too much for Shep. More moisture filled his eyes. Even the thought of the chooze money, still safely locked in the cab of the truck, was not enough to console him.

Eddie felt sorry for the sad man with the disfigured, crusty-looking raccoon face. His red and raw sunburned skin was shedding like a lizard. It wouldn't surprise him if the guy's facial injuries had been caused by an attack from one of the dangerous-looking demonic creatures. Eddie was more than relieved to no longer be locked in a trunk with the smelly wet bodies and mini Godzillas.

Now it was clear. He should have joined the chess club. Lesson learned. Choose your friends wisely, and above all, listen to your mother.

31

RUNNIN' WITH THE DEVIL
~ Van Halen ~

Shep was beating himself up. *If only . . .*

Alternative scenarios were speeding around in his head like Richard Petty's Ford at Daytona. His two favorite gals were gone. Carmen had reunited with that dullard coma-induced Enrique. Josephine was MIA. His dream businesses had gone bust before they even started. Juan was no longer talking to him. His hairless pets had been kidnapped. His lizard supply was somewhere in Miami with a bunch of degenerate assholes. All he had was the chooze money.

Shep didn't know that by the time the frat boys reached Florida City, a hostile mutiny had occurred in the Cutlass. His treasured collection of reptiles was dumped in the Burger King parking lot along with Brother Steve. New nonnative wildlife, heading toward the Everglades, were making themselves comfortable in their new habitat.

Shep thought long and hard about his next step and how to control his galloping anxieties. Pythons normally retreat after a filling meal to relax and digest. He didn't smell any putrid snake regurgitation. That was a good sign that Josephine's feeding had probably been successful. One thing about snake barf. The odor was unmistakable. He had to assume she was tucked away, resting happily.

As a responsible pet parent, he had a last look around. He didn't want to be busted by big, burly, former Marine Mel. Thinking ahead, he unlocked the windows of the men's room so he would have the ability to sneak back in later that night for a reconnaissance mission. No one would be the wiser that eleven-foot Josephine had gone AWOL.

Shep drove off, patting the suitcase next to him. The balm of the chooze money was easing the pain. With the chooze people at his place, he hoped Deep Dive wouldn't mind if he crashed on his couch. He badly needed some shut-eye.

Deep Dive hadn't been asleep long before he felt a smack on his feet. "What the hell are you doing here?" he asked.

"I vacated my pad. A Mr. Chooze man paid me a visit," Shep said, patting the suitcase next to him.

"No kiddin'. Wow! You're one lucky bastard. How much is there?" Deep Dive asked, evaluating the ratty plaid tweed Hartmann suitcase.

"Dunno. Haven't counted it yet. Probably more than I make in a year. I've had too much going on. Except for this, my life's in the crapper."

Deep Dive looked again at Shep, practically hugging the suitcase. A chooze suitcase? They were known to be hefty. Hmm, could the Hartmann pull him out of his own hole? This could change everything.

"Hey, I've got your back, man. You know I'd do anything for you. You're my bro."

That's what Shep was worried about. He wasn't so sure about Deep Dive, considering the events of the past few days. He nodded anyway, pulling the suitcase tighter to his body. Deep Dive was already far too interested in it.

"Not to bust your balls, but you stink like monkey butt."

Shep smelled his armpits. More like onions, he thought. Or maybe snake poop.

"The shower's all yours. Use the striped towel. I only used it twice," Deep Dive said. "Ya know . . . why don't I put the suitcase in my closet for safekeeping?"

He patted Shep on the back and without asking lifted the plaid tweed suitcase with buckle straps out of his friend's hands. Instantly, he liked the weight and feel of it. It felt, how would one say, moneyed.

"Trust me. It will be safe there. Anyhow, sorry to cut things short, but I got to go to work. The Pink Flamingo is calling." Deep Dive headed toward his bedroom closet. A big smile was spread across his face. He now had options.

Deep Dive couldn't wait for the Wilkie mess to be sorted. He had had his fill of retail tourons. Shutting his bedroom door, he anxiously unzipped the suitcase. It was one of the most beautiful things he had ever seen. Stacks of green bills held together with rubber bands. Yes, siree . . . lots and lots of green. This was even better, significantly better, than the gift from Jesus. No conversion to cash was required. Free untraceable money. It was too good to be true. He zipped it back up and placed it in the back of the closet. He was giddy with excitement. He was almost out of the woods. So close . . .

The suitcase changed everything. He didn't want to beg the Wilkies for mercy ever again. And now he wasn't going to. After the way he was horribly treated, he wasn't giving them one fuckin' dime. Or his boat.

And if the Wilkies wanted the square grouper bandits, have at it. Now that he was sure the girls had done him wrong it was no skin off his back if Hibiscus and Micki got the full Wilkie heat. At least the target would be shifted away from him. In his head, it was clear. If the girls hadn't stolen the bales from his boat, all this would never have occurred. Why should he have to suffer the consequences of the girls' devious actions? Payback couldn't happen fast enough.

Deep Dive just had to find his hula girl keychain and take back what was rightfully his, plus, of course, Shep's cash-filled suitcase. Then it was time to hightail it out of the Keys for a fresh start in Bimini. A place where he would be respected and appreciated for the man he was. He had never been to Bimini, but he knew plenty of people who had. From everything he had heard, it was just as warm and almost as beautiful as the Keys. And dock space was said to be a lot cheaper.

There was, however, one tinge of regret. Sticking it to Shep. They had been friends for so long, but what choice was there? Shep's miracle suitcase was going to give him safety and a new life free of the Wilkies. Shep would understand. He would bounce back. He always did.

Feeling good about how it was going to turn out, he promised himself he would make an extra special effort to be nice to the tourons today.

☘ ☘ ☘

"Who does he think he is, treating me like he has? I'm over it," Shep said to himself. He looked out the window to make sure Deep Dive had driven off. He walked to the closet, pulled out the suitcase and placed it on the bed. Shep zipped it open, caressing the rubber banded money rolls.

"Whoa, buddy. This really is a lot," he murmured. Rumors about the amount of cash the chooze people handed out were not exaggerations. Mr. Chooze man had been more than generous. There was a lot there. He could count it later.

Shep knew Deep Dive all too well. He would not let him screw him over again. He rummaged through the closet, looking for what he needed. Voilà!

He emptied the suitcase contents into two flowery pillowcases. Now he just needed something to replace the bills with. Shep had to get the weight just right to avoid drawing suspicion to the switcheroo.

How about that, asshole!

32

INSTANT KARMA

~ John Lennon ~

Growing up on the same street, Shep and Deep Dive had been friends for as long as either of them could remember. Four years older than Shep, Deep Dive had been like a cool older brother to Shep, who grew up in a house full of estrogen. They were bros. A bossy big brother/pesky little brother dynamic—with its share of ups and downs. Shep idolized him and emulated him even when Deep Dive treated him like a second thought.

Shep's memories of their time together were by and large fond ones. They'd first fished together when Shep was only eight. They'd caught their first lobsters together a year later. As true lobster mobsters, they would cover a dock with their catch in the days when restrictions on how many you could take were much looser and rarely enforced.

Stone crabs were even more prolific. During the season, their traps were always filled. They made good money with the local restaurants.

Their first scuba dive with Deep Dive's dad had taken them out to the beautiful clear waters of Alligator Reef to see the underwater wreck just two hundred feet from the lighthouse. It was an unforgettable moment so special yet typical for kids growing up in the Florida Keys.

Deep Dive and his dad also taught him how to use a Hawaiian sling for spearfishing. It took him a bit to get the hang of it, but eventually he did. Spearing the tourist in the hand was truly an accident. A beginner's oopsie. Luckily for them, the blood in the water panicked the tourist, giving them time to disappear from the scene. The overly dramatic screaming tourist feared every shark in a fifty-mile radius was on its way after getting a whiff of fresh Northerner blood.

Deep Dive even taught Shep how to be a man. Spying on his older friend through the back of his foggy car window, Shep figured out what his mother refused to talk to him about.

These were wholesome childhood memories that Shep would not forget. The guys had been through a lot together and shared a deep bond. Nevertheless, the last few days had been horrendous. Much of it was caused by Deep Dive. The old ties were fractured. Shep knew his buddy all too well. That was why things would work out much better if Deep Dive could not easily open the suitcase.

At the hardware store in Tavernier, Shep purchased a lock. Deep Dive didn't need to know that Shep's chooze money had been replaced.

Before leaving the apartment, Shep left a short note thanking Deep Dive for his hospitality and accepting his offer to keep the suitcase for safekeeping until the chooze man cleared out and he could return to his own house. The note explained that for extra safety, he had added the lock. Shep acknowledged how lucky he was to have such a good friend who would help look after the suitcase. Blah, blah, blah. The yellow-lined paper was positioned so it would be easily seen on the cluttered kitchen counter.

Shep grabbed the two cash-filled pillowcases and drove to Barry's house. His one remaining true friend. Depressingly, Juan's house was now off-limits.

※ ※ ※

Too embarrassed to seek professional help for his personal infestation, Rico had to find a way to rid himself of the bloodsucking beasts before heading back to the Keys. The only sure way was to make sure the tiny *bastardos* had nothing to hang on to.

Shaving cream and a razor were in his hand when he was distracted by a TV commercial for Nair Hair Removal Lotion with baby oil. The bathing-suit-clad gals singing and dancing on a giant shaver got his immediate attention. *Drop the blade, babe. Put the Nair there. Gets rid of hair in minutes!* He loved the song, the message and particularly the promise of quick, gentle hair removal. The girls in heels and pink bathing suits were an extra treat.

Perfect. He needed no convincing to ditch the sharp razor. Removing hair with a lotion that contained baby oil sounded divine. Within the hour he had purchased a pink-and-white bottle of Nair.

Although heavily accented, Rico considered his English to be good. His skills had greatly improved since his arrival in America, although reading remained a struggle. Anyway, Rico found reading a waste of time. Most things were intuitive. He skimmed the package directions. Nair promised good results. What else did he need to know?

In a few short minutes, a lathered-up Rico learned what else.

Nair recommended a pre-use patch test to check for possible irritation or allergic reaction. Other warnings were also bypassed. Do not apply to aggravated open skin. Do not use Nair on your genitals or anus. Particularly the anus.

Reading also would have disclosed that depilatory creams scorch the hair in a way that can also burn sensitive skin. Rico's skin was already highly tender in the nether region from scratching himself raw.

The bottle also cautioned the importance of hand washing with soap and water before touching anything else.

Midway through a generous application, Rico was distracted by *The Price is Right* Showcase Showdown, his favorite part of the popular TV game show. He unconsciously stroked his mustache, scratching his head for imaginary crabs while talking to the screen and offering advice to the contestants.

Contestant Two had a distracting bounce. A lady with large floppy breasts, which overshadowed her large floppy red velvet hat and blue "Pick Me" T-shirt, jumped up and down in excitement, producing a lot of wiggly-wobbly.

She was desperately playing to win a new car when an unbearable sudden burning sensation jolted Rico to reality. His crotch and now hairless butt were on fire. He ran to the tub, turned the water on full blast and jumped in, hoping cold water would relieve the pain. Panicked, he splashed his entire body, trying to remove any trace of the hair removal lotion.

By the time his thoughts were together . . . too late. Disgusting clumps of black, disintegrating black hair, not just from his private parts, were floating on the water.

Somewhat cooled down, Rico climbed out, dried himself off and peeked into the mirror. He was still itchy and very sore. "*¡Joder! ¡Qué mierda!*" That was one commercial that had not exaggerated what its product could do.

Mirror, mirror on the wall. He was no longer the most beautiful of all. Scraggly patches of his movie star lush hair and mustache mocked him. He resembled a doll that a toddler had taken scissors to. Without his full bushy mustache to distract the eye, Manny Mendoza's primitive dentistry skills were on full display. "*¿Por qué yo?*" he screamed, scaring his cats.

Time was running out. He still needed to hurry back to the Keys to pluck his beautiful flower and collect from the Wilkies. Maybe he'd wear a hat.

He would never know whether Big Floppy Boobs won the car.

※ ※ ※

Bartender Juan's Tiki Juice was legendary. Now, Juan just wanted to move forward. Let the whole mess be a distant view in his rearview mirror. He was focused on his new cocktail creation—the Kick-A-Butt. He knew it was going to be a hit. A potent knockoff of Long Island Iced Tea but with triple the amount of white tequila.

But, as we all know, it takes a good deal more than great mixologist skills to be a man.

You see, Juan had one major problem. He was a bona fide chickenshit.

He saw it as being in his best interests to remain silent about his role in triggering the Wilkie fiasco. His theft of the square groupers from the engine room of Deep Dive's boat had set everything in motion. Now there was no point in telling everybody. The past couldn't be changed. What was done was done.

He called Barry and hesitantly offered to chip in a few dollars to help pay for the TR7 repair. For appearances's sake, it was the least he could do.

Even though Barry was the driver who backed into the front of Sam's shiny red car, Barry found Juan's measly offer more than annoying. What a cheapskate. A true friend would at least offer to pay half.

Barry headed to Septic Baron's office to ask sister Roo for an advance on his next paycheck.

"Really, Barry? You've got some nerve coming in here asking for money. Maybe if you worked nine to five like the rest of us and stopped spending your money on booze, weed and women, you wouldn't be so damn broke. I'm not giving you a dime, loser."

Barry flipped her the bird. He'd have to hustle his dad.

🌿 🌿 🌿

"Girls—hey, girls," Pearl called for the twins as sweetly as she could muster.

"What is it, Nanny?"

"Your daddy, uncle and me, we need your help tonight with—"

$ea Weed | **175**

Belle cut her off before Pearl could finish. "No can do. I've got a date tonight. So does Tinker. What about Tiffani? Can't she do it?" Belle did not want to miss her rendezvous with a fat cat from Fort Lauderdale.

Pearl needed the right bait. Tiffani was not it. She hesitated. How to answer politely? She couldn't disrespect Sam's princess, her own granddaughter.

"I need you, girls, tonight. Your cousin doesn't have the right tits or ass for the job."

"Do we have to?" the twins whined. A steely Mama Pearl glance gave them the answer.

"Okay. So what's in it for us? You better make it worth our while." The twins realized the family needed them for something big. They were a hot commodity. No family discount would be applied. Their assistance would most certainly not come cheap. The apple didn't fall far from Pearl's side of the family tree.

🌿 🌿 🌿

Hibiscus was drained. After finding Auntie Peg and Funcle Paul at her house the night before, she made a fast break to her friend Betsy's house, where they stayed up most of the night gossiping and trying out new makeup and hair looks. She was hoping her parents' close friends would be gone by the time she returned home. No luck. Hibiscus was now hiding out in her room away from the clutches of her family's unexpected visitors.

"Hello? Are you still there?"

Micki had hung up on her. Hibiscus sat on her bed, mulling over the details of the heated conversation. She was surprised by the turn the call had taken. They didn't often argue, but today they had and not over something trivial like borrowed clothes or cute boys.

Micki was finished with the square groupers and the boat. No ifs, ands or buts. She was done with the lies, the deception and the stress.

She didn't have the nerve to go head-to-head with the awful Wilkies. Her thoughts were solely focused on winning the conch fritter competition.

"How many times do I have to tell you? You're being stupid," Micki said. "Don't you see the danger you're putting yourself in? Look what they did to Shep and Deep Dive. The truck explosion . . ."

Yes, but why couldn't Micki see the positives as well?

Micki had persisted. "We all know Deep Dive can be a jerk, but throw him a lifeline. He's got everything to lose. Do what's right. Hand the crap back to him. Or just leave it anonymously at his doorstep. I really don't care. Just get rid of it. It's not worth it."

Hibiscus struggled to understand Micki's logic. How could anyone relinquish so much money? Sure, some bad things had happened, but wouldn't giving up *The Reel Upside* calm things down? It made sense to hand over the boat to the Wilkies. What was the big deal? The boat was old and ugly. It needed serious upgrades and some moderate rehab. Deep Dive could eventually buy a new one. With the boat gone, the girls, Hibiscus in particular, would be free of the whole mess, no longer culpable—for anything.

But returning the square groupers? Give up her future cash cow? If she returned the weed, everything would just remain the same. Same old, same old. Nothing appealing about that. The bales were the key to fulfilling her dreams. The more she fantasized about the perks, the more the pendulum swung toward an enticing payoff.

Hibiscus had been Deep Dive's good friend. She was the one who had retrieved the boat, hidden it and landed him the job at the Pink Flamingo. What was that worth? The square groupers were more than a fair payment. But, alas, for some people, you could never do enough. What an ungrateful asshole he had become.

Hibiscus got off her bed and stood in front of her mirrored closet doors, admiring herself, striking a few modeling poses before continuing to argue her case. She was working overtime to convince herself to keep the golden goose.

Her reflection stared back. No response.

She sat down on the floor and faced the mirror to continue her conversation with herself. "Micki wants nothing to do with it. No one else knows I have it except the mystery dumper. Whoever it was that put the pot back on the boat obviously didn't want it. By definition, the square groupers are mine to keep. Right?"

But who was she turning into? She no longer recognized herself. Her greed-riddled thoughts didn't sit well. Would it bring a lifetime of deep shit karma? Even though Deep Dive wasn't her favorite person, would it be right to stick it to him? It was fun to dream of what an enriched bank account could bring, but, as Micki told her, bad mojo was not to be fooled with.

Acting with ill intentions means problems will follow. Her chin was a case in point. Small pus-filled pimples were popping up on her face. The Clearasil wasn't working. It was time to recognize that her negative actions were unfavorably impacting her photogenic face. She needed to return the bales to clear the bad energy. She was dreading it. But better late than never. Hopefully, no one would notice one of the bales had been sampled. And her skin would clear up.

Hibiscus stood up and opened the closet doors. Something was amiss. Trepidation set in.

"Where is it?" she screeched. The bales were no longer in the corner where she had neatly stacked them next to her shoes.

33

PURPLE HAZE
~ Jimi Hendrix ~

Stan and Patricia giggled in the Pink Flamingo storage room like two cheeky schoolgirls. Much of Wednesday night and predawn Thursday were a blur. They had no business being at work.

Sixteen hours earlier, Peggy and Paul, their former roommates and best friends from the Mother Earth Intentional Living Commune, had paid the Dubickis an unexpected visit. It didn't take long for the reunion to run off the rails.

Peggy had always been a bit of a wild filly. Unpredictable. But you could always count on her to get the party started. Good-time Paul was no wallflower either. As Stan and Patricia liked to joke—two P's in a pod. And if Patricia was feeling particularly frisky—three P's in a pod. The two old friends never disappointed with their kooky antics.

Paul and Peggy had recently returned from Peru where Paul had attended an intensive one-day "How to Become a Shaman" program. He was proud of his certificate of completion and was excited to introduce his friends to the Sacred Plant of Vision, ayahuasca. Evolved from indigenous cultures, it was a powerful psychoactive brew used for healing spiritual and physical maladies.

Paul had trouble remembering the exact ratio of stalks of the *Banisteriopsis caapi* vine to the leaves of the *Psychotria viridis* shrub to make the hallucinogenic concoction, but he figured he was close enough. The timing of the full strawberry moon was perfect for a shamanic ceremony. It would be a profound spiritual experience. Remembered for a lifetime.

The two couples sat in a circle as Paul poured the ayahuasca tea. In a high pitch, he chanted "Ikaro" to attract healing spirits. Thirty minutes later, all four were in various stages of undress, howling at the moon. The get-together had lifted off into another dimension.

Hibiscus, after a long day of work, pulled into the driveway. Spotting the four adults prancing around the yard chanting, she instantly put the car in reverse and headed to the sanctuary of her friend Betsy's house. Hibiscus wasn't interested in joining their questionable festivities. She'd return the next day after they had whatever it was out of their system.

Stan, Patricia, Peggy and Paul's animalistic howls slowly morphed into oohs and aahs as the rays from the beautiful vibrant pink moon cast swirling multicolored auras off the top of the water. Before too long, the hypnotic beat from the dancing waves distracted them, summoning them toward the dock.

Below the dock, manatees were happily swimming, unconcerned about dodging boat propellers. Patricia noticed them first. Thankfully, ayahuasca gave her the ability to speak manatee. The largest one winked and waved at her with his glowing, flashing flipper. In a soft singsong voice, he spoke to her. The big manatee said he and his family were hungry for seaweed.

She understood what they meant—sea weed, not seaweed.

Fortunately, Hibiscus had four nice bales in her room.

Before too long, Peggy, Paul, Patricia and Stan were sitting quietly on the wooden dock, soaking in the beauty of the kaleidoscope vibrations whizzing around them. The manatees' plea for food became stronger.

"Feed us," the manatees chanted. With a bale on each lap, the three P's and Stan fed their new friends dinner.

The manatees danced and grinned big happy smiles. It was a joyous time. Kumbaya.

34

THE GREAT PRETENDER
~ The Platters ~

A visit from Peggy and Paul always ended in chaos. It was a guarantee.

Damn them! Hibiscus frantically ran down the outside stairs. She found Paul peeing in the bushes. It was an environmentally friendly thing to do. Fresh urine was a nutrient powerhouse for plants and Paul was always happy to give back. It was the least he could do.

"Paul, what have you done?" Hibiscus yelled.

Paul, stunned, looked at her and quickly zipped up his shorts in mid-stream. "Sorry, nature called."

"I don't mean that. How could you!"

Paul was confused. He was sure he had cleaned the poop out of the pool. Everybody knew Ayahuasca could be unpredictable. You never could tell how the body would react under its mystical spell. It was understandable Hibiscus would be upset. Never mind. She'd get over it. Paul unzipped his pants again and finished what he started.

Hibiscus jumped into her yellow VW Rabbit, put it in gear and peeled out, shooting jagged white pea rock into the air as she sped off to the Pink Flamingo. Her parents had a lot to explain. Hopefully she wouldn't run into Deep Dive. She couldn't bear to face him.

The Rabbit's tires screeched with her arrival at the Pink Flamingo. Deep Dive saw her storming up to the door and opened it. He would have preferred to smash the glass door in her face. Not wanting her to know he was on to her, he smiled his best Welcome Aboard boat captain smile.

"What up?"

"Do you know where my parents are?" Hibiscus looked away as she asked. She felt a jittery nervousness the moment she saw him. It was not the right time to come clean. Hibiscus still held on to hope the four missing bales had only been moved to a new location in her house. She continued to avoid eye contact.

Okey-dokey... What's with her? he wondered. Casually he said, "Don't take this the wrong way, but your folks have been acting stranger than usual. I think they're in the storage room again." He pointed to the back of the store.

Since opening the store that morning, Hibiscus's father, Stan, hadn't stopped jabbering about something Deep Dive couldn't pronounce while praising the Colombian ganja he and Patricia had been sampling. The two Dubickis were totally stoned. Babbling complete gibberish.

Deep Dive didn't want to hear anymore. Their midnight skinny dip session with the manatees and being one with the strawberry moon was bullshit mumbo jumbo. His ass was on the line. That was the real story.

Hibiscus speed walked through the T-shirt aisle, the storage room firmly in her sight. Her first inclination was to barge in, but with those two she hesitated. Hibiscus tapped on the door to give them fair warning. The door cracked slightly open. Hibiscus could see her father's eye. "Honey bunny! Come in, come in." Stan swung the door further to let her into the space. At least they were dressed.

"What in the hell is going on? What are the two of you up to?" It was probably for the best to have the conversation in a private area—away from Deep Dive.

At the other end of the store, a customer approached Deep Dive. "Excuse me, sir. How much is this T-shirt?"

He didn't have time for this shit. He had eavesdropping to do. "It's free. Bug off."

Deep Dive moved as close to the closet door as he quietly could. The damn Dubickis! What were they doing in there so secretively? Were all three in it together to screw him over? Maybe Micki played no part in all of this. He could faintly hear Hibiscus's voice.

"Did you take my stuff? Yes or no?"

Patricia was gnawing on a Tootsie Pop, like a peckish squirrel, trying to get through the hard candy coating to the chewy chocolaty center. What could her daughter be so agitated about? The tone of Hibiscus's voice was making her uncomfortable. Patricia didn't like confrontation. That sort of bad energy zapped her good juju. She chewed harder.

The lasting effects of the ayahuasca and perhaps some other ingestible goodies were messing with her head. In the blink of an eye, she had gone from a state of joyful euphoria to a sudden state of paranoia. Her trip was not ending smoothly. She needed to take the edge off. Maybe one more toke before going back to work would right the situation. She grabbed the last half of a joint from behind Stan's ear. "Light her up, chuckle buns."

A distinct odor was escaping from under the door. The store's patchouli incense didn't disguise what was happening. It did not go unnoticed by Deep Dive.

"Are you joking? Is that from my stash?" Hibiscus asked. "It smells like it!" Colombian Gold had a very distinct aroma.

"Honey . . . we wouldn't invade your space without asking. Dad found this leftover grass in his pocket this morning."

"Leftover?"

"Hmmm, I'm not sure. Stan?"

Stan sought clarity from his foggy brain. Had Patricia invaded Hibiscus's personal space? Scattered images from the full strawberry moon ceremony darted in and out of his consciousness. He vaguely remembered feeding the manatees. Oh, dear . . .

Deep Dive's concentration was broken again. "Hello! Anybody working today?" A man was holding a pair of Ocean Pacific swim trunks.

What was with these tourons disturbing him? Didn't they see he was in the middle of something? Fuck it. Deep Dive had heard enough. It was obvious now. Fake "sweet" Hibiscus had been the mastermind of his destruction. Tonight couldn't arrive fast enough. "Hey folks, take whatever you want. It's on the house." He stormed out of the store.

Hibiscus followed a few minutes later. She didn't notice Deep Dive was no longer behind the cash register. She wasn't even aware of people walking out with armfuls of unpaid merchandise.

She rolled down the window and sat in her car, trying to contemplate her next move. "What am I going to do now?" Hibiscus was stuck. No ideas flowed. Just utter panic. The lifeline she could have offered Deep Dive was now permanently cut, like an umbilical cord. No way to reattach it. Deep Dive was dead meat. She prayed the mystery dumper wouldn't out her.

35

LIAR, LIAR

~ The Castaways ~

Feeling extremely betrayed, Deep Dive drove to the Dubicki house to retrieve what was rightfully his—the square groupers and *The Reel Upside*. There was one overwhelming problem. He needed the hula girl, the one married to his boat key.

He turned the front doorknob to open it. Paul stood in a flowing indigo-and-green robe with a parrot feather crown on top of his long, graying locks. Crouched on the back of the sofa, Peggy was smiling like a Cheshire cat. Strange music and unfamiliar odors filled the room.

"I've stepped into a madhouse." Something was very off about these people.

"Greetings, fine fellow. Who might you be?" Paul tapped Deep Dive on his head with a wand-looking thing.

Deep Dive hadn't expected anyone to be there, particularly somebody like this. "Um . . . um . . . my name is Shep," he lied. "I'm here to pick up some things for Hibiscus. You haven't seen a hula girl keychain by any chance, have you? She said it might be in her room."

Before he could make it past the entryway, Peggy sprung off the couch in his direction. She circled him with a burning sage bundle, focusing her energy on his face.

"Shhhhhep," she breathlessly chanted. "Enter with love and light." She hugged him tightly before releasing him. "Let me purify you. Your chakras are not in balance."

She blew the sage smoke into his face, into his eyes and up his nose. Deep Dive coughed. These out-of-towners were frigging crazy.

"I gotta get cracking, folks. Places to go, people to see." Deep Dive gave them a thumbs-up sign and an awkward grin. He walked towards Hibiscus's room.

"We are not folks," Paul called after Deep Dive. "We're Shaman Paul and Peggy. We want to share our love. Peace be with you,"

Whatever. Deep Dive walked into Hibiscus's room, covered wall to wall with film posters. He began rummaging through her stuff, starting with her dresser drawers. Various-colored bikinis crammed the drawers. He continued digging through her personal items. Nothing. He lifted her mattress. Nada. Where the fuck was the key? His bales?

A resin-caked bong filled with dirty, skunky water sat on the nightstand. He picked it up and poured it onto her pillow. It felt good to release some of his pent-up anger.

The closet was next. "Damn, she sure owns a lot of shoes for a Keys girl." No boat key or bales anywhere. Maybe *The Reel Upside* held what he was looking for. He should have started there.

The thought of having to pass Peggy and Paul again creeped him out. He looked out the window to see if he could evade them. Hell no, too far down. He bit the bullet and strolled through cuckoo land once more. Eyes closed, they were now sitting cross-legged on the floor, crystals in hand, rocking back and forth. Deep Dive crept his way past them, quietly opened the front door and escaped to his boat.

The Reel Upside looked lonely and sad. She never should have been ripped from the docks of Paradise Isle. Or hidden away in the mosquito-ridden mangroves on the bay side. The injustice the Wilkie devils had inflicted on her paint and her name was painful.

Deep Dive jumped on board. He desperately wanted to find what he was looking for. He patted her side. "Don't worry, baby. You'll be more appreciated in Bimini." That was when he spotted a few windblown stray cannabis buds scattered on the deck.

No, no, no! What's this? It did not look good. His heart racing, he scoured every inch of his boat, hoping to find the four bales the buds belonged to. The bales had to be there—a potential Hail Mary for Shep. Without the bales, he had no choice but to screw his buddy and take the suitcase. The only thing of interest on the boat was an old pair of frilly red panties from a conquest many moons ago. No key or square groupers anywhere.

He badly needed *The Reel Upside* key. Ideally, he would have been able to sail into the sunset with the chooze suitcase, bypassing the Wilkie meet-up. Without it, there was no chance of an early escape to Bimini. He would have to face the scumbags unless someone could get the key to him.

He had several more hours before the handoff. It was just enough time to get a drink at a place where an easily manipulated friend would be sure to show up. All he had to do was play it nice and cool until he would sucker punch them all.

Deep Dive was rolling out of the driveway as Hibiscus rolled in. Mutual surprise. Alarmed, she tried to look unruffled. She slowed her car as she hesitantly waved to him.

"Deep Dive, what are you doing here?" she asked through the driver's side open window. "Aren't you supposed to be at work?" Her mind was whirling. Why was he here? Was he on to her?

Caught off guard, Deep Dive blurted the first thing that came to his mind. "Your mom sent me to pick up a pair of underwear." He lifted the panties he found on the boat and waved it in the air, immediately regretting it.

"Gotta go." He stepped on the gas and sped off. Then it occurred to him. He had forgotten to ask for the key to his boat.

"Shit! Shit! Why didn't I get the key?" Deep Dive banged his head on the steering wheel.

Hibiscus watched the car swerve as he drove off.

"What the hell? This is getting weird. My mom doesn't wear underwear."

36

I'LL GET YOU

~ The Beatles ~

Hibiscus parked next to Peggy and Paul's Chevette. "Crap, they're still here," she mumbled. Opening the driver's door, she scanned the front yard before running up the front steps. She was not in the right headspace to deal with them right now. The quicker she could get to her room, with the least amount of small talk, the better. No luck. The moment she opened the door, Peggy wrapped her arms around her and clutched Hibiscus to her bosom.

"Paul, our cutie patootie is back. Give me some sugar." The hug lasted longer than Hibiscus liked. A fly trapped in a sticky spiderweb. She tried to pull away before Paul could get in the action.

"Do you know how to disco?" Peggy asked.

Hibiscus groaned. Not this routine again. It was too late to make a break for it. Peggy had already grabbed her hand.

Kicking her legs like a Rockette, Peggy started prancing. "Dis go here, dis go there. Put more leg into it," she sang, giggling herself silly.

Hibiscus pulled away, heading toward the hall.

"You missed your friend. What an unusual aura."

"Friend?" That might be a bit of a stretch right now. "Did he say why he was here?"

"He said he had to pick up some things for you."

"What do you mean? My things or my mom's?"

"Paul, do you remember what Shep wanted?" No response. Silence. He was in a trance, stirring a big pot on the stove. His simmering concoction flooded the house with an odd smell. A mixture of sticks and swamp.

"Earth to Paul. Hellooo." Peggy clapped her hands together to get his attention.

"I'm not sure. His energy was not very welcoming. He might have mentioned something about a hula girl." He licked the wooden spoon he was using and placed it on the silver-and-gold speckled aqua Formica counter next to a tall thermos.

"Wait, what? Shep? When was he here?" Hibiscus was confused.

"Are you teasing me?" Peggy laughed. "Stop it. You know—the handsome young man, with the detoxing skin, who just left."

Hibiscus had heard enough. Shep and Deep Dive were both dealing with funky skin issues right now, but the visitor who'd just left was most definitely not Shep. She couldn't even respond to Peggy. She went to her bedroom and shut the door.

"What in tarnation!" She noticed immediately he had left a fuck-you present on her pillow. Deep Dive was sending her a clear message.

Hibiscus unzipped her navy LeSportsac purse and peeked in. Topless hula girl was still there. "He needs to be nicer to me." She zipped her bag back up.

She was dreading the call to Micki. How was she going to tell her the square groupers were gone? Like really gone. Deep Dive had been at her house snooping around, pretending to be Shep. He was on to her. His parting gift was a clear indication he was not amused. Friends don't dump dirty bong water on your bed—even as a joke.

Frantically, she picked up the handset and dialed Micki's number. No answer. She looked at the time on her nightstand clock. "Fluck a duck!

Why am I the one stuck with gettin' Deep Dive's floating piece of junk to The Conch? Where is she?"

She opened her bedroom door and shouted at Peggy and Paul. "Did Micki call me today?" There was no reply. The house was quiet. She looked out her window. Paul was up a coconut tree attempting to pick an unripe green one, while Peggy splashed around the pool like a wounded flailing fish.

"Crap, Micki's probably at work already. I don't want to take the boat by myself."

What choice was there?

37

WHIPPING POST

~ The Allman Brothers Band ~

Deep Dive had time to kill. What better place than the bar at Peter, Dick and Willy's?

"Tommy Boy, one more." He pointed to his empty glass and stuffed his mouth with a handful of barbeque-flavored peanuts.

Chuck came over. *Looks like Pearl let him off easy*, he thought. "Nice to see ya, Captain. Not on the watah today?"

Chuck obviously didn't know *The Reel Upside* was currently on a brief hiatus. "Hey, Chuck. *The Reel Upside* is getting a little work done. She should be out and about real soon."

"Supah. What else is happening? Anything new and exciting?" Chuck was fishing. He wanted to find the reason for Pearl's interest and, more importantly, the meaning of the Polaroid picture. A couple more drinks would loosen Deep Dive's tongue.

"Barry! Barry! Barry!" the regulars chanted as the younger Baron sauntered in. He shook hands as if he was running for mayor and sat down with Deep Dive and Chuck.

"Mr. Chuck Feelers, my man. Hey, Deep Dive. The eggy fart smell is a lot better today. Just a slight whiff when you walk into the parking lot." Barry looked around. "Business doesn't seem to have suffered any."

Without asking, Tommy the bartender placed a draft in a frosted glass in front of Barry. Without hesitation, he gulped the ice-cold beer, wiping the foam from his upper lip. "Mother's milk."

Deep Dive clinked Barry's glass with his own.

"What's eating you?" Barry asked. "Aren't you supposed to be at the Pink Flamingo today?"

"About that . . ."

Chuck had been around long enough to realize he didn't need to be a part of this conversation. It looked like Pearl had struck after all. He moved on down the bar, wiping it clean. He would grill eagle ear Tommy as soon as he could.

"Bro, what's goin' on?"

It was time to work the sympathy angle. Implement the best buddy code. "Hibiscus screwed me. Royally. I'm pretty sure she stole the square groupers. I thought she was my friend." He looked at Barry with the saddest look he could muster. Which was difficult because he was seething inside. It was time to play Barry like a fiddle.

Barry looked stunned. "Hibiscus? Our sweet Hibiscus? You sure she has enough brain cells to plot something like that? Doesn't sound like something she would do."

"Yup, I know. I found some buds lying around the deck of *The Reel Upside* and overheard her being all sneaky with her parents. Think clearly. Who the hell would leave good-quality buds lying on a boat? Someone who has future money to throw around. That's who! She's one hundred percent suspect number one."

"Shit, man. That's cold. Whatcha gonna do?"

"I don't know what to do. You feel my pain, right?" Deep Dive looked like he desperately needed a friend.

"For sure."

"I need some help, man. You've always been such a good and loyal friend." He was laying it on thick.

"Anything, dude."

"You think you could call Hibiscus and offer to get my boat to The Conch?"

"You don't want to do it yourself?"

"Hibiscus won't give me the key," he lied. Deep Dive tried to force a tear. "I just can't believe she did me wrong. How can I possibly face her? Who knows what else she has up her sleeve? I'll owe you big-time if you can do this one favor for me."

Deep Dive grabbed Barry and hugged him. "Oh, one more thing. We haven't had this conversation. You haven't seen me."

"Gotcha. No sweat, dawg. I'm on it. Wait a sec. What about the bales?"

Barry and his damn inconvenient questions. "It's all good. Luckily, a buddy of mine is giving me a loan to cover the loss. I'll meet you on The Conch dock. Ten thirty, okay? You got nothing to worry about." Deep Dive had become a very proficient liar.

Satisfied with Deep Dive's plan, Barry walked over to the pay phone. He noticed Jenny's number had been crossed out. Someone wrote underneath. "Don't bother calling. She's not a good time. Her husband ain't either."

꽃 꽃 꽃

Hibiscus was picking out an outfit when the phone rang. It jolted her. She hoped it was Micki. It wasn't. Barry's voice was on the other line.

"Whatcha doin', girl?"

"Gettin' ready for work. What's going on?"

"Work, huh? You need help getting Deep Dive's boat over? I gotta be there anyway. I owe those shitheads money for their car."

"Really? Oh my gosh! You're a lifesaver. That would be so rad." His offer was music to her ears. Sweaty, sticky and messy windblown boat hair was not a great combo for tips. Even with a good outfit on.

"I owe you one! I'll leave the hula key chain on the dash."

Barry had now scored two IOUs.

Hibiscus felt an immense sense of relief. Thanks to Barry, she'd be fresh as a daisy and not a clammy mess.

Hibiscus removed her tank top and electric-blue Stubbies corduroy shorts and changed to her best tip-producing outfit with the very low-cut white top and her best black miniskirt. White pumps made the look pop.

Thanks to her parents, she'd be needing those tips now.

38

SOS

~ Abba ~

By the time Hibiscus arrived at Conch on the Bay, the lunch crowd had dwindled to a half dozen day drinkers. It was an unexceptional Thursday. No different from any other. The late-afternoon lull would soon be over. The dinner storm was brewing on the horizon. It was going to be a busy evening. In more ways than one.

Hibiscus arrived, plunking the hot tea thermos on the counter. She had been polite when Paul handed it to her, giving no indication that she had zero intention of touching any of his strange brew.

As a former midwife trainee, Paul had helped deliver Hibiscus in a teepee at Mother Earth Intentional Living Commune just outside of Pittsburgh. A couple of months later, the town folk ran the group off, unnerved by the members' strange practices. The eclectic group of misfits scattered across the country looking for like-minded, enlightened people.

Because of his strong ties to the Dubicki family, he couldn't stand idly by when he sensed a disharmony within her soul. As any loving shaman funcle would do, he wanted to ease her inner turmoil. It would be irresponsible of him to ignore her disrupted chakra frequencies. When out of balance, a person becomes out of tune. Things start to go awry spiritually, mentally, emotionally and physically. Hibiscus needed an emergency reset. Meaning well, he sent her to work with a warm freshly brewed thermos of Sacred Plant of Vision tea. After a few sips, she'd be right as rain.

🌿 🌿 🌿

"Mel, where's Micki?"

He flipped a greasy burger on the griddle, a toothpick dangling from his mouth. "Out back."

Micki was squatting on a three-legged stool, peeling some of Idaho's finest. The Conch's made-from-scratch french fries were highly popular. So much tastier than the mass-produced fries from the chain restaurants. Over several years, they'd earned both kid and drinker stamps of approval.

She glanced up at Hibiscus with a questionable look. "You're early. Where's the boat?"

"I tried to call you. We gotta talk. Something's happened. It's important."

Micki gave her an inquisitive look. "Yes . . .?"

"I don't know how to tell you this." She paused. "It's gone."

"What's gone? The boat?" Micki's eyes widened.

"No. You know, the stuff. It's gone, gone. Never to be seen again. I don't know what to do."

"Whoa, back up. You mean . . .?"

"Stan and Patricia and their two crazy friends. They did something with it. I don't know exactly what, but it's definitely not there anymore."

"You sure?"

"Oh, yeah. All that was left was half a joint. And they smoked it."

"Hibiscus, come on. That was a lot of grass. You telling me the truth? You know how I feel about all this."

"God's honest truth, I don't have it! I admit I wanted to keep it, but I changed my mind. I swear. I was going to call Deep Dive and fess up. Now I'm too scared to tell him the stuff's really gone. He'll never forgive me. Anyhow, I think he's on to me."

"How do you know?"

"He dumped bong water on my pillow."

Micki put down the potato peeler. "Aye yai yai. I don't know what to say. You're freaking me out. I don't think he's going to be able to get out of this mess. You too, if he has proof you had the weed." Micki sighed. "And the boat?"

"Barry's bringing it over tonight. He called me when I couldn't reach you."

Micki looked at her friend. "It should never have come to this. We should have fessed up when the square groupers reappeared. He won't forgive us. Get another peeler. Help me out here." Micki needed time to process it all.

While Hibiscus was in the kitchen, Micki noticed Shep nosing around the building, lifting various items up and peeking underneath. "Hey. What are you doing here?"

"Busted." Shep laughed nervously. He didn't want anyone to know that his pet python in charge of vermin control was on an uncontrolled walkabout. "Just checking things out. I need to make sure Josephine is doing her . . . I mean, did her job. Are you happy with the quality of her work?"

"I guess. Maybe there are fewer rat droppings. Thanks for checking, though."

She couldn't believe she had agreed to another of Shep's harebrained ideas. Did he ever do anything right? Maybe that was why she had a soft spot for him. She had a heart for screw-ups.

Micki looked at her old high school friend. She wanted to broadcast the latest disaster to Shep but thought it best not to. She didn't want to involve him any more than he already was and Deep Dive needed to hear the bad news first. She'd let Hibiscus make that call. It wasn't going to be pretty.

"Hey, Shep. Lend us a hand." Hibiscus tossed her peeler at him as she exited the kitchen door.

"Well, um, sure, I guess. I don't have anything else going on right now." He sat on the ground next to Micki, pulling a dirty potato out of the bag. As he peeled, he kept a sharp eye out for unusual movements around the building.

"Shep, you don't happen to know where Deep Dive is, do you?" Hibiscus asked.

He shrugged his shoulders. "Pink Flamingo?"

"Most definitely not there."

"Maybe at home?" Shep hoped he wasn't. He didn't want Deep Dive shimming open the lock on the suitcase.

The three sat peeling and cutting potatoes, wondering if revealing their secrets would do more harm or good or potentially something else, while Deep Dive waited at Peter, Dick and Willy's plotting his revenge.

At the Baron office, Barry was attempting, one more time, to plead his case for an advance on his paycheck.

Juan was passed out on his living room couch, after testing too much of his Kick-A-Butt drink.

Along the roof line, Josephine sunned herself. She was resting up for the evening buffet.

39

DA' YA' THINK I'M SEXY
~ Rod Stewart ~

Rico was in a rush, looking for a classy cologne and a debonair hat to cover his now-bald head. He wanted to look and smell tiptop for his beautiful blossom, Hibiscus. The Nair had left a lingering sulfur smell on his body. Rico scanned the shelf, looking for a good-quality men's cologne. Advertised as earthy, primitive and fiercely masculine, Musk by English Leather was the winner. A generous splash would mask all unpleasant odors.

Heading to the Eckerd's checkout line, he spotted a box of Russell Stover chocolates – reduced by a dollar. "*¡Perfecto!*" The line was longer than he had the patience for. He had a place to be and people to see. He stuffed the chocolates and cologne down his pants, plopped the hat on his head and walked out. But not unnoticed. The nice older lady working the cash register took one look at the strange-looking man and decided it was probably best to let things slide.

The standard summer afternoon shower was just letting up as Rico puttered down General Douglas MacArthur Causeway in his beaten-up white van. Stopping at a red light, he grabbed a bucket of flowers out of the hands of a Cuban street vendor. The vulgar language hurled at Rico stopped when he pulled out his pistol and aimed at the man's crotch. Rico had a jam-packed night ahead. He didn't have time for any of the street vendor's silliness.

Rico looked forward to the evening. He was going to woo Hibiscus the right way. Flowers and chocolates, the world's top two aphrodisiacs, always did the trick. Other than liquor, of course, which admittedly was quicker. Mitzie, his latest regret, could never resist.

If he arrived early at The Conch, there would be time to stake the place out, make the moves on his Barbie princess and then collect for Mendoza. Packing heat meant playtime with the Wilkies was over. Time to crack some heads. One of the perks of his job.

He glanced at himself in the van mirror. Hairless didn't look too bad. Just different. The Panama hat was a sexy touch. It pulled together his new appearance. He would definitely catch her eye.

꧁ ꧁ ꧁

"I hate it! I look ugly!" Tinker exclaimed.

"It does make your butt look big."

Tinker flashed her sister, Belle, a hateful look. Nanny Pearl could not have picked two uglier outfits for the evening's commitment.

"Zip it! I don't wanna hear any more squawking outta you two. Y'all hear me?" Pearl's petulant granddaughters were getting on her nerves. She had had her fill of them.

"Yes, ma'am." In sync, they both stuck out their tongues as Pearl turned her back. Nanny could be so annoying.

"Nanny, can't we please wear our Dolfin shorts?" Belle pleaded. "These crochet hot pants are really itchy." It hadn't dawned on the girls that the silkiness of the polyester-and-nylon Dolfin shorts would not relieve them of the itch they shared with Rico.

"If they were good enough for catching a man in 1970, they're good enough now."

"We look like hookers."

"What's your point?" Didn't the twins fully understand their assignment? They needed to grab Rico's undivided attention. It wasn't that complicated. "Fluff up your hair some more. It looks too flat. I wish y'all would have permed those limp noodles like I told ya to. C'mon, girls. The higher the hair, the closer to heaven."

Belle grabbed a comb and teased her sister's bang. "Ouch, you're being too rough," Tinker fussed.

She picked up a can of Aqua Net and handed it to her sister. Belle shook it and sprayed enough hairspray around her sister's head to form an invisible impenetrable shell. A cyclone wouldn't budge a single strand.

When they glanced in the mirror, what they saw was not their best look. Their matching bangs resembled a cockatoo's raised head crest. Pearl flashed them a thumbs-up and pointed to the Mary Kay makeup kit on the counter.

"Full war paint."

40

IS SHE REALLY GOING OUT WITH HIM?

~ Joe Jackson ~

Rico pulled into the dusty parking lot, looking for the first empty spot he could find. Conch on the Bay was thriving on a busy night. In the rearview mirror, he glanced at himself one more time, making sure nothing was stuck in his teeth or hanging from his nose.

Without a care, he roughly opened the van door, slamming it into the passenger side of an expensive Mauritius blue BMW 635CSi, leaving a hefty ding and some chipped paint. He grabbed the wilting flowers and chocolates. Hopefully the chocolates weren't too melted. His air conditioner had blasted out its last bit of cold air months ago.

Through the large windows, he could see his alluring flower blossom pouring a cup of coffee for an overly friendly gringo. She giggled. *No es bueno*. But that could easily be fixed.

Many of the customers glanced his way as he strolled in. His new look was eye-catching. Pleased with the vibe, he headed toward an empty table. Holding the bouquet of flowers ever so gently, he nudged the cup of hot coffee on to the man's lap. The man yelped and shot straight up as the scalding liquid touched his skin.

"Dammit!" he yelled. "You clumsy—"

"*Ay, amigo.* So sorry." Rico smiled an unsettling smile. Unnerved by Rico's treacherous look, the young man thought it best to accept the apology.

"No biggie." He fanned his wet pants, attempting to quickly cool his crotch.

"Wise boy." Rico winked at him and patted the man forcefully on the back. Rico's .38-caliber side piece did not go unnoticed.

"Check, please." The young man bolted toward the exit.

Rico plopped down, positioning himself to face the parking lot. He could see when the Big Pine people arrived. He wanted no unexpected funny business from them.

He took off his hat and waited. Betsy approached the table. "Hi, welcome to Conch on the Bay. Would you like a drink while you look over the menu?"

"Where is my Hibiscus? I want her to serve me." He tapped the chocolates and flowers.

"Sorry, sir. This is my section."

Rico opened his wallet, pulled out $20, and handed it to her. "This is Hibiscus's table now. Okay?"

Betsy held out her hand. It would cost him a little more than $20. Understanding her hesitation, he placed another Jackson in her hand.

"Hibiscus will be right with you." Betsy walked toward the kitchen, cash in hand. "Stupid horny men . . . ," she muttered, disgusted but pleased with the quick money.

"Mr. Clean is here to see you, Hibiscus. Man, oh, man. You've got a doozy waiting for you.

"Which table?"

"You can't miss him. Trust me." Betsy laughed. She made an animated Bugs Bunny face, squeezing her upper lip around her two front teeth.

Hibiscus sashayed toward Table 8. She spotted the back of the man's bald head. She was puzzled. Who was this guy?

Cautiously, "Hello?"

Rico turned as soon as he heard her soft, alluring Marilyn Monroe voice. It was the sound of an angel, her eyes as blue as a precious stone, perfect melon breasts and long slender legs that could wrap around him and squeeze him right. Her extremely low-cut white top and black miniskirt, offset by the white pumps, dazzled. Her smile could melt an iceberg in seconds. She was as close to a perfect ten as anyone could get. She was even more delicious than he remembered.

"For dju." Rico handed her the chocolates and flowers.

Hibiscus racked her brain. Who was this weirdo? An audience member from the last bikini contest? "Thank you . . . um . . ."

"Rico, at djour service, *señorita.*"

"Oh, Rico. Yes, of course. You look so . . . different."

"Dju like?"

"Uh-huh." *Oh, heck no,* she thought. *Not in a million years.*

This guy was creepy as hell. She hadn't noticed his teeth before. His missing mustache had done wonders for him. Struggling not to look uncomfortable, she flashed her best big tip smile.

"Here, touch." He grabbed her hand and placed it on his head. "Smooth as a snake." He hissed at her playfully. Rico had a feeling she was digging him.

She removed her hand and giggled playfully, wiping her hand on the side of her black miniskirt. "What can I get you?"

Rico licked his lips in a suggestive manner.

He was taking too long to order. "Do you want me to pick something for you? Tell you what! Let me surprise you." Hibiscus wanted a quick turnaround for Table 8.

"*Sí.*" Rico liked where this was going.

"I'll be right back." She couldn't get away from the table fast enough.

Micki and Betsy laughed as Hibiscus walked into the kitchen. "Who's your boyfriend? Micki asked. "Hubba-hubba."

"Not funny. Vomitrocious."

"What's the deal? Inquiring minds want to know." Micki and Betsy were very curious.

"I dunno. I guess he likes me. Whip up the most expensive thing on the menu. If I gotta deal with him, I want a big tip."

As the night went on and the customers started clearing out, one persistent customer with a bald head remained. He was locked in. He had no plans to go anywhere anytime soon.

"It's getting late. Would you like your bill?"

"No. Not really. I want dju." His eyes scanned her from her top to her bottom.

"Rico, I really appreciate the chocolates and flowers, but I gotta close up. I'm going to have to ask you to leave. Some other time, okay?" If Mel hadn't left already, she would sic him on Mr. Creepazoid.

Rico was thrilled. Hibiscus was interested. *¡Fantástico!*

She handed him his restaurant receipt. He grabbed her hand and kissed it. Hibiscus twitched with disgust as some of his saliva drooled onto her skin. Rico opened his wallet. He reached for her hand once more as he stroked her fingers lewdly with badly worn paper currency. "Dju keep, my enchantress."

"Okay. If you insist."

On the bright side, gross guy was an outstanding tipper. What's not to love about a couple of hundred-dollar bills?

41

DEVIL WOMAN

~ Cliff Richard ~

"Chop-chop! Let's go!" Pearl beeped the horn of her rusty gold Chevrolet El Camino. A wave of cigarette smoke wafted out as Sam opened the passenger side door.

"What the hell ya doin'?" barked Mama Pearl. "Git in the cargo bed. Earl, you too."

"Really, Mama?"

"Yes, really. You want the girls' hair messed up? Look how purty they look."

A proud Earl agreed. Sam thought his mom's idea of beauty was purely subjective. He looked at his brother. "Wipe your nose. You're disgusting."

"I c . . . c . . . can't help it. I have a cold." Earl wiped his dripping nose on his shirtsleeve.

"Belle, hold my beer." Pearl put the truck in gear and headed north with the heavily made-up twins sitting next to her while an annoyed no-neck Sam and gangly Earl were tossed around the back like balls in an unstable pinball machine. Sam held on to his precious Polaroid camera, always the perfect fit with his Hawaiian shirt.

Mama Pearl switched off the truck lights as she approached The Conch. With a sudden jerk of the wheel, she pulled into the parking lot of the Sizzlin' Pepperoni next door. It was the only place in the Upper Keys to score a freshly made pizza. Having closed an hour earlier the place was totally dark.

"Damn it, Mama!" Sam grabbed his bumped shoulder. "Whatcha doin'? This wasn't part of my plan."

"Quiet, boy! This ain't gonna spoil nothin'. I don't want nobody to see we're here." She turned to the twins and stuck her finger in their faces. "You two stay in the truck until I need you."

"What she say?" an irritated Belle asked, pulling the left side of her Walkman headphones from her ear. She nudged her bored sister.

"Stay put. Turn that racket off. I need y'all to listen out for the signal."

"What was it again?" Tinker asked.

Pearl's patience was nearing zero. "How many times do we have to go over this? For crying out loud! The peacock call." She quietly made the noise as a reminder. How was it possible she had contributed genetically to this bunch of nitwits?

Pearl signaled for Sam and Earl to climb out of the back of the truck. "Follow me. Let's check the place out."

As soon as Nanny Pearl was out of sight, the headphones returned to their ears. The Walkman cassette players were cranked to the max.

The waning gibbous moon was playing hide and seek behind the clouds, appearing every so often to illuminate the ground below. The only other light source came from inside The Conch. Pearl and her boys quietly made their way over to the restaurant. They crouched behind a white van to peer into the restaurant's window without being spotted. In the dark, the old Sears name was not visible under the white paint.

Pearl wondered why the restaurant was still open. Inside, a bald man was kissing the hand of a waitress. He needed to be gone before Rico showed up. The fewer eyewitnesses, the better.

Pearl got up and motioned her boys to head toward the empty dock. The ever-hungry tarpon splashed around, waiting for a handout in response to the vibrations on the creaking wood boards above them. In the distance, the Wilkies could hear the approaching sound of a boat engine. Hallelujah. Deep Dive was earlier than anticipated.

They didn't realize Deep Dive wasn't driving the boat.

Deep Dive had also thought about arriving early and positioning himself to strike when the moment was right. Punctuality, however, was not his strong suit. He pulled into the pizzeria parking lot. He parked away from the El Camino when he noticed movement inside the cab.

"Dammit! Couldn't those kids have found a different place to neck?" Rudely inconvenient. Now he'd have to walk further than he wanted.

Grabbing his knapsack and the chooze suitcase, the puny gold lock wobbled back and forth as he slogged toward the bay. Adrenaline was rushing like a fire hose through his system. Everything was about to change. Everything.

Getting closer, Deep Dive spotted the Wilkies on The Conch dock. *Those bastards. How am I going to get on the boat without being seen?*

The Reel Upside's purr was getting closer. A quick decision was needed.

Hide in the dark, murky water surrounding the mangroves? What about saltwater crocs? The apex Keys predators generally avoided people. Night was when they cruised mangrove swamps and estuaries looking for a juicy morsel. Chances of meeting one, however, were slim. They were so seldom seen they were on the endangered list. There was occasional talk of sightings in Blackwater Sound, but he'd lived in the Keys his whole life and had never seen one. The fact that tarpon were on a crocodile's menu probably worked in his favor.

It was time to stop putzin' around. Deep Dive headed toward the mangroves. He'd wait until the boat was docked and the assholes were distracted before making his move.

As it turned out, crocodiles were not his biggest challenge.

Saltwater mangroves were home to prolific, highly aggressive mosquitoes as well as teeny biting insects known locally as no-see-ums. Mosquitoes and the little black flying shits relentlessly dive-bombed him, kamikaze style, loading him up with itchy bumps.

With every bite, he wanted to scream. The constant buzzing in his ears was driving him mad. He was a sitting duck, unable to swat the bloodthirsty barbarians away. Any movement would draw attention to his location. *C'mon, Barry. For God's sake, hurry.*

Barry was relieved as *The Reel Upside* approached the dock. Navigating the shallow bay side at night was tricky for even the most experienced boat captains. He had never driven anything larger than a skiff.

His run through the infamous Toilet Seat Cut, a narrow pass lined with toilet seats and lids embossed with personalized messages that celebrated birthdays, engagements, anniversaries, graduations, drinking sessions and other events, was nerve-racking. Fortunately, it was high tide. Nevertheless, *The Reel Upside*'s bottom scraped sand several times. What if he had gotten stuck? He was mentally spent.

In the dark, he could barely make out three figures standing on the dock like Russian stacking dolls. A petite figure, possibly a woman. There was a more squat person somewhat resembling a fireplug. And finally, a figure that reminded him of a praying mantis.

None of them resembled Deep Dive. Crap! Who were these people? The small one was waving him in.

Shifting into neutral, Barry gilded slowly in, neglecting to throw the rubber guard bumpers over the side. *The Reel Upside* bounced against the dock. Deep Dive, knee-deep in the mangrove water, cringed. Would the abuse of *The Reel Upside* ever end?

Sam grabbed the line as Barry threw it. "Well, look who's here. Poop boy himself. Where the hell's the captain? We want our money."

Barry had the same question. Where was Deep Dive? He didn't want to be alone with these inbreds. "He should be here any minute. He's got your dough."

"Well, good news for him," Sam replied. "What about you? Is there good news in store for you?"

Earl chuckled when he heard his brother's question. It seemed the appropriate time to flash his revolver. Sam stroked his Polaroid.

"I hope you haven't forgotten you got a debt to clear up yourself."

Barry cursed the day he'd met Deep Dive. Deep Dive should have been on the boat handling everything while Barry lounged on his couch watching TV. Barry had no good thoughts about Juan either. Where the fuck was he? Why was he doing everybody's dirty work?

"I have it. Can I get off the boat? I don't feel so hot." His nerves had gotten the best of him. His dinner was making its way north instead of south.

Sensing it was best to give Barry some space, Pearl, Sam and Earl moved out of the way. With the boat securely tied up, the foursome headed to the parking lot where they expected to greet Deep Dive.

Predictably, the twins had not followed directions. They were thirsty and hot. The crochet pants itched more than ever. Waiting for Pearl's signal inside an air-conditioned building was much more logical than waiting in the hot, stuffy El Camino. Just common sense. Lately, their aging nanny seemed to be lacking in that department.

An animated scene unfolding inside The Conch stopped the three perplexed Wilkies dead in their tracks. The bald guy, Belle and Tinker were shouting at each other. Hands were flying wildly in the air.

The twins and the customer were getting reacquainted.

42

MR. BAD LUCK
~ Jimi Hendrix ~

Misfortune is gregarious. Bad moments rarely show up alone. More often than not, they bring unwanted company.

But as uncomfortable as they can be, troubles can also be ridiculous. That makes it even worse for the unfortunate victims, particularly when the misfortune is outright laughable. The poor victim also becomes the butt of the joke and is then squeezed into afterthought status. That can be even more painful than pain itself. Thursday night's escapades at The Conch underscored the point.

With things rapidly slipping out of her control, Mama Pearl's outdoor whisper voice escalated into a peacock-like wail as her slender, wrinkled body shuddered with frustration.

The girls ignored her signal, the screeching peacock call. After all, they had their own priorities. In particular, they didn't appreciate being accused of giving Rico the crabs. That one-nighter asshole had some nerve, thought Belle as she resisted the urge to scratch her lady parts. Instead, she tugged on her outdated crochet hot pants, hoping an adjustment would bring some relief.

The commotion was Deep Dive's signal to make his move. He waded into the warm salt water with the knapsack on his back. The precious tweed Hartmann suitcase was balanced precariously on his head. With each step, his feet were sucked deeper into the soft mangrove mud. His right hand reached up to hold his bright future firmly in place. Above all, the suitcase had to remain dry.

As he inched closer to the back of the boat, the water was above his head. Deep Dive could no longer stand. Struggling to swim with one hand, he reached *The Reel Upside*'s dive platform. But he was unable to grasp it firmly, and the suitcase slipped from his head and splashed into the water. Frantically, he grabbed the slow-sinking case, lifted it out of the water and, with an effort that could only come from desperation, heaved it onto the boat.

The splashing and subsequent thunk caught Earl's attention. "Something's g . . . g . . . going on d . . . d . . . down there." He gestured back toward the boat. Barry peered back into the darkness. He hadn't noticed anything unusual. His only thought was how quickly he could get the hell out of there.

"Tarpon, dingleberry. Didn't you see the sign? Stay focused," said Sam.

"*Keow . . . Keow . . .*" Pearl's screeching secret peacock call was a last attempt to get the twins' attention. Failing to do so, she shouted at Earl. "Git your damn girls in order, now."

Sniffling, he trudged toward the entrance to the restaurant. He could not think of a worse time to have a cold. He stuck his finger on the left side of his nostril and blew with as much force as he could muster. The snot from his right side shot to the ground. Before he had a chance to switch sides, the sound of a boat engine distracted him. He turned to look.

A soaking wet but elated Deep Dive cranked up *The Reel Upside*'s diesel engine. "Sayonara, suckers," he yelled over the noise. He was free. Free with the chooze money. On his way to Bimini. Freedom! He was good-looking, rich, single and headed to an exciting new future.

Dashing from the parking lot back to the dock as quickly as his short, stubby legs would permit, Sam pushed Barry out of the way. The Polaroid camera bounced, hitting his chest with each stride, his Hawaiian-style shirt flapping in the wind. Earl followed, his long strides enabling him to overtake his squatty brother.

In the parking lot, Barry looked at the wrinkled prune next to him, pulled a fat envelope out of his back pocket and threw it at her feet. Like a cheetah, he bolted toward US-1. He had never moved so fast. His payment to fix the TR7 was cleared. He urgently needed a chilled beer.

By the time Sam reached the dock, it was too late to stop what was in motion. Deep Dive and *The Reel Upside* were out of reach. Only smelly traces of diesel exhaust remained as the boat slowly chugged out of sight.

"W . . . w . . . want me to shoot him?"

"Earl, you ding-a-ling! You want to draw more attention to us? Your girls are doing a fine job of that. We need to straighten that shit up before Rico arrives."

Sam's future depended on it. He exhaled audibly in a long, weary, deep breath.

The two Wilkies walked back to the parking lot to a fuming Mama Pearl.

"It's gone," said Sam. "Somebody took the boat."

A low, raspy growl rose from Pearl's throat. She was not in a forgiving mood. "You fatheads!" She was holding a tamarind tree branch in her bony fist. It was the perfect size, weight and shape for a switch.

"Sam, git that bald guy outta there and start positioning the girls. That Rico could be here at any minute. Earl, go around to the back of the building. See who else is around. We're running out of time before that asshole Colombian gits here." She attempted to give the boys a motivational swat across their backs. Sam and Earl jumped too quickly for the switch to make contact.

Sam could hear arguing as he opened the restaurant's front door. The bald man turned and looked directly at Sam and smirked. Sam knew who those mismatched teeth belonged to. Over the last couple of days, they had featured all too often in his nightmares.

"Rico . . ."

Two young women who looked somewhat familiar and uncomfortable, sat quietly next to each other in a booth watching the confrontation between Rico and the twins.

"¡*Silencio!*" said Rico, trying to quiet the angry twins. "Where djour manners? Look! We have a guest." Rico pulled out his gun and waved Sam in. Instinctively, Sam raised his hands.

Hibiscus grabbed Micki's arm. What the hell was going on?

From the parking lot, an enraged Mama Pearl watched the scene unfolding through the open window. "No one messes with my kin without regrettin' it," she said. "That rat bastard has double-crossed us and sent an accomplice. I'll show him who's in charge." With the switch still in her hand, she scampered around the back and silently entered the kitchen door. Earl was drinking from a tall silver thermos.

"What the hell you doin', Earl?"

"I'm d . . . d . . . drinking some hot tea, Mama. Thought it would make my c . . . c . . . cold feel better." He stuck his finger into a bowl of spicy and sweet conch fritter batter and licked it.

Pearl shook her head. "Your brother is about to get his head blowed off and you're having a tea party? I oughta . . ." She lifted the switch and stopped herself. "One of Rico's guys is in the dining room with a pistol."

"Sh . . . sh . . . shit."

"¡*Ándele!*" Rico gestured with his pistol in the direction of the kitchen. "Señor Sam and dju dirty goats, go." In disgust, he spat on the ground. His tone flipped, softened. "My flower, and djour pretty *amiga*, please follow. Into the kitchen. Oh, and lights off. *Gracias*."

The dining area went black. From the street, Conch on the Bay looked officially closed.

Earl was sweating. He was beginning to feel a little woozy. The tea was already having an effect. "Mama, they're coming in here."

"Hide, you big dodo. Shoot the bastard when I give the signal." Petite Pearl squeezed herself inside a bottom kitchen cabinet, pushing paper products aside. Earl hid behind some brown cardboard supply boxes. With her tobacco-stained chicken-toe-looking pointing finger, she propped the cabinet door slightly ajar. She needed a clear view.

Rico entered, holding Sam at gunpoint. He motioned toward the cabinets. "Señor Sam, take a seat here, on the ground. Put djour back to the cabinets. Keep djour hands up."

As Sam lowered himself down into a sitting position, he slid his back against the cabinets, shutting the partly opened door on Pearl's face. Sam faintly heard a familiar whisper behind him. "Fucker."

Ah, the comfort of a mother's voice.

Rico kicked the stick out of Sam's reach. "Tsk, tsk. Dju be a good boy."

"Who do you think you're talking to, you ugly one-inch-pencil-dick moron?" said Belle.

"Yeah," Tinker chimed in. "You don't know who you're foolin' with."

Rico lifted his shoulders and tilted his head. Translated, his movement implied the question, *What dju talking about?*

"You're makin' a big mistake. We're Wilkies," the twins declared.

Rico looked at Sam, then the twins. How could he have been so stupid? He slapped his own forehead. The conniving sisters had tricked him with drunken revelry at the Tiki Shak. Lured him back to the motel with their wicked ways. They had desecrated him in more ways than one—resulting in his hairlessness. What a fool he had been.

"Dju two. Go." He opened the walk-in fridge, motioning the twins in.

"You can't make us," Belle said defiantly.

He aimed his gun at Tinker.

"All right already. Keep your panties on," Belle said. She nudged her sister. The girls walked into the cold food locker, purses in hand, cursing as they went. "Asshole."

Looking over at Hibiscus and Micki, he said, "I'm sorry, my love, but I have business I must do. Please, this way." Rico shuffled backwards keeping his gun pointed at Sam.

He opened the undersized staff bathroom and politely motioned Micki and Hibiscus in.

"Dju wait here. I shall be quick. Then we can enjoy"—he winked—"nice alone time." He blew Hibiscus a kiss.

A scared Hibiscus bobbed her head in hesitant agreement and latched on to her friend. As soon as the door shut, they locked it and looked at each other. "Crap, Micki! I don't know what the hell is going on. This guy's fucking crazy."

"You really don't know this guy?"

"Hell no. The guy belongs in the circus. How are we going to get out of here?"

Micki scanned the small bathroom. There was only one door. Out of all the bathrooms in the joint, this was the only one without a window. "I hate to say it. We're stuck."

She hoped whatever was going on in the kitchen would soon resolve itself. Besides safety, there was one other thing on Micki's mind. Her freshly made competition batter. She had finally achieved the perfect consistency and flavor profile. In the evening's excitement, she had left the bowl sitting on the kitchen counter. Would the mixture spoil?

Micki had a thought. Maybe she should poke her head out and ask Rico nicely to refrigerate the batter. It would be an understandable request. The start of the Conchy Tonk Festival was less than twenty-four hours away.

43

STAND AND DELIVER
~ Adam and the Ants ~

A serious Rico hovered over Sam, who was sitting on the floor, his back to the cabinet door. "What dju have for me? Boss no happy."

Sam needed time. He hoped Rico would provide him with much-needed details about the head honcho. "Yeah, of course. About your boss..."

Before Sam could angle for info, a box toppled to the ground. Earl popped up from behind the stacked boxes, his hands positioned in a karate strike pose.

"Hong Kong Phooey, quicker than the human eye. Hi-yah!" He lunged forward.

Even though the room was spinning, Earl had assumed the persona of the beloved cartoon character Penry Pooch who transformed himself into a superhero to solve crimes. The fluorescent lights twinkled and flashed an indecipherable Morse code, disorienting him. Nevertheless, Earl was feeling like a million bucks. It was the best tea he had ever tasted. He delivered a quick kick into the air and a hand chop for emphasis before falling on his ass, giggling like a thirteen-year-old waiting for her first date to pick her up.

The warm earthy-tasting tea had worked wonders, even relieving him of his nagging cold symptoms.

Trapped in the cabinet, Pearl was confused. She attempted to open the cabinet door. Feeling the door pushing on his back, Sam, bewildered by Earl's erratic behavior, moved to the left, enabling Pearl to crack the cabinet door open.

Looking on, Rico still didn't get it. He hadn't asked for much. All he wanted was a drama-free night, a quick handover of goods and some lovin' in the back of his van.

But it wasn't working that way. His tidied-up van, spritzed and freshened up with his new cologne, would very likely see no action. Distracted and frustrated, he turned to face a strange scarecrow-looking man holding a disfigured hand up to the light. He seemed to be inspecting it. A pistol appeared, dangling precariously in his other hand.

"Whaddya know . . . I got two missing fingers." Earl laughed at this known and obvious discovery.

In an instant, Sam grabbed Mama Pearl's switch and raised it in his right hand, ready to strike. As if on cue, an impish Pearl popped out of the cupboard like a jack-in-the-box toy, squawking like a deranged peacock.

"Earl, *keow, keow!* Shoot!"

Mechanically, Earl raised his right hand and pulled the trigger. He fired and dropped the gun, mesmerized by the beautiful flickering rainbows flaming out of the backside of the bullet. "Cool . . ."

The switch flew from Sam's hand as the .38-caliber slug decimated his thumb and pointing finger. "Fuuck," he screamed in agony and terror as bits of pulverized fingers ricocheted and blood splashed around the kitchen.

Hearing the shot and blood-curdling scream, Micki and Hibiscus crouched between the wall and toilet bowl, seeking porcelain-level protection. "Head down," said Micki, staring directly at the mold peeking out from under the rim. The toilet needed a good scrubbing.

Rico awkwardly dove for the dropped gun, slipping on the goopy bloody mixture splashed on the patterned harvest gold linoleum floor, hitting his head with a whack on the stove.

His lights went out.

Pearl swiftly removed her well-worn baby-blue Members Only jacket, wrapping it around Sam's right hand to stop the bleeding. Two fingers had evaporated.

"For Pete's sake. Lift your hand," she said.

Sam tried to raise his hand above his head. "Higher, boy!" his mother demanded.

"I'm gonna kill you, Earl!" Sam shouted. With his good hand, he attempted to wipe off the blood-splattered Polaroid.

"Hey, we're twins!" Earl gleefully shouted. He waved his three-fingered left hand. His stutter was gone.

Sam, in shock, and Pearl, dumbfounded by the last three minutes, stared at Rico lying facedown on the floor, splattered in red.

"Hey, that guy looks like a hot dog with ketchup, minus the bun," blurted Earl. He stepped over Rico and reached for Sam's camera. "Let me take a picture."

"Mama, get him out of my sight before I strangle him."

"Catch me if you can." Earl farted and ran.

Pearl took a deep breath before raising her voice.

"Shut up, pinheads! I need to think."

"What's goin' on out there? Let us out!" Belle demanded, banging on the walk-in refrigerator door. "It's as cold as a witch's tit in here."

Pearl walked over to release her granddaughters from the freezer. Belle and Tinker strolled out—lit Virginia Slims in their right hands and packets of chilled lobster tails and filet mignon in their left. "Oh, that's so gross. Is he alive?"

Pearl felt for a pulse. There was still life in the bastard. "Yup. Let's tie him up. I don't want him goin' nowhere." Mama Pearl nudged him with her foot.

The color had drained from Sam's face. His hand needed to be treated. An unconscious Rico also needed to be dealt with. Adding to the chaos—a discombobulated, high-as-a-kite Earl and two waitresses locked in the bathroom. Only one person known to Pearl had previous experience with troublesome situations like this one. Chuck Feelers.

"We got a shitstorm that needs fixin'. Girls, go fetch Chuck. Hurry!"

The ayahuasca was turning on Earl. His initial psychedelic visual hallucinations and feel-good vibes were gone, replaced by unpleasant symptoms—vomiting and diarrhea. "Mama, I don't feel so good. Oh, boy. I think you're right. A shitstorm is a comin'."

It wasn't uncommon for those using ayahuasca to experience both positive and negative effects from the brew.

"Outside, now!" Pearl shrieked. There was enough in the kitchen to clean up.

Earl squatted, positioning himself behind the metal garbage cans, dealing with multiple bodily explosions.

Rico needed to be shut up before he came to. Using aprons and kitchen twine, Pearl hogtied him then removed one of her shoes and pulled off a low-cut tennis pom-pom sock. She rolled it into a ball and tried stuffing it into his mouth, but something kept snagging it. It was a poorly made denture retainer-looking thing. She removed the contraption, putting it in her jeans shorts pocket.

Tiny but mighty Pearl dragged Rico into the dark dining area. She needed a visual break from his ugly mug. Chuck could take care of the problem à la Bum Farto after he stitched up Sam.

Micki got up and walked to the door, unlocking it. Cracking the door open, she shouted, "Can someone put the large white bowl of batter in the fridge? I'd really appreciate it." She quickly pulled the door closed and locked it. "Don't look at me like that. I don't want to give anyone food poisoning, do I?"

Hibiscus shook her head in disbelief.

Pearl looked at the large plastic bowl. She was dumbfounded. Why anyone would want to save batter with bits of Sam's fingers in it was beyond her. She put the batter in the kitchen fridge. It was the least of her concerns.

44

ABRACADABRA
~ Steve Miller Band ~

Chuck had never found the Wilke twins particularly likable. Tonight was no different. Banging on the door, waking him from his sleep, was a very loud Belle.

"Mr. Chuck! Wake up! Nanny needs you." She pounded furiously on the door of Chuck's small apartment located directly above Peter, Dick and Willy's.

In Boston, the apartment would be called a studio. For Chuck, it was the ultimate bachelor pad, conveniently located just above the store, so to speak.

The living room, bedroom and kitchen were combined into a single room with a separate bathroom. The walls were decorated with framed pictures of Sinatra's Rat Pack depicting the stars performing in Las Vegas. The dwelling did not scream typical tropical Keys. If anything, it was more midcentury Palm Springs desert.

The evening's scotch still lingered, initially relegating him to a snail's pace. Too much had given him a mild case of Irish flu. He turned on his bedside table lamp, grabbed his toupee and rolled out of bed.

"Ladies, please. My head. I'll be right theah." He plucked his bathrobe off a chair. What could Pearl possibly have gotten herself into at this hour? It would likely not be pleasant.

Opening the door, he wasn't sure what to make of Belle's appearance. There was something uncannily familiar about her look. Perhaps it was the crochet shorts. Belle's grandma had always filled them out nicely. Back in the day.

Tinker blew the horn of the El Camino. She leaned over to the passenger side and rolled down the truck window. "C'mon, Belle! Move it. We need to get the lobster tails and filet mignon on ice. You want to be able to sell this shit or not?"

"Hiya. How can I help you, dahlin'?"

"Nanny's in a jam. Daddy shot Sam's fingers off. And there's an asshole rolled up like a Cuban cigar. She needs you, fast like."

"What? Wheah the hell is she?"

"Conch on the Bay. The kitchen." Belle turned and began to walk down the outside concrete stairs. "She said hurry. You'd know what to do."

Belle got in the truck, turned up the radio and headed home with her sister, their heads bobbing along to Sister Sledge's "We Are Family." Let Mr. Chuck deal with the fallout. They were tuckered out. They could find a hungry buyer later.

Chuck didn't like what he heard. The kitchen? He dressed quickly, grabbing the emergency kit kept under his bed. A not-so-quaint leftover from his old life. He opened his beaten-up brown leather doctor's bag to check the contents. A small hand saw, duct tape, pliers, a tube of Colgate toothpaste, a sewing kit, a flask, some other miscellaneous items and his untraceable 1939 Luger, a 9 mm toggle-locked recoil-operated semi-automatic pistol carried by the Germans in World War II. For most owners, it was a precious collector's item brought back by a GI after the war. For Chuck, it was simply a tool in his toolbox. He hadn't fired it since 1976, the year Bum Farto went missing. Farto was one of only three people who heard the shot.

Chuck's joints ached. He was getting too old for a cleanup call. He limped down the back stairs to his shiny black 1960 Cadillac Eldorado Brougham. He got in and gently placed his bag next to him. Action was necessary without delay. He sped down the highway. Sinatra had a way of doing things "my way." So did Chuck. It was his anthem.

※ ※ ※

Shep drove to The Conch. The restaurant's front lights were off. The place appeared to be deserted. Time to find Josephine without anyone being the wiser.

He strolled to the side of the building, hoping the bathroom window was still unlocked from the other night. Ta-da! Luck was on his side. With a flashlight in his back pocket, he pulled himself up and squirmed his way through the small window. Shep landed with a plop on the black and white tile floor. "Josie, Josie, where are you?" he whispered.

Shep exited the bathroom. His flashlight flickered as he turned it on. He banged it with his hand. Light. An unusual putrid odor filled the air. He flashed his light around the room, suddenly stopping. The light reflected off two sets of eyes. Shep had finally found his pet and business partner, Josephine. She was not alone. Her new friend wasn't moving.

Wrapped tightly in her coils was the vile iguana murderer from the Tiki Shak. His face was unmistakable even without the bushy mustache. Josephine's torso and tail tangled tightly around his neck, his eyes wide open, bulging, frozen in a look of disbelief. Strangely, he had a pom-pom tennis sock in his mouth. The purple pom-pom jutted out like he was blowing a grape-flavored Bubble Yum bubble.

In a panic, Shep shut off the flashlight. This was not an ideal situation. He had to get his thoughts together, quickly. Gathering up courage, an uneasy Shep walked cautiously toward his snake and the body. "Josie, you've been a bad girl."

He grabbed a fork off the table to poke Rico's leg. No movement. Deduction confirmed.

"Dead," Shep mumbled. "He's definitely dead. But, as God is my witness, he deserved it. He really did. If he hadn't been such an asshole . . ."

"Josie, you know it's funny how people look when they're dead. I mean, I've never seen a person as dead as this guy, but just look at him. He left this world with a surprised look frozen on his face. For the life of me, how could he have been surprised? A smart person would have seen it coming."

Folks would not take kindly to a murderous python. Shep needed to protect his misunderstood pet at all costs. It was a guaranteed death sentence and bad for his fledgling business model if anyone found out what type of mischief Josephine had been up to.

"If he stays here, they'll be looking for the killer. But . . . but, one of the things everybody knows is that without a body, there is no murder. Without a body, there's just a missing person. Right, Josie?" He had to dispose of her handiwork.

From the kitchen, he heard voices. He wasn't the only one at The Conch. Shep froze, unsure. He had to move quickly. But where?

🌿 🌿 🌿

"What took you so long!" Sam yelled at an unusually disheveled Chuck as he entered the kitchen.

Pearl slapped her son upside his head. "Mind your manners, boy."

"What the hell is going on?" said Chuck. He looked over at angry no-neck Sam holding a bloody wrapped hand above his head.

Chuck reached for the hand. "Let me take a look, son."

"Don't call me son!"

Sam yelped as Chuck unwrapped his hand. "Impressive! That was some solid shooting." Chuck had done a lot of "target" practice in his time and was impressed at how cleanly Sam's thumb and pointing finger had come off. "Who did this?"

"My fuckin' brother."

"Yaw lucky he didn't take yahr eye or something worse." He studied Sam's hand more closely. It needed more than light stitching, but it was doable. He'd dealt with much worse. The late Sean O'Reilly's shot-off butt cheek had been a real humdinger. He dug through his bag and handed Sam two 10 mg Valiums and a flask.

"Staht drinking. This isn't going to be fun. Pearl, tidy up while I get this show on the road. I want this place spotless. Everything needs a good wipe-down. Hand your ma yahr camera."

Sam reluctantly gave the Polaroid camera to Pearl.

Pearl didn't often follow orders, but in this case, she listened. One person she trusted implicitly was Chuck. She agreed. Morning was a-comin'. There was to be no trace of the Wilkies or anything else.

There were two remaining loose ends. The girls and Rico. She also wasn't sure what had turned Earl into a crazy person. That had to be sorted out.

"After you finish in here, there's somethin' else that needs lookin' at."

"What's that?"

"I got two gals locked in a bathroom and another bigger problem that needs some Bum Farto-style attention." She moved her head in the direction of the dining area.

"Do I have time to stitch yahr boy up before taking a gandah at what's behind door two?"

"Sure. He ain't goin' nowhere. He's a bit tied up anyhow."

"The ladies? How much did they see aw heah?"

"They were in the head before the shit hit the fan."

"Hmm . . . let me think while I work."

"Son, you want me to take a picture?" Pearl asked.

Sam glared at his mother. She noted the look. Pearl would let that photo op slide.

Nevertheless, two photographs were nonnegotiable for the Wall of Shame. A reminder of what could happen if you didn't toe the Wilkie line.

Earl's poor aim and unexpected, bizarre antics could not be dismissed. You just didn't shoot at family members willy-nilly.

Mama Pearl never spared the rod. That was what was wrong with the world. A good thrashing and a little public shaming never hurt anyone. How else could someone learn? There had to be consequences. It didn't matter if it was Earl or Rico. And that Colombian asshole had messed with the wrong clan.

Pearl walked outside, looking for Earl. Splashing sounds against the metal garbage cans led her directly to him. He was squatting, squeezing out leftovers. She lifted the camera to her eye. "Say cheese."

"Cheese?"

Click. The camera whirred. The photo did not capture Earl's best angle. It wasn't intended to.

Before heading back in, Mama Pearl detoured down to the dock. She had something for the tarpon. Digging into her shorts pocket, she threw Rico's retainer to the fish. With a splash and a gulp, it was gone.

Pearl tapped lightly on the bathroom door as she passed by. "Psst . . . best you shut your traps and stay put. Unless you want an unkind visit down the road."

Micki and Hibiscus received the message loud and clear. The toilet bowl still needed cleaning.

Sam continued to whine as Chuck stitched his hand.

"Boy, buck up. Don't be such a blubbering baby." She shook her head.

"You got something he can clamp down on?" Chuck asked.

"Yup." Pearl took off her remaining sock and in her nurturing motherly way jammed it into Sam's mouth, patting him on his head like a dog. "You got this. Make your Daddy proud." She pointed upward, looking at the ceiling.

※ ※ ※

Josephine was not letting go of her new prized possession. No matter how hard Shep pleaded or tugged. He had no other option. He dragged his stubborn but beloved python and Rico's corpse across the floor toward the entrance door.

The slight movement of unlocking the door made the bell chime ting-a-ling ever so lightly. Shep's hand shot up like a bolt to silence it.

What could he stuff into the bell to shut it up? Necessity being the mother of invention, he felt around under one of the tables. Shep peeled off a piece of hardened chewing gum, popped it into his mouth and munched on it until it softened. Definitely peppermint Carefree. He pulled the softened gum out of his mouth and molded it around the clapper. Then he quietly opened the door into the darkness of the parking lot. It worked. Oldest trick in the book. No sound from the bell.

Shep grabbed a large piece of coral rock to hold the door open.

With Rico being pulled by his feet, the irritating pea rock gravel rubbing against Josephine's scaly body finally convinced her to release her prize.

"Josie, wait here. I'll be right back." Shep dragged the body to his truck. Rico's body made a crunching sound as it was schlepped across the pea rock. He leaned Rico in a sitting position against the back of the truck.

Shep climbed onto the truck bed. Grabbing the ties around the body, he pulled it up until it was completely in the truck. He was breathing heavily. Hauling around a dead body was tougher than it looked in the movies.

He ran back to fetch Josephine.

Shit! Gone! Why did pythons have so much difficulty with the "stay" command? In the dark it was impossible to spot her. Shep was about to turn on his flashlight when a light in the dining area flicked on. He'd have to come back later.

With his truck lights off, he put it in neutral and pushed it onto a quiet US-1. There was never any traffic this time of morning. Sunrise was imminent. He pushed the truck further down the road until The Conch was no longer in sight.

Shep fired the engine and headed up the road to the Crocodile Lake National Wildlife Refuge in north Key Largo, which had recently been established to protect and preserve critical habitat for habitually hungry American crocodiles. It was the logical place for Rico. Hit men probably used it all the time.

45

CRAZY TRAIN
~ Ozzy Osbourne ~

"Let me look." Pearl was impressed with Chuck's work. "You still got the touch, my dear." She reached out and patted him on the shoulder.

Sam's hand was now Frankenstein-ish, but did it matter? It was not like he was ever going to be a hand model.

"Thank you, milady." Chuck took her hand and kissed it.

Even in his loopy state, mushy talk between Chuck and his mama disgusted Sam. "Gross, get a room."

"You ungrateful little dung beetle. You better straighten up real quick like. I'm not havin' that kinda talk."

An exhausted Chuck moseyed into the dining area and turned on the lights. "Okay, let's see what we have heah."

He glanced around, looking for the "problem" that Pearl needed fixing. What was it?

"Let's give him a full Farto," Pearl said as she sauntered in behind Chuck. Standing next to him, she surveyed the room. Something was missing.

"Who?" said Chuck.

"Rico." A breathless pause. "Mother trucker, where's that pig's sphincter?" she shouted. "He must have escaped."

The front door was wide open. A good-sized coral rock held the heavy glass door in place. She ran out toward the parking lot. Like a hunter tracking game, she followed the drag marks from the front door to a solo purple pom-pom. The only evidence Rico had ever been there. She was perplexed. There was no sign of kitchen twine or aprons. Pearl continued to scan the area for any other trace of the asshole.

Pearl stooped down and picked up the purple pom-pom and dusted it off. It would be a great addition to her latest crochet project. Waste not, want not.

She suddenly jumped, reacting to unusual movement in the sea grape shrubs under the large front window. "Shit balls. A frickin' monster anaconda. Move, move, move!"

Pearl nervously stared at Josephine, stretched out and enjoying the moment. She had long outgrown aquarium life. Josephine was already enjoying her new freedom, life on the open road.

Chuck pulled out his 9mm Luger and pulled the trigger, attempting to fire at the large python. It was a moment with an important reminder. Guns not regularly cleaned and oiled have a way of not firing when you want them to. With enough excitement for one night, Josephine quickly and safely slithered off into the dark, looking for a nice place to call home. The Everglades was calling.

Relieved the snake was gone, Sam, Pearl and Chuck went back in and took one last look around. The kitchen was spotless. Their cleanup job was impeccable. Chuck had even filled in the small bullet hole in the wall with toothpaste. Ingenious. Highly professional. The bullet hole imperfection blended nicely with the rest of the wall.

A pantless Earl stood before Chuck.

"Is he going to crap in my backseat?"

"Nah, he's got nothin' left in him. He's as empty as a politician's promise." Pearl fashioned a diaper out of her bloodstained Members Only jacket. "Here, wear this. Just in case," she said, handing it to Earl.

Earl, holding the sides of his newly formed adult diaper, shuffled slowly toward the car. What a long, strange trip the day had been. He wondered if he was coming down with the Philippine flu virus he'd heard about on TV.

"What about those gals in the bathroom?"

"No time now to worry about that. I reckon them girls are gonna hush up after I remind them nicely like. I think they're gonna listen up just fine."

Pearl rapped on the bathroom door for the last time. "You saw and heard nothin' tonight, got it? I'd hate for somethin' to happen to those pretty faces of yours . . . you mind your own business and I'll mind mine. I'll call us square. We on the same page?"

"Uh-huh." The reply came easily from Micki and Hibiscus. They were fully aware of the hell the Wilkie clan could unleash.

"Looks like you two got brains after all."

Pearl returned to the Cadillac. A grinning Sam was sitting in the front passenger side. He had coveted Pearl's preferred seat. In the rear, an odorous Earl smiled at his mom and patted the seat next to him. His front tooth was missing.

"Sorry, Pearl. I couldn't stop Sam from walloping his brother. Guess theyah even now," said Chuck.

"Where's the tooth?"

"Right here." No-neck Sam held it between his two fingers, dropped it into his mouth and swallowed it. A clear statement. An eye for an eye, a tooth for a tooth.

"Move over, baboon stank ass. I need some space." Pearl pushed Earl closer toward the car door away from her. She still wasn't sure if he was right in the head. She still hadn't made the connection with the tea in the thermos.

As Chuck pulled out of the parking lot, a suddenly stutter-free Earl remembered something.

"I know that white van . . . Sam, you got a quarter? Sing us a song." Earl laughed at the joke at his brother's expense. With his good hand, Sam reached over the seat to shut his brother up.

Pearl grabbed Sam's arm and dug her nails into his skin. "I'm gonna jerk a knot in your tail. What now?"

"Rico's van," Sam unwittingly divulged.

"Well, I'll be." If his van was still parked, where was that slug Rico? It dawned on her. The twins had done their nanny proud. It was the only possible explanation.

Pearl tapped Chuck on the shoulder. "Stop the car. I got one more thing to do." Pearl didn't like loose ends.

Chuck yawned. He just wanted to get home for some quality shut-eye before the Conchy Tonk Festival began. He had judging to do. But he wouldn't say no to Pearl.

The three occupants of Chuck's Cadillac watched as Pearl climbed into the van. With a little bit of old-fashioned engineering known to any 1970s-era car thief, the engine came to life. She motioned for Chuck to follow. Barely able to see over the steering wheel, tiny but mighty Pearl pressed the accelerator and headed toward the fancy new Winn-Dixie in Marathon. It seemed like a good enough place to park an unwanted white van.

※ ※ ※

Summoning the courage after hearing nothing more, Micki and Hibiscus cautiously emerged from their small bathroom cell, keeping an ear out for the Wilkies. The place was empty. Even that gross, baldy Rico was gone.

To their surprise, the kitchen was spotless. It was cleaner than they had ever seen it. Micki opened the walk-in fridge and was even more surprised to see her container of conch fritter batter. She sighed with relief. The batter wouldn't have to be remade from time-consuming scratch. As an added bonus, the place was quiet. Mr. Clean and the Wilkie family were gone.

An old Polaroid camera had been left on the counter by the door. Hibiscus pressed the round button. It still worked. "I can get pictures of you on stage!" *Or, even better*, she thought, *some artsy bikini shots of myself.*

Micki smiled as she imagined her big win.

✿ ✿ ✿

Hours later, to Deep Dive's initial shock and then embarrassment, amused Bahamian customs officials in Bimini opened the Hartmann suitcase to discover it stuffed with his prized eight-year collection of *Hustler* and *Oui* magazines.

46

MY WAY
~ Frank Sinatra ~

Once a year, the Friends of the Keys Conch Society hosted the Conchy Tonk Festival, showcasing the beloved tropical marine mollusk that was such an integral ingredient of Keys life.

What began as a friendly conch-cooking competition between local restaurants expanded over the years as the event grew in popularity. Cookery categories were added including Best Conch Fritter, Best Conch Salad, Best Conch Chowder and Best Specialty Conch, along with the highly coveted Best in Show, highlighting the best conch recipe out of all the categories.

Front-page recognition and bragging rights for the winners drew locals and visitors alike to their restaurants' dining rooms.

New this year was a car show with five classic Keys cruisers (the prize going to the ugliest still-running clunker), a performance by the Bushwhackers and vendor booths led by the Pink Flamingo. A vendor booth previously scheduled by Shep for his pet iguana collection was empty.

Other fun and dependable activities returning to this year's Conchy Tonk were the conch-blowing contest and the crowd favorite, the conch fritter eating contest.

Walter and Pookie Jones, a visiting couple from Canada, using a new and perhaps unorthodox technique for the conch-blowing portion, performed a conch-shell-and-vocal duet that drew cheers and laughter from the crowd and impressed the judges enough for them to take home a win.

The judges included the mayor of Monroe County, a beloved local artist, a leading fishing guide, a popular guitarist, a peace activist, a leading real estate broker as well as Kimbo and Chuck. After the notorious 1977 conch fritter shakedown, the judging method remained under a microscope. Local hearsay claimed Big Ol' Grouper restaurant was caught bribing the judges with free beer and $20 bills. To correct any perceived unfairness, a blind taste test was now in place.

Fourteen restaurants were entered, the largest group the contest had ever seen. No two establishments prepared conch in quite the same way. Tastes and cooking techniques varied. Last year's winner and the reigning champ Jake Schmidt represented Seafarer's Delight. He stood smugly confident he had another win in the bag. At one point he was seen winking at Kimbo.

Micki and the other contestants stood by nervously as they watched the judges sample the variety of conch fritters laid out in front of them. A smile. A grimace. A look of satisfaction. A wince. Every expression, every chew, every movement of the jaw was intensely scrutinized and analyzed by the anxious contestants.

Kimbo was certain entry number three was Micki's. The fried balls tasted and looked very similar to the ones she had eaten at The Conch a couple of days earlier. She scored those fritters a one out of five and scribbled a snide note – "terrible texture on the palate." In addition, she was sure Jake had winked at her seven times.

As it turned out, Kimbo had misread all the signs. Jake would not be pleased with her comment on his entry.

Believing it was Jake's, Kimbo aggressively advocated for number seven.

It was, in fact, Micki's best effort ever, a perfect conch fritter, a golden-brown crispy ball of deliciousness with a tender conch meat filling, light and airy with a hint of sweetness and a touch of spice.

But it was a good deal more than just the crunchy outside texture, the fluffy core and the spicy *je ne sais quoi* that clearly set her offering apart from all the other entries. It was the secret definitive accent provided by bits of Sam's thumb and forefinger.

For Kimbo, an unbelievably great taste!

The votes were tallied. "We have a winnah." Chuck announced.

"Numbah seven! Micki Wilson from Conch on the Bay!" The crowd burst into applause. Micki grinned and waved. Hibiscus clicked the Polaroid. Kimbo frowned.

Victory never tasted so good.

EPILOGUE

Tying up a few loose ends.

* Cuban refugee Carlos Suarez made it to Key West, where he is living the American dream. Happily married, he is co-owner of two bars, three tourist attractions and four houses with his brother Jorge. He still hates snakes.
* Edward "Eddie" Lambert IV made headlines in the chess world when he was accused of using vibrating anal beads to beat a top-ranked opponent in a national championship tournament.
* Peggy and Shaman Paul moved to a premier Active Adult Retirement Community located in southwest Florida. They made lots of new friends. The neighborhood continuously makes news for having the highest STD rate in the state—maybe the world.
* Respected business owners Patricia and Stan Dubicki established a manatee rehabilitation facility after a family of bloated manatees mysteriously beached themselves at the Islamorada Sandbar. The cause of the unusual behavior remains unresolved.
* A frugal Betsy eventually bought Chuck out. As the proud owner of Peter, Dick and Willy's, she still employs eagle ear Tommy to keep her abreast of all the Keys gossip. She always keeps a bottle of Visine in her office.
* Sick of dealing with her imbecile brother and the smell of Lysol, Roo left the septic business when the municipal sewer system came to the Keys. She now runs a successful Fortune 500 company.

- Barry inherited the Septic Baron. It went bankrupt after the sewage system was installed. Even restaurant grease trap pump-outs weren't enough to save it. Barry went on to open a tattoo parlor in Atlanta. Much of his work has been prominently featured on the highly popular TV show, Tattoo Nightmares.
- Pearl and Chuck ended up at the Happy Life Assisted Living Facility in Homestead before being kicked out for bad behavior. Pearl stabbed her roommate, Doris, with a crochet needle after she turned off the TV during an episode of *General Hospital*. Chuck was accused of knocking up Nurse Tammy. DNA results are still pending.
- Tinker married a secret Everglades celebrity—Sasquatch of the Everglades. She runs airboat tours selling $1 bags of lima beans to bait the elusive "humanoid," thereby leading to "sightings" for the tourists. Local lore claims the omnivorous swamp creature loves the legumes. Pabst Blue Ribbon works as well.
- Belle married Billy, the nephew of the mayor of Everglades City and a notorious local drug runner. They were only married a month before an anonymous tip-off led to the arrest of her new husband and several friends and neighbors in the small, sleepy fishing village. She now manages a very lucrative operation. The source of the tip-off remains undisclosed, but Nanny Pearl would be proud.
- Tiffani never did get her Disney wedding. She settled for a Southern belle-themed wedding at Cypress Gardens. She was thrilled with how the corset and crinoline accentuated her tits and ass.
- Deep Dive spent several years in the Bahamas. At one point he was attacked by wild swine at Pig Island. He carries permanent facial scars to this day. He treasures his collection of water-damaged Hustler and Oui magazines. The Reel Upside is still running.

* Hibiscus's dream white bikini poster was produced by Drooling Fred in 1982. It was an immediate hit with junior high school boys in Key Largo. She went on to marry the head dolphin trainer from Seas of Wonder and became a Weight Watchers coach after her fourth child was born.
* Micki was never able to recreate the original *je ne sais quoi* flavor of her prize-winning conch fritters. It stumps her to this day. She did, however, set up her own successful food truck business – The Rolling Conch. She considered reuniting with Juan, but ultimately decided he was too much of a pansy-ass.
* In desperation, Juan married Jenny after calling her number on the wall at Peter, Dick and Willy's. The marriage didn't last. He finally settled on a simpler life on the seven seas as a popular bartender on the lower deck of one of the world's largest cruise ships, happily serving his ever-popular Tiki Juice in a specialty cup with a grinning lobster and the ship's logo topped with a Bacardi 151 rum floater and garnished with a bright red cherry, a slice of lime and the predictable small multicolored umbrella. Many former passengers showcase their collection of grinning lobster cups.
* Micki was not the only Wilson to win a prize. Michael's newspaper won accolades for its exposé on the mysterious retainer with two prominent mismatched front teeth found inside Scarface the Tarpon after a touron illegally caught him in the no-fishing zone at Conch on the Bay. When it was picked up by the National Enquirer, the story was an instant sensation with soccer moms and other grocery store customers all over the country.
* Gerald flunked out of husband training. Kimbo shacked up with Jake and opened Conch Balls on a Stick, a direct competitor of The Rolling Conch. She's still a bimbo.
* Sam and Earl renamed themselves the Three-Fingered Bandits. With Mama in her new digs, the brothers finally acted on their

dream venture—strip club boat charters. After his ever-trusty Polaroid camera was lost, Sam upgraded to a Polaroid SX-70 Land Camera Alpha 1 Gold Limited Edition. He became a keen documenter of men gone wild. Blackmail kept the brothers' new business venture cash positive. The Organ Grinder charter boats receive consistent one- and two- star reviews. Earl still has three unused sticks of dynamite in his shed.

* Shep married Carmen after Enrique finally died from his garden injuries, thus becoming Juan's least favorite stepfather. With the benefit of the "chooze" money, they opened an iguana pet shop and iguana training center until success overtook them when the Keys were overrun by the scaly reptiles. Locals, upset with iguana poop on their docks and the decimation of their prized hibiscus flowers, finally had enough. The county forced him to shut it down.

* Señor Mendoza never learned what happened to Rico. Marty the diaper man constantly asks about him. Rico's pets, found almost starved to death, were taken in by Mitzie. She now has twenty-seven cats.

* Josephine made it to the Everglades, reuniting with her long-lost sister, Shep's other former pet python, Isabelle. She became a highly prized consort for dumped males. Josephine is the proud mama of thousands of babies destroying the national park's wildlife.

* The Crocodile Lake National Wildlife Refuge in Upper Key Largo has been an enormous success in producing an ever-growing population of healthy, well-fed crocs. They are no longer classified as endangered.

THE END

About the Authors

Liv and her father Frank have written an off-the-wall novel with a "nostalgic" look back at the old Keys, a place dear to their hearts. Representing two distinct generations with different life experiences, their blended skills bring an unusual perspective and touch to the story.

In the early 1980s, Liv would day trip to the Keys from Miami looking for the perfect place to park her beach chair. She was drawn to the slow-paced, laid-back lifestyle and beautiful scenery.

After college, Liv traveled the world and returned to paradise a few years later with a husband in tow. It wasn't long before they added two Conchs (and later a Jersey boy). Her time as a third-grade teacher at the local elementary school caring for the class project, a small python, provided inspiration for part of the story.

Frank N. Hawkins, Jr. lived with his wife in Tavernier for twenty-two years. As an active member of the community he served on the boards of the Florida Keys Electric Co-op, the Upper Keys Rotary Club and the Islamorada Fishing Club. He is also a founding contributor and former board member of the Keys History and Discovery Center and a Founders Level contributor to Baptist Health Mariners Hospital.

A former spy, foreign correspondent, corporate executive and international businessman, Frank is the author of the highly rated thriller *The Zurich Printout* and the gripping adventure novel *Ritter's Gold*. He also privately published his memoir *Risks, Gateway Moments and Unrivaled Travel*. He's been to a lot of places you've never heard of.

Frank has no idea how his daughter managed to conjure up all the characters and the plot of *$ea Weed*. It's probably best for a father not to know how much of the story is true.